The Rake Gets Ravished

He hesitated when he saw her. One of his dark eyebrows lifted, but he otherwise gave no reaction. He seemed very . . . calm. No outrage over confronting a veritable stranger in his room.

Perhaps he was accustomed to finding strange women in his bedchamber. A powerful, wealthy man like him—handsome, no less—likely had women pelting themselves at him at every turn. She distinctly recalled what the woman downstairs had said to her.

Most women who are looking for Silas Masters know what he looks like. That is why they are looking for him.

That was when she knew exactly what to do. As scandalous and shameful the notion. She had to do it.

"Hello," he murmured. He managed to even look . . . *bored*. Apparently her presence here did not merit a noteworthy reaction from him. "Lost, are you? This is not the ladies' retiring room. Was that not where you were going earlier? I think you mentioned that."

She nodded and made a mild sound of agreement. "I am not lost."

"No?"

"No," she affirmed with a fortifying lift of her chin. "I am right where I want to be."

By Sophie Jordan

Sophie Jordan

The Rake Gets Ravished

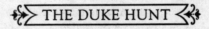

THE DUKE HUNT

AVONBOOKS

An Imprint of HarperCollinsPublishers

THE RAKE GETS RAVISHED. Copyright © 2022 by Sharie Kohler. All rights reserved. Printed in the United States of America. No part of this book may be used or reproduced in any manner whatsoever without written permission except in the case of brief quotations embodied in critical articles and reviews. For information, address HarperCollins Publishers, 195 Broadway, New York, NY 10007.

First Avon Books mass market printing: February 2022

Print Edition ISBN: 978-0-06-303567-6
Digital Edition ISBN: 978-0-06-303569-0

Cover design by Nadine Badalaty
Cover illustration by Alan Ayers

Avon, Avon & logo, and Avon Books & logo are registered trademarks of HarperCollins Publishers in the United States of America and other countries.

HarperCollins is a registered trademark of HarperCollins Publishers in the United States of America and other countries.

FIRST EDITION

Printed in Lithuania

22 23 24 25 26   SB   10 9 8 7 6 5 4 3 2 1

For my dear aunt, Linda Haynes: healer, adventuress, matriarch, world traveler, caregiver, and friend. A true heroine in every way.

The Rake
Gets Ravished

Chapter One ❧

*H*er corset was killing her.

Mercy Kittinger fidgeted on the well-worn velvet squabs and tried to adjust the boning digging into her ribs. The modiste she had visited upon her arrival to Town insisted the contraption fit her properly and that it did wonderful things for her shape.

Mercy would not know. She was accustomed to the comfort and ease of her own modest garments. She lived on a farm. She never gave a thought to her shape. Nor did anyone else.

Her days were about function, about taking care of her sister and the house and the staff and making certain everyone was fed and everything was running smoothly. That was her life and she liked it very well.

And up until last week everything had been running smoothly.

Then her brother had arrived home. Her feckless, spendthrift wastrel of a brother. Her twin. Not that that bred any special loyalty within him.

Now she was here, doing what she always did—cleaning up Bede's messes.

Mercy paid her fare through the hatch to the cloaked driver and stepped down from the hansom cab. Squaring her shoulders, she faced the building and shivered in the night—a shiver that had naught to do with cold. On the contrary. It was a pleasant evening. Only the task at hand was unpleasant.

She grasped a handful of her silk skirts as she started up the steps to the impressive brick edifice. It was one of the nicer houses in the modest neighborhood. Brightly lit with outside sconces. The three-storied house was no home, however. It happened to be one of London's most notorious gaming hells and where her foolish brother had lost everything. She suspected a great many foolish men lost their fortunes in this place. But as her brother's fortune was *her* fortune, it fell to her to reclaim it.

Nodding once, she entered the building, determination fueling her steps.

The place was busy. She was not the only one entering through its front doors. Nor was she the only woman beneath its roof. There were several ladies, all attired in much the same manner she was.

Just as she had hoped, she did not attract an inordinate amount of notice in her scandalous gown.

She was merely another body. Another person getting lost in the revel.

When Mercy had visited the modiste, she requested a gown befitting a woman of looser inhibitions. It had hurt to part with the precious coin, but she had no choice. She knew she could not wear anything from her modest life. She would be playing a role, and it was not a game she could lose. Too much depended upon it.

The dressmaker had not even blinked at the request. The lady had obliged, attiring her in the requested level of bawdiness. She had plumped Mercy's breasts that were on indecent display, the areolas of her nipples very nearly peeking above the edge of stiff black lace, and proclaimed, *"Magnifique!"*

More indecent than the front of her gown was perhaps the lack of sleeves. The whisper of wind over her bare shoulders and arms felt wicked and wholly unfamiliar as she wove through the crowd of tables and bodies. It was as though an entire swath of fabric were missing from her gown.

She felt virtually naked.

One thing was certain. Women of looser inhibitions did not dress for comfort.

Mercy longed to finish this evening's unsavory business and return to her life.

She assessed her lively surroundings. After

emerging from the darkness of the night, her eyes did not need much time to adjust to the indoors because the gaming hell was kept in dim lighting, the lanterns and sconces burning low.

Dozens of tables occupied the main room, which might have acted as a ballroom were this a traditional home. But there was nothing traditional about this scene.

Various card games were being played out. The players ranged in age and gender. Some of the faces were tense; others loose and jovial, flushed from an excess of spirits. Liveried servers wove through the rooms, quick to indulge, keeping glasses full to the brim. A small dais at one end boasted a string quartet.

Idly, Mercy wondered where her brother had sat when he was here. Which table had he occupied whilst he gambled away their lives?

Was the man who owned her family lands here even now? Sitting at one of these tables, taking the livelihood from another wretched soul as easily as he had taken it from her brother?

She'd known it had been an easy task. She knew that because she knew her brother. Many an evening had she played whist with Bede after dinner. Always *she* won. She won and she had no special training at cards. She had only ever played with family or, infrequently, with Imogen. What made the fool think he could win against the seasoned players of a gaming den? With the *owner* of this gaming hell, no less? She might be the best card player in her family, but she had no such illusion that she could stroll in here and handle herself against this veteran crowd.

She would reclaim her home, but not in a traditional game of cards.

No, her methods would be more questionable than that.

Mercy reached out to touch the arm of a woman who had just finished topping off champagne to the occupants at a table.

"Pardon me? Is Mr. Masters in the house this evening?"

The server looked her over from head to toe in a slow perusal. "He is here most every evening," she answered as though that was widely known information. "And day."

That information matched what she had been able to learn about Silas Masters. He kept no other address. This place was his sole residence. He worked and dwelled here.

Mercy nodded slowly and glanced over the room, pretending that she felt no real sense of urgency and was not on the verge of breaking any laws tonight. "Ah, and might you point out the gentleman to me?"

"You don't know him by sight?" The woman looked amused as she asked the question.

"Um, no."

"Interesting." Again with that almost smile.

"What is?"

"It is just that most women who are looking for Silas Masters know what he looks like." Her lips curled in a full-fledged smile now. "That is why they're looking for him."

Mercy shifted on her feet nervously. "Well, I don't know . . ." Her voice faded as the woman raised her hand and pointed.

Mercy followed her direction to a second-floor balcony and the small group sitting there looking down upon the ground floor as though it was their small kingdom.

Mercy's gaze skipped over the gray-haired gentleman and the lady, settling on the man at the center of the trio. He acted as a magnet, sucking in everything—especially her awareness.

"That's him, there. Nice, hm?"

Yes. That was him. Silas Masters. She had deduced as much. "Oh," she breathed.

"Oh, indeed," the server chuckled.

Mercy nodded, understanding at once why women might wish to seek the company of Silas Masters.

Aside from his apparent fortune, he was quite

something to behold. He possessed the kind of dangerously good looks one might expect from the owner of a gaming hell . . . or the gatekeeper to an antechamber to hell.

Thick dark hair longer than fashionable fell past his ears, and yet this man made it look good. Enticing. A style all of his own. Other men might attempt to replicate the look but they would only look foolish and unkempt.

It was the whole parcel of him. Hair. Face. The impressive breadth of his shoulders looming above the balcony. A closely trimmed beard dusting his jaw and cheeks. Sensually curving lips that promised sinister delights.

From across the distance the color of his deeply set eyes was indeterminate beneath the dramatic slash of thick eyebrows, but Mercy imagined them to be equally dark. They were certainly intense as they looked down on his domain.

She thought they fixed on her, but in the dimness it was only conjecture and a vague . . . sense. Her imagination was running wild. She was one person in a room full of people. Why would he be looking at her?

"He is a sight to behold, no?" the woman asked as though she could read Mercy's mind.

She nodded once in agreement, aiming for an unaffected air. "An attractive gentleman."

"Shall I inform him you wish for an audience with him?"

"No," she was quick to answer. Perhaps too quickly, but her pulse jumped at the notion of an encounter with Masters. That was to be avoided at all costs. "That's not necessary."

"But I thought you wished to see—"

"Might you direct me to your ladies' retiring room?" She needed only to establish his presence, mark his location so that she could safely go forth on this evening's enterprise, and now that was done. Stealth and strategy were required. He looked quite comfortable up in his perch. The night was still young.

Now was the time to strike.

The woman shrugged and then motioned toward a door on the other side of the large room. "Through there. Second floor."

"Thank you." Turning, Mercy started across the room. She tried not to look his way again. No easy task when she knew he was up there watching. She was hoping to achieve an air of covertness. Gawking at the man would not accomplish that.

She wove through the room, taking her time, forcing a sedate pace, stopping occasionally to observe a game or two as though she was interested in the play. She did this in case she was being watched. Or perhaps so she would not *become* watched.

She had to resist her instinctive urge—which was to dash for the door leading to the second floor and locate Silas Masters's private rooms, where she assumed he kept all his important documents. She hoped she was correct on that score. She *had* to be right about that. Otherwise she did not know what she would do. Fling herself at his feet, pleading for mercy? That did not seem like a promising plan. He had looked hard and uncompromising from her one glimpse of him . . . not the manner of man given to compassion.

She was close now. The door loomed ahead.

She sidled past a table of gentlemen playing a particularly lively game of whist. A combination of shouts and applause erupted. One of the gentlemen tossed down his cards with a fierce exclamation. Groaning in defeat, he leaned back in his chair. As he stretched his arms wide, his hand bumped into her while she attempted to pass the table.

He shot a foul glare over his shoulder. Clearly he was in a bad mood over his poor luck and thought to vent his spleen on the person who dared to step in the path behind him.

Unfortunately, she was that person.

His venomous look shifted as he assessed her, transforming into something speculative and fairly lecherous.

"Hallo there, lass." A meaty paw reached for her

and snatched hold of her wrist, stopping her in her tracks.

Reminding herself that she had no wish to call attention to herself, she forced a smile on her face and resisted recoiling in outrage.

"Come here, lovie," he continued. "Cheer a fellow up, won't you?" His thick sausage fingers tightened their pressure around her, digging into her skin.

She felt the forced smile on her face turn as brittle as glass. "As tempting as the invitation is, sir, I must decline."

"Aren't we the lofty one?" He gave a hard tug and she went tumbling. "Never met a female here who wasn't open to a little fun."

"Ooof." She plopped unwillingly into his lap.

His arms came up around her waist and there was no hiding her outrage now. She was not accustomed to being manhandled. Things like this did not happen back home. Back home she was accorded respect.

"What's the matter, lass? My coin isn't good enough? Are you not here to work?"

She sucked in a hot breath. Well. That was rather presumptuous of him. He thought her a courtesan? Certainly not every woman here was plying her trade. And even if she was, a courtesan, undoubtedly, had her standards and did not have to tolerate him.

"Unhand me, sirrah."

Instead of following her command, his beady little eyes lowered from her face to her daring décolletage.

She rested a hand there, her fingers pressing into her soft flesh. She knew she should not appear so modest, so skittish beneath his insulting regard, but she could not help herself. His gaze felt like a snake slithering across her bare skin.

He tsked and dared to touch her, peeling her hand off her chest, flinging it away as though it were a pesky crumb. "None of that now. Do not hide such a bounty of loveliness from Howie." Presumably he was Howie.

Enough. She ground her teeth and surged up, determined to free herself from his lecherous advances.

"I am certain there is another lady about only too happy to entertain your abundant charms."

His eyes narrowed. Apparently he did not appreciate her forcefulness. Bullies never did appreciate someone with a backbone. She was yanked back down with jarring force and his hand came up to roughly fondle her breast.

She gasped and reacted. All attempts to appear

at ease in this wildly strange environment with this awful wretch vanished. Ease did not exist. There was only instinct.

Her hand flew, her palm connecting soundly and very satisfyingly with his cheek. The sound reverberated through the air. All the gentlemen at the table froze. Even the people in the vicinity of them stopped to gawk in their direction.

Blast it. She had created a spectacle.

A stark red handprint began to take shape on Howie's face.

"Oh," she breathed, dread consuming her, but not regret. She could summon none of that sentiment for putting a stop to his groping.

He lightly stroked his wounded cheek. "You little tart!"

She took advantage of his astonishment and vaulted to her feet. Her action revived him from his frozen stupor. Shaken from his astonishment, he clamped down on her arm. He, too, jumped to his feet, overturning his chair with a clatter and only drawing more attention to them. *Splendid.*

Exclamations erupted all around them, but Mercy did not look anywhere save Howie. Her handprint became less visible as angry red suffused the rest of his face from the flare of his temper.

"How dare you? Who do you think you are?"

His fingers tightened painfully on her bicep and he gave her a hard shake that rattled her very teeth.

"Unhand me before I—" She did not get the rest of her words out.

"Hold there." A large hand closed around Howie's shoulder. She followed that big hand up its arm to the face of the gentleman intervening.

Him.

The one who held her life in his hands.

The one whom she was here to rob.

Howie twisted around with an ugly snarl that quickly faded to a squeak when he saw who stood behind him.

Mercy swallowed back her own pitiable squeak at Silas Masters's sudden appearance.

This was not supposed to happen. She was not supposed to meet him. She was not supposed to come face-to-face with him.

In and out. Undetected. That was the plan.

The blood drained from Howie's face. "Masters," he acknowledged in a voice that had lost its edge and was no more than a whispery tremble.

"You know I have no tolerance for disorder in my club, Bassett," Masters said, and the sound of his growly voice made her knees go weak. Made him all the more real.

"Y-yes. Of course," the man stammered, releasing her as though the touch of her now burned him. "P'raps you should have a word with your girl here then."

"I am not anyone's *girl*," she objected.

"You're *here*," Bassett said with heavy accusation, "and dressed like a trollop."

"What does the manner of my dress signify?" she demanded. "That it is acceptable to grope me? That I invite your attentions?"

"Precisely." He spat the word without shame.

"Precisely *not*," Masters intoned in his deep yet soft voice—a voice that nonetheless shouted of authority.

Even if he were not the proprietor of this club, this man commanded deference. She doubted anyone ever challenged him.

He continued, "The women here are not in my employ and even if they were, I would not require them to suffer your or any man's attentions."

Bassett blustered and waved at her with contempt. "I have a right to courtesy and respect from this—"

"There you are wrong. The women who patronize my club are guests here just as you are. They should be able to stroll across the floors of this house free of molestation. Since you cannot afford a lady that modicum of courtesy, you have no right to respect and are no longer welcome here."

Mr. Bassett blanched. *"Ever?"*

"You shall have to find other diversions to amuse yourself. Elsewhere."

A long stretch of silence fell.

"What? Now? I must leave?" Mr. Bassett glanced wildly around him as though any of the many faces staring back at him might offer an alternative solution. His face flushed an even deeper red and his eyes suddenly looked watery.

"Indeed." Mr. Masters nodded his dark head once, decisively. "Do not cause further spectacle, man. Have some dignity and take your leave."

With a baleful glare cast her way, Mr. Bassett gave a grunt, followed by a nod, and stormed off through the room, dodging people and tables with angry movements.

The gentlemen at the table whom he had been playing with resumed their game of whist as though nothing untoward had occurred. Apparently he would not be missed by any of them.

Mercy turned her gaze on Masters to find his attention smoothly trained on her.

"Thank you," she murmured.

"You seemed to have the situation well in hand, but my apologies. You should not have been accosted."

"As you said, it was no doing of yours, sir." She swallowed, but it felt an impossible task. There was no ridding herself of the giant lump in her throat. "You need not apologize."

He inclined his head slightly. "Everything that happens under this roof is my responsibility."

Everything?

It was precisely the reminder she needed to put aside any softening she felt over his display of gallantry.

By his own admission, everything that occurred here was his responsibility, including the ruination of a family. *Her* family. *Here.* Under this roof. Had he no care for that? For *all* the families he had ruined, because there were undoubtedly many more. More reckless brothers. More selfish fathers. More ruthless takers like Silas Masters.

With her heart freshly hardened against him, she closed herself off to his outward courtesy and handsome face. Many a lady would doubtlessly simper when presented with such a darkly pretty man. Mercy, however, was made of sterner stuff.

As a guardian to her younger sister—true, Bede was their sister's legal guardian, but it always fell to Mercy to act as mother and father to Grace—Mercy had to be immune. There was only room enough for one husband-seeking, stars-in-her-eyes dreamer in the Kittinger household.

Grace's arrival had been a surprise to their parents. It had been a surprise to all, in truth. At the time Mama was no young woman set to the task of delivering babies, and the birthing of twins had nearly finished her a decade before.

Unsurprising then, perhaps, that she had never recovered from Grace's birth, sadly languishing . . . withering, really, until her broken body finally surrendered to death's embrace two years later. Even before Mama's demise, it had fallen to Papa to see to his three children—or rather, it had fallen to Mercy.

Only a young girl herself, Mercy had stepped forward and taken the reins as lady of the house. Papa had managed the farm and she managed her baby sister and rascal of a brother. At least until Papa sent Bede off to school. At that point her brother belonged to the world and his own many foibles.

Ever since Grace's birth, Mercy had put family first. She had not approached adulthood with the hopes that other young women harbored. She had a farm to run, a family to oversee and a young sister to bring up whilst her brother followed his own merry pursuits.

It was a relentless and grueling task, ushering a young girl into womanhood. Especially when one did not rely on servants and governesses and ladies' maids for assistance. It all fell to Mercy. Everything fell to Mercy.

Mercy had not the leisure herself for merry pursuits. There were no courtships or dalliances or even flirtations that one might expect for an unattached lady. Those adventures were reserved for other young ladies. Ladies like her young sister—or so Grace hoped.

Grace hoped for a great deal. Dances. Parties. Teas. Catching the eye of a handsome young gentleman. She begged Mercy for a trip to Town where she might enter the marriage mart on a broader scale—as though they were good *ton* and not simple gentry.

Mercy fixed her attention on Silas Masters's face, continuing to tell herself not to be swayed by all of his masculine beauty. Grace would have melted into a puddle at his feet. He was not like the country gentlemen in their sphere. Not in the least.

Bede should have warned her.

When her brother first told her of The Rogue's Den and of the proprietor, Silas Masters, he merely described him as ruthless, intimidating and powerful. A very rich man without mercy.

Without mercy. She remembered that specifically because Bede had used her name. The irony had struck her at the time as her brother continued talking, bemoaning this wretched owner of a gaming hell who would take everything from him so callously. From *him*, Bede. No mention was given of Mercy or Grace and what they stood to lose.

And yet Mercy had vowed that she would go to this club and face the purportedly ruthless man himself if need be. Of course, she had hoped it would not come to that.

She would somehow reclaim their lives. She would succeed and not be deterred by Silas Masters's lack of compassion or, as it would turn out, by his dark good looks.

"If you would pardon me, I was on my way to the ladies' retiring room."

His gaze held hers, perhaps a bit too long. As though he could smell the subterfuge on her person. Perhaps he thought her suspicious or simply up to mischief in his establishment. She certainly felt suspicious standing there in her newly acquired gown that felt like someone else's skin on her.

But that was silly. She took a gulping breath. She was being overly anxious. He had no reason to suspect she was anything other than a lady-about-town, here for diversions just like everyone else.

Even though she was not like everyone else. Far from it.

She was in this lion's den to thieve.

To steal from the lion himself. She would not go home empty-handed.

Chapter Two 🖎

As Mercy moved along the second floor it became clear that Silas Masters's private rooms were not on this level.

There were retiring rooms for both ladies and gentlemen and more rooms where private card games were being held. She knew the house boasted three stories and she suspected his rooms were on the third floor. It was an easy matter to deduce which door led upstairs. The one marked No Entry felt like a good choice.

The merry sounds of the revelers faded as she opened the door and ascended the steps. With a racing heart, she turned the latch of the door at the top and stepped out onto a thickly carpeted corridor.

It was quieter up here, far away from the world below. Her muffled tread whispered on the air as she tried first one door, peering inside. Then another door. Nothing. Darkened bedchambers both with minimal furnishings.

She tried yet another door. It opened to a well-stocked library. No desk though, so she doubted any important papers or documents were kept there.

The next door opened to another bedchamber, this one more opulent with double doors leading out onto a balcony. Those doors were open. An evening breeze came through, gusting the curtains in great billows of fabric, like sails on a ship.

The bedchamber touted not only a colossal four-poster bed, but a large fireplace, too. A wingback chair and sofa were strategically positioned before the hearth that crackled with a low-burning fire.

The sofa loomed invitingly with a fur blanket tossed haphazardly over one side as though someone had cast it off when interrupted from a nap.

Her gaze skipped away from the tempting scene, scanning the rest of the chamber, landing on a mahogany desk. A bookcase crammed full of leather-bound volumes occupied the wall behind it.

She approached the desk in a rush of whispering silk. It was not simply for appearances. It served a function. There were papers and correspondence organized on its surface. An ink pot and quill. Letters opened and unopened, arranged in stacks.

Circling the desk, she eyed the surface for a moment before setting her hands to it.

She was systematic in her search. She did not want anyone to know someone had been here, rifling through items.

Every pile of papers she touched, every ledger or journal she examined, she made certain they all went back in their proper place, as though she had not been here at all. She was, in effect, *hopefully*, a ghost.

At the start of this mess she had conceived a plan that would run smoothly and without complication. She envisioned that she would drift in and out of The Rogue's Den undetected, no one the wiser.

Meeting *him* had not been in the plan. Already her scheme had not gone as intended. She was supposed to be invisible. But that did not mean it was ruined. That did not mean things could not go smoothly from here out.

From what she had gathered, Silas Masters made a lucrative business accruing debts from men like her brother—foolish and reckless men. Men who doubtlessly had dependents: wives and children. Or, as in Bede's case, sisters.

Her indignation burned anew—not just at what Bede had done, but at the mercenary Mr. Masters. Where was his honor? His sense of culpability? Had he no shame over ruining innocent lives?

Finished examining the top of his desk and finding nothing that resembled what she was searching for, she eased into the great leather chair and turned her attention to the drawers.

She opened one and flipped through stationery and envelopes.

It had not even been a week since her brother gambled away the family farm beneath this very roof. Certainly Masters still had Bede's voucher in his possession. She winced. Unless he had turned it over to someone else. An agent or a secretary. Someone to begin the process of confiscating her home . . . her life.

"No," she whispered fervently to herself with a hard shake of her head. That was not happening. "It's here. It has to be here."

She could not consider the alternative. The alternative led to homelessness. Penury. Aloneness.

The bottom right drawer was deeper than the others. It stuck a little as she tried to open it, forcing her to give the knob a hard tug.

It opened with a rattle, revealing a small lacquered chest inside.

She lifted the box out of the drawer and set it carefully on the desk before her. Hope hummed over her skin.

She anxiously flipped the clasp and lifted the lid. A dozen pieces of paper filled the box. She picked one off the top and scanned it, releasing a relieved gust of breath as she registered it was a voucher for a racehorse owed to one Silas Masters, dated three days ago.

She tossed it aside and quickly began rifling through each and every slip of paper until halfway through the pile and she stopped flipping.

With a shaking hand and a sinking stomach, she raised the paper to eye level.

She recognized her brother's familiar looping scrawl at once. They actually had very similar penmanship. She had always credited it to a condition of sharing a womb together. She scanned the words confirming that he had signed over all their property, land and house and objects therein.

She should feel only elation at the discovery of it, but this was irrefutable proof. No more holding out hope that it was all a mistake, that her brother was less than perfidious. There was no denying it now. Seeing this evidence of his recklessness in bold ink fired her ire all over again.

"Blasted fool," she muttered as she folded the document into tiny fourths and tucked it into the reticule dangling from her wrist.

With no voucher bearing her brother's signature, no court in the land would honor Mr. Masters's claim on her home.

A satisfied smile curved her lips. She had done it.

Now, however, was no time to relax her guard and revel in her relief over her triumphant find. She had to get out of this place posthaste.

After securing the chest very correctly back inside its drawer, she eyed the desk one final time, assuring herself that all was in order and it appeared as it had upon her arrival to the chamber.

Nodding, she rounded the desk and advanced a hard, swift line toward the door, ready to escape through the house and out into the night, so that she could return home knowing it was *still* her home and it always would be.

Mercy was approximately three feet from the door, from freedom, when the latch started to turn.

She froze.

Everything seemed to slow even as her heart took off like a galloping horse in her chest.

Pressing a hand over her pounding heart, she looked frantically to her left and right, searching for an escape, a place to hide.

The bureau was on the far side of the chamber. Much too far. She doubted she could reach the drapes in time. And hiding beneath the desk seemed like a bad idea. What if he decided to take a seat there?

Helplessness rose up inside her. A thick sob threatened to spill out of her throat, but she forced it down. She held back the sound, and held herself together . . . just as she made the decision to stand her ground.

She lifted her chin and waited for the door to open. It only took moments, a mere blink, but time crawled interminably as she waited for *him* to cross the threshold.

It would be him. She knew that.

The door swung inward and Silas Masters stepped inside his private rooms. *His* rooms. Except *she* was here. Standing where she should not be—in the middle of his room with no explanation for her presence.

No explanation *yet*.

Her thoughts churned feverishly, seeking a reasonable story to give.

He hesitated when he saw her. One of his dark eyebrows lifted, but he otherwise gave no reaction. He seemed very . . . calm. No outrage over confronting a veritable stranger in his room.

Perhaps he was accustomed to finding strange women in his bedchamber. A powerful, wealthy man like him—handsome, no less—likely had women pelting themselves at him at every turn. She distinctly recalled what the woman downstairs had said to her.

Most women who are looking for Silas Masters know what he looks like. That is why they are looking for him.

That was when she knew exactly what to do. As

scandalous and shameful the notion. She had to do it.

"Hello," he murmured. He managed to even look . . . *bored*. Apparently her presence here did not merit a noteworthy reaction from him. "Lost, are you? This is not the ladies' retiring room. Was that not where you were going earlier? I think you mentioned that."

She nodded and made a mild sound of agreement. "I am not lost."

"No?"

"No," she affirmed with a fortifying lift of her chin. "I am right where I want to be." Her voice sounded pleasingly coy even to her own ears.

He canted his head and crossed his arms over his chest. "And where is that?"

Must she say it directly? She swallowed thickly. He certainly did not make seduction an easy matter. Or perhaps she was just very bad at it. She winced a bit at that possibility.

She considered him for a moment, wondering if she was really doing this. Was she really willing to offer herself on a platter to him so that he did not discover her true purpose in his rooms?

She did not fool herself into believing it would be a small matter. If he accepted her invitation she would be in that bed with him. At least she assumed it would happen on the bed. Her experience was limited, but she knew things. She might be from the country, but she was no sheltered maid.

She grew up on a farm and spent a goodly amount of time around livestock. She understood the mechanics involved. Not to mention, she was well-read. More well-read than she ought to be. In fact, her choice of reading material would horrify all of Shropshire. No one would expect it of her and perhaps that was part of the thrill of finding herself in this moment, in this place . . . with this man.

Her gaze fixed on the bed for a prolonged moment, visualizing herself there with Silas Masters. It was not a terrible imagining.

If he took what she was offering him, she would be a maid no longer—not that she was saving herself for marriage. There was no prospect of matrimony on the horizon for her. She had no inclination toward marriage when she had been eighteen. Now at six and twenty, she *especially* was not so inclined. Marriage suited some people. Very well. *Most* people. She had long ago decided, however, that it did not suit her.

Wrong or right, that made the notion of an affair with this man more than palatable. She would finally learn what it was like, what all the fuss was about . . . and in the process she would provide herself with an excuse for her presence in his rooms.

He moved deeper into the chamber, past her,

stopping before a tray with a decanter and glasses. She eyed his lean length as he poured himself a drink and lifted it to his lips with easy, languid movements.

She continued to watch him as he drank, his throat working in an appealing manner before he turned his attention back to her. "You don't want to be here." He stated this very matter-of-factly. "You don't even know me."

Frowning, she glanced down at herself. Did she present as a demure, chaste lady that needed ushering away? "Do I have to know you?"

He took another drink and considered her again slowly, pensively. "So we were introduced downstairs and now you are here to what? Seduce me? Am I to believe that of you?"

Yes. She had to make him believe it. Otherwise he might start looking for other reasons to explain why she was standing here, and that could not happen.

"Is it so very unbelievable?" Her smile felt nervous and shaky on her face and she willed it away. Willed her expression into something mild and relaxed . . . the countenance, hopefully, of a bold woman at ease engaging in casual peccadilloes.

"Must we be longtime acquaintances?" she added as she took a steadying breath. "Would that be so shocking? There is"—she paused, searching for the word to best explain what she was feeling, what swirled thickly on the air around them—"heat between us. Surely you feel it, too."

"Heat," he echoed, the word rolling off his tongue as if it were something alien.

"Yes. I thought, well . . . downstairs . . ." Her voice faltered and she hated that. She sounded unsure and without confidence. Two ingredients that did not fit with the persona she was attempting to project. If she was playing the role of seductress she should be more comfortable with herself and the words she was spouting.

"You thought there was heat," he finished, a thread of skepticism still humming beneath his words.

"Yes." She nodded slowly, propping one hand on her hip. "Did I imagine that?"

He eyed her slowly, up and down, and she managed not to fidget under his regard. "I am sorry if I misled you. You are not . . . to my taste."

She flinched.

There was no *not* reacting to that.

It hurt. It stung. She could not help wondering what was to his taste. If not Mercy, what then? *Who?*

She had not considered the chance of rejection, and she should have. How blindly arrogant could she have been?

She was no model of charm. She was no raving

beauty. Oh, she was not hideous, but she knew beautiful and she was not that. She had never had suitors beating a path to her door.

Of course a man who looked as Masters did was accustomed to beautiful women. Women who far outshone her. Now she felt a fool. A great fool.

"Oh." She smoothed a shaky hand down the front of her gown. "I see."

Indeed, she did see.

For all she knew he was a married man. Or attached romantically. Perhaps he believed in fidelity. Some men did. Her father had been one such man, faithful and devoted every day of his life to Mercy's mother. That would make his rebuff sting less.

She suffered an internal sigh. Now she was simply looking for a way to spare her own feelings.

"I am flattered." He smiled a pitying smile and that was salt in the wound.

It was really too much.

"Very well. Your loss." She hoped that sounded flippant. Like a woman accustomed to casual liaisons—to the occurrence of them and the rebuffs. "I am sorry to have invaded your space," she murmured and made to exit, her face still burning with the sting of rejection, a part of her relieved and a part of her not. That other part of her, the part of her *not* relieved, was markedly disappointed.

So much for her gown. Her fist twisted in her skirts, eager to be rid of the scandalous frock. She would burn the thing when she reached home. She supposed it was not tempting enough after all. Or rather the woman inside it was not.

She had to pass him to leave and she hated having to do so with this shameful heat crawling up her face and the air trapped tightly in her chest.

It would be awkward, however, to take another route—a less direct route. She was not going to circle around and walk between the sofa and fireplace. That would hardly appear the behavior of a confident woman. She would look more like a skittish animal.

She struggled for a careful breath and advanced, walking inches from him where he stood.

They were not touching. Not so close as that, but close enough. Their arms brushed, the fabric of his jacket a whisper against her skin as she walked past.

"Wait." His deep voice dropped on the air, filling the scant space between them. "Don't go."

Chapter Three ❧

$\mathcal{M}$ercy had just passed him when he spoke the words. They echoed in her ears.

Wait. Don't go.

She stopped but did not turn around. He did not need to see her face again. He did not *get* to see her face again. Not as it was. Her heat-radiating face was not his to behold. It was her shame. Hers alone. A private thing.

"Yes?" She tossed the question over her shoulder.

Mercy heard the rustle of movement. *His* movement. He was coming closer. She felt him right behind her. His breath directly on the back of her neck.

It took every bit of restraint inside her, but she held herself still. She waited. Waited for him to do whatever he was going to do . . . say whatever he was going to say, so that she could leave this place unscathed—at least physically—and never come back.

She was rooted in place and it was because of him. Because he had changed his mind about her leaving—at least momentarily.

Why was he keeping her here after he had rejected her and sent her on her way?

She stared ahead. The door loomed. Roughly a dozen feet. She simply had to reach it. Pass through its threshold and she was free.

The voucher burned like a living torch inside her reticule, searing into her hip. Had he sensed it there? Were his suspicions roused? Was that why he had called out to her? Would he make an attempt to search her and her bag?

Her hands were shaking in front of her and she clasped them together tightly, telling herself to get a hold of herself. Now was not the time to unravel. Her nerves were getting the best of her.

She had done nothing to give away her true purpose here. He merely thought her a woman after . . . well, after *him*.

He did not hold her captive. She could keep moving. She should. She doubted he would stop her. He had declined her offer of herself, after all, even if he had just told her to wait and not go.

She was not tempting enough. She should be relieved instead of unaccountably hurt. And disappointed. Very well. *Crushed* would be an apt description.

It was nonsensical though. She was free. She need only put one foot in front of the other and she would be liberated. Mission completed. A success. She could return home and forget all about this aberration.

Suddenly it was more than his breath on her neck. His nose grazed her nape. A hiss escaped her at the physical contact.

"You smell like . . . oranges."

"Oh." Her breath shuddered out of her chest. "Yes." She knew that.

She spent a good deal of time in her beloved orangery. It was what she did—aside from seeing that the farm ran smoothly. The orangery was her pet project. Tending to her trees and experimenting, creating creams and balms and soaps from the fruit and zest of oranges. She tested the products that she sold in Shropshire and local fairs and market days on herself, naturally.

"Oranges," he murmured again and there was a touch of marvel in his voice. She heard him inhale—*felt* it.

His nose shifted, slid over her skin, and she shivered.

She held her breath for a long moment before releasing it. "Do you like . . . oranges?"

"I was a lad the first time I tasted one. It was quite the luxury. A rare treat. I had never even seen an orange before my mother gave it to me one Christmas morning."

"I am sure you can have all the oranges you want now."

And if she meant something more than oranges, something like *women* who were more to his tastes, then she was certain he caught her meaning.

She did not know this man—not really—but she knew enough to know that he was keenly intelligent. It vibrated from him. Gleamed from the deep pools of his eyes. It was one of the things that made her so on edge around him. His ability to look at her and see more than she wanted him to see. At least it felt that way.

The longer she remained in his company, the more likely it was that he would discover her true purpose here. It certainly seemed like a law of probability.

It should prompt her to flee, to tear herself from the fan of his warm breath on her neck, from the sensation of his nose inhaling her skin, and go.

Now. At once. Immediately.

"I can," he agreed in that deep voice that made her knees go weak. "Oranges are no longer so . . . unattainable." Even that simple word—*unattainable*—felt laden with erotic promise. "They are well within my reach." His nose and mouth nuzzled her then and she released a ragged puff of breath. "But it is the sweetness of the memory, no?"

Why did it feel like he was talking about something other than food?

He went on, "The delicious smell that brings it all back and makes your mouth water?"

She made a garbled sound of assent and turned around to face him—which was, yes, the opposite of fleeing.

The opposite of smart and sensible and self-preserving.

The opposite of modest and lackluster Mercy Kittinger.

He was directly in front of her. The air sawed from her lips, as though she had run a great distance and could not recover her breath.

She sank her teeth into her bottom lip until she tasted pain. Releasing it, she asked, "Do you want a sampling . . . of oranges?"

His eyes, intent and deep, peered into her face and she felt certain he could see everything then, into her very soul, beyond the surface of her skin and flesh and bones to the truth.

Hopefully, the foremost truth he read on her face was how very aroused she was and not that she had stolen a voucher from his desk. *Not* that she was a thief.

"A sampling of oranges?" he husked as though

contemplating that. "Is that what you will taste like?"

There was a decided shift in the air. A change in the room's atmosphere, in his eyes, in the way he looked at her, in the way he watched her. Even his mouth looked different as it shaped and formed words. Softer. Touchable.

Kissable.

Now she had snared his interest.

She was not certain how she had accomplished such a feat, but that lessened the sting of his earlier rejection a modicum.

"Yes," she answered, committed to the role she had assumed. She would see this to the end.

"Oranges. Unusual perfume for a woman."

"I am an unusual woman."

His lips twitched as though amused. As though he doubted that about her. It was irksome. "Are you then?" he queried.

She moistened her lips, hoping it was an enticing measure and she did not look like a cow back at the farm licking its lips with an enormous and inelegant tongue. "I think you are coming to realize that I am." He had stopped her from leaving, after all—and sniffed her neck. That had to signify something.

"Perhaps," he allowed, looking contemplative and not so amused anymore.

A sudden rush of nervousness assailed her, but fortunately it was not stronger than the other feelings besetting her, primary of which was the desperate desire to not get caught. Mixed in there with that overriding compulsion, however, was a fair amount of arousal.

Yes, she knew enough to recognize that particular sensation. Her mind stored a wealth of knowledge on the subject of arousal. She might be a virgin, but she was no novice. Indeed not.

When Bede left home, she naturally gave his room a thorough cleaning and discovered a plethora of books. Novels, memoirs, collections of the most graphic content, including illustrations of equal lewdness. She should have been appalled. She should have burned all of them like a proper lady would have done.

Instead she had pored over them, practically memorizing the erotic stories and illustrations of fornicating couples.

She kept them still, all these years later. In her bed at night, by candlelight, she read those pages and studied those images until she knew all there was to know about copulation. All the various positions . . . all the places that mouths and tongues could be placed. To say nothing of hands.

Her hands had mimicked and learned from the books, fondling herself, bringing herself to gasping, writhing pleasure in the privacy of her chamber.

She would close her eyes and imagine her hands belonging to someone else. It was always a faceless stranger. A man with big, solid hands and a hard cock.

A man, she realized, not unlike the one standing before her.

She moistened her lips. He was terribly exciting. Strong and beautiful to behold. It would be no sacrifice on her part to join him on that bed. She could finally satisfy her desires and rampant curiosities with a partner.

It would no longer be *her* solitary hands wringing pleasure from her body. She could use him for that. When would she ever get another such opportunity? A chance to escape the shackles and responsibilities of home and engage in a wild romp where she could exercise all her lustful fantasies and bone-deep longings.

If he was willing, of course . . . and it sounded like he just might be.

Perhaps, he had said.

With her heart in her throat, she lifted her hand from her side and placed it on his chest, palm down over his heart. The beating thump rose up to kiss the pocket of her palm. "Do you want me to stay after all then?"

Breathe, Mercy. Breathe. Do not behave as though this were so out of the ordinary.

Even if it was.

She gazed at Silas Masters's face, at his shadowy features, waiting for what the final verdict would be.

"Why don't you show me what you would like to do?"

"What I would like to do?" she echoed uncertainly. She did not want to mistake his meaning.

"To me. Yes. You said you felt heat between us. Then show me." He lifted one shoulder in a shrug. "What do you do with this heat?"

What do I do with this heat?

As though this was a normal occurrence for her.

As though seducing a man outside the realm of her fantasies was a regular event.

She supposed it was a good thing that she had convinced him of that. He believed her capable of seduction.

She quickly fortified herself with the assurance that she was not *in*capable. She had ideas. Plenty of them. Her imagination was ripe and she had years of reading and practice—if only with herself. She had been warming up for this for a long time even though she never realized it.

She was ready.

As ready as she would ever be. And if she

wasn't, she had to press on. She had to put aside any reservations and do this. She flexed her fingers against his chest, the joints bending as though she were preparing to play an instrument. And in a manner, she was.

She enjoyed the sensation of his chest. She could only imagine she would enjoy it more if there were no barriers of clothing between them. If she could see him, feel him, a real flesh and bone body.

She licked her lips and added a second hand to his chest. But this time she did not demurely hold her hands in place. No, they moved. Emboldened, she went at him like he was a present to be unwrapped, peeling off his jacket, his vest. His garments hit the floor with force. Her greedy hands kept going in a feverish flurry.

She seized his shirt, grasping twin fistfuls of fabric and pulling it over his head. He neither helped nor hindered. Simply stood and allowed her to undress him like the great present he was.

And he was undeniably a present.

She did not harbor unreasonable expectations. Granted, the male figures in Bede's books were all magnificently proportioned with mythical godlike physiques. But she knew the reality of man skewed more toward pudding paunches. At least that was what was prevalent in Shropshire.

Except this man and his figure looked promising. There was no hint of a pudding paunch on him. Indeed not.

Her eyes widened as she assessed him, her gaze skimming, sliding over the hollows and curves of his taut skin. He had muscles under all that lovely flesh. Even as he stood before her that skin rippled and moved over muscle and sinew and bone and she wanted to explore all of him with her hands, her lips, her tongue. He was a powerfully built man. The sight of him was much more gratifying than all those exaggerated illustrations. This man was real and he was hers to have. Her belly tightened.

Her hands dove for the front of his trousers. Her fingers dipped and curled inside, sliding down against his lower stomach, her nails lightly scoring the smooth skin. There was the barest sound of his breath catching. She felt it more than she heard it. Just as she felt his gaze drilling into her. He watched her with intense eyes and it was too much.

That face, those eyes, his body.

She could take no more.

She eagerly yanked on his trousers and the motion caught him off balance. He stumbled forward a step, bringing them almost flush. His eyes flared wide as her hands worked feverishly between them, tearing open his trousers and shoving them down. Down to his knees. Down to his ankles.

She was squatting now, awkward perhaps with her gown puddling around her and his feet.

Her mouth sagged open on a silent gasp. There, at her eye level, was his cock. It was big and getting bigger before her very eyes.

She had seen a naked man before. Naturally. She had grown up in a household with a father and a brother. It was she at the end who nursed her father in his final year. And she and her brother had been brought up together.

There were also the illustrations in her brother's books—though they bordered on the absurd. When she pored over those erotic books she thought that the depictions of the male member were more like something that might belong to an elephant. Thankfully, Silas Masters did not have one of *those*. Although he was impressive.

"Why do you look so . . . relieved?" he asked in that voice that would forever remind her of a growly wolf.

She wet her lips. "You're just—" She stopped herself from blurting out what she was truly thinking. *You don't have an elephant cock.* "Better than I imagined."

All of him really. Truly. He was *better*.

More beautiful than anything that existed in her fantasies. Goodness, she had kept her fantasy lovers faceless for a reason—because she did not even have a partner in mind. No one around Shropshire had ever struck her fancy to such a degree that she fantasized about a specific individual.

That would no longer be a future dilemma for her. She would have plenty of fodder for the imagination. This man would fuel her for years to come.

"I would be interested to hear about these . . . imaginings of yours. Are they specific to me? Hmm. I think not. We just met. I gather these are long-standing."

"Well," she began rather breathlessly. "*Now* they are specific to you."

He smiled then, slowly and beguilingly, and her stomach pitched. The sight of it on his handsome face was a mysterious thing. Those unfurling lips were like a forest on a moonless night, with all kinds of magic humming below the surface, out of sight, but real and present. As real as the nose on her face.

Her gaze dropped from his eyes to his manhood. He was inches from her. Her lips so close, her nose even closer. So close she could smell him, the male musk of him, a faint aroma of salty skin, soap and the heady scent of leather.

He had grown even bigger. Still nowhere in the vicinity of the illustrations she had studied for so many years, but he was not without intimidation. He would still have to go inside her and that looked as though it might hurt.

Very well. Not *have to*. She wanted him inside her. That cock buried deep. She wanted this. She was salivating for it.

She had created this entire scenario and not even fled when the chance presented itself.

The prospect of them joined together, of him moving inside her, made her belly squeeze. The core of her tightened and throbbed between her legs. She longed for it, for that part of him to fill her. Even if a small inner voice told her this was madness and she should flee.

Even the thought that there would be pain at the start did not deter her. The prospect was too thrilling, and she was no young maid anymore. Women her age were married with children— veterans in the matters of the flesh. This moment was long overdue. She did not want or need marriage or children, but she *wanted* this. She needed this.

Her gaze hungrily traveled over his swollen member. *That*. She needed that beautiful instrument.

She would finally have something to fill the ache, and that had her trembling with anticipation. With that thought fueling her, she reached up and wrapped her fingers around him.

He gasped softly. She sent him a quick look, gratified at the expression of rapture on his face.

That look was enough to motivate her. Not that she needed further incentive.

Her gaze shot back down to her hand wrapped around his member. Nothing could have prepared her for the sensation of his skin, so soft, like silk. But there the softness ended. He was hard and pulsing under that satiny texture.

She stroked him in long pulls that soon had the breaths shuddering out from him and his hips thrusting up into her hand. She had never felt so powerful. So in control.

Her own breath came out faster. The ache between her legs intensified until she felt the familiar build of her own climax. That was shocking. She did not know it could happen so quickly. He had not even touched her yet. She was doing all the touching—and to him, not herself as was usually the case. She was ready to explode from this alone.

She felt like she was someone else in this dress, in this room, with this man. Even the very air she inhaled felt different, tasted different. Not like oxygen at all but something bred of desire and instinct and the thrill of danger and the forbidden.

She closed the last bit of distance separating them and pushed forward and licked him. Once. Twice. Three deep savoring licks to the plump head of him.

The blood simmered in her veins. She had played this countless times in her mind. She had read about it in her lurid books, observed it in the illustrations, but now she was doing it and it felt surreal. This seeming lack of reality emboldened her.

She savored the head of him between her lips, loving him with her tongue like he was the sweetest lolly, before she sucked him in deeper, her cheeks hollowing out as her mouth slid down the full and considerable length of him.

Recalling everything she had ever read, she worshiped him with her mouth until he seized her by the arms and hauled her to her feet.

"What are you . . ." Her voice faded away. His eyes felt like hot pokers on her, sizzling her skin, robbing her of speech.

Breathing heavily, she held his stare. His gaze fixed on her lips, his fingers following, landing there, thumbing over her swollen flesh, sliding back and forth as though needing to feel her cock-bruised mouth for himself, needing to verify the evidence of her desire.

He moved then, his hands hooking beneath her arms. He lifted her off her feet and in a few short strides carried her to that giant bed of his where he unceremoniously dropped her on it in a flurry of skirts she detested and wished were gone.

He had his own demon garments to shed. He kicked at the trousers trapping his feet, giving a curse as he went down.

She released a small yelp and sat up, peering down over the bed where he had disappeared from sight.

Suddenly he popped up, fully naked and free of his garments.

She giggled and a grin broke across his once serious features. That grin was breathtaking. Her chest ached just looking at it.

Her hands flew to her laughing lips as he hopped down onto the bed beside her, his dark hair tossing carelessly with his actions. The sound of her own laughter astonished her. She had not heard it in a while and the sound was rusty, like a knife blade that had long since gone dull. She had not realized that. Had not realized how very grim and cheerless her days had become. All work. All rote and no spontaneity. No levity.

Not only did mirth feel strange in this moment of passion with this stranger, but it felt wrong. She had always imagined passion to be a very serious matter. Intense. Consuming. Splendid, yes, but not a humorous undertaking.

As quickly as it arrived, however, the light-hearted moment passed.

His smile faded. Things suddenly felt very serious as he crawled toward her on the bed. Intense. Consuming. Splendid. It was all of that and more as he came over her, reminding her of a great predatory cat.

Except she was not prey. Indeed not.

In this, *she* was the initiator and the creator. It had been her fantasy for years and if it was to be only this once, this single time . . . then she would make certain the experience went according to her every wish.

Chapter Four &

*M*ercy did not flinch or shy away as he came over her. Not in this, a situation of her own making. She would not permit maidenly virtue or convention or her button-down upbringing to get in the way of having this for herself. And this was for herself—even if she needed to do it, even if it was necessary.

"You're a bold lass. Very sure of yourself, are you not?"

She looked up at him. "I know what I like."

Strangely that was the truth of it. She had years ahead all to herself, an old maid alone in her house, for surely one day Grace would leave, and Bede could never be expected to stay. Her future loomed . . . alone. Alone in her bed. Alone with her wicked books, perfecting the art of her own climaxes. She did, indeed, know how to achieve her own pleasure, but now she had this man with whom to do it. For one night at least.

She licked her lips, tracing the upper one slowly before her tongue darted over the bottom. "Don't you?" she asked, staring at him beneath half-mast eyelids. "Know what *you* like?"

He considered the question for a moment before answering, "I thought I did, but now you're in my bed."

Ah, yes. She was not to his tastes. He had said that. It had rightly stung.

She pulled a pout and dragged a hand across her amply displayed bosom, noting the way his eyes followed the path of her hand and she felt instantly gratified. Presumably, he was not immune to the sight of her.

"You wouldn't normally want me in your bed?" She felt giddy and breathless as she coyly posed the question.

He responded by placing two hands on either side of her head on the bed and lowering himself until his nose grazed her cheek. He inhaled her again. "Like I said, I have my preferences."

"I recall. And I am not to your preference." She arched an eyebrow, that scaldingly embarrassing moment fresh in her mind.

"How quickly you have convinced me otherwise." He shifted slightly and the heat of his naked body radiated over her.

She smiled. "I am persuasive in that way."

"Then don't let me stop you. Keep persuading."

She wiggled under him, hoping to gain a little room between them, just enough room to maneuver. "I am vastly overdressed. Do you want to help me correct that? I am more persuasive with my clothes off."

Where did these words come from? Who even was she? Her face burned. She had no notion where such skill for provocative repartee originated, but he did not hesitate to oblige.

His hands made quick work of the buttons on her gown.

First her dress came off, then her corset, her chemise, petticoats and drawers. All was removed, soaring through the air like birds in flight, until she was as naked as he was.

His eyes moved over her feverishly fast, missing nothing.

Watching him watching her was its own form of delicious torment. His eyes went dark, fathomlessly deep, intense and impossible to decipher. His nostrils flared and she swallowed thickly, feeling caught, pinned as his gaze touched her everywhere . . . breasts, belly, the juncture of her thighs.

She had never felt so . . . examined, so seen. There was no hiding. Fire lit a path everywhere his gaze tracked.

She couldn't stand it. As blistering as his gaze

felt, she needed actual contact. She needed his touch. The feel of his hands on her skin.

She squirmed under his regard, whimpering and reaching for him, desperate to get to it.

She didn't reach him before he reacted, moving, hauling her to him.

The two of them came together, bare limbs sliding sinuously against each other—and there was that tempting cock of his.

Her hands greedily seized it, both palms wrapping around it this time, anxious to have him shuddering under her hands again—eager to feel that silken steel in her grip.

"Whoa, there." He plucked her hands off him. "I shall spend myself before we have done even half the things we want to do."

She made another dive for him. "But I want—"

"No," he said emphatically, dodging her and rolling her over so that she could not take him in her hungry fingers again. "Show me something else you want."

She paused. *Something else?*

Her gaze skipped from his eyes down to his inviting mouth nestled in that darkly lush, well-tended beard. She could freely touch him there now. He would permit that.

She did just that. Ran her fingers through the short bristles, marveling at the softness.

She brought her face closer to the soft pelt, nuzzling him like a purring cat, imagining the sensation of his bearded face elsewhere, *everywhere*. On her breasts, her belly, the insides of her thighs.

He felt marvelous. She brought her lips to his cheek, nibbling toward his lips. Her tongue darted, testing, stroking, licking.

Her open mouth traveled along the hard line of his jaw. Excitement continued to twist inside her and she nipped that jaw before going down to his bare neck, his skin so hot and velvety and delicious against her tongue.

He groaned as she continued to explore him, savoring him, getting herself worked into a frenzy in the process.

She sat up higher, pushing against his broad shoulders. He fell on his back as though she were some powerful creature he was helpless to resist. She straddled him and settled her aching woman's core directly over the ridge of his cock, aligning him perfectly with the weeping crevice between her folds.

Reveling in her control over him, she tossed back her head, sliding along him, the wet friction offering no resistance as she worked over him, gasping when the head of his cock bumped into that sensitive button nestled at the top of her sex.

She went deeper then, grinding down on him

until moisture rushed between her legs, soaking them both. His hands came down on her hips, gripping her tightly, his fingers digging into her flesh as she rode toward her climax, recognizing the sensation as it built inside her.

She dropped her hands on his solid chest, using him for leverage as she barreled closer and closer, rubbing herself over the length of him as his hot eyes burned into her, watching her as she chased after her pleasure—and finally reached it.

She arched her spine and came apart, pushing her palms down on his hard chest as an exultant shout bubbled up inside her.

He held himself still beneath her as she broke and shattered over him, her head flung back as she cried out.

She had never made a sound whilst in the throes of passion before. Of course she had always been alone in those moments, her face turned, buried in her pillow. Even if she had not been concerned with staying quiet for fear of her sister overhearing her, she had never felt like this, never felt so wrecked, like she was flying out of her skin. Never had she made a sound above a gasp or even felt compelled to. Her climaxes had been so *controlled* by comparison.

There was nothing controlled or mild or manageable about this. She dropped her head back down and fixed her gaze on him with incredulity.

His own stare moved over her like a hungry touch. She grasped one of his hands on her hip, peeling it off her and placing it on her breast.

She held his hand there, molding it to her, guiding him to squeeze the aching mound. He didn't need prompting. He readily clasped her breast and leaned forward, pressing his mouth to the valley between her breasts. Starting there, he kissed her, loving her with his tongue, grazing with his teeth as his hands continued to knead and play and fondle her.

His fingers found her nipples and rolled and pinched them, pushing her right back to that razor-sharp edge. Already. So soon. Again. She did not think it possible. Every inch of her shook and convulsed.

She had never wrought more than one release from herself in a single night, but his broad palms over her, on her, working her into a frenzy was too much.

With a sobbing cry, she fell over him, pushing him back down on the bed. Her hands dove through his hair, grabbing fistfuls of the strands as she crashed her mouth over his.

She did not even care that she was inexperienced at this part of the intimacy game. In the privacy of her bedchamber, she had not managed to perfect the art of kissing and she knew she was clumsy and inept. She had never kissed anyone on the mouth before, but she was driven by raw primitive need.

She had to kiss his beautiful mouth.

Her lack of experience did not seem to matter to him. He met the wild collision of her kiss with an open mouth and questing tongue. The desperate mating of their lips, tongues and teeth was all consuming. Without dignity. Without restraint or ease. Intimacy—kissing specifically—did not, she dimly realized, need to be neat or skilled or gentle. It was better this way. Like this.

This way it was perfect.

The wilder, the better. The more primal it all felt. The more . . . right. *Honest.* Perhaps the only honest thing between them. The only honest thing about this night.

She dragged her fingers from his hair to his face, her nails clawing through the soft pelt she wanted to rub all over her body.

They were both breathing hard through their noses and around the breaks in their ravenous and unrelenting mouths.

The impossibly hard length of him still slid against the wet seam of her sex. She rolled her hips, ground down, seeking pressure.

Just a slight adjustment. A lift and push and he would be home.

She would be fully seated upon him. *Full of him.*

She reached between them, seized his cock, closed him in her hand, wrapped her fingers around the rigid rod that jumped and pulsed in her grip. He groaned and she gave another squeeze of his manhood, ready to feel his hardness inside her. She was so wet and so ready.

Raising her hips, she dragged the tip of him along her, up and down, until he trembled beneath her. And that was something. A very heady something, emboldening her further.

She poised him over her opening, played with him just a little bit, dipping and easing him inside her channel.

She trembled, too, her thighs quaking from holding herself above him and from the restraint it took to not sink down on him.

"Please," he choked, begged.

He begged.

And that was the very last thing she could endure. It was like something out of a dream. Out of one of her fantasies. This beautiful man was begging for *her* when the only thing she wanted was *him*. Her core ached, clenching with fiery need. There was no sense waiting another moment.

Her hips moved, seeking, lowering herself down

until she was completely and blissfully impaled, his member wedged fully, pulsing inside her.

A broken gasp wrenched from her lips. Their heavy breaths merged, mingling between them, warm and thick as vapor.

He was inside her.

Bigger. Harder than she had imagined, than she dreamed. It was done. She was a maid no more.

There was no regret. Only delight.

She moaned at the stinging pleasure. The burning stretch of her inner muscles felt good. Pleasure throbbed between her legs, any pain residual and fast fading away. Apparently her body had been waiting for this. For him.

His strong fingers grasped her hips, anchoring her above him as he surged all the way inside her, pushing impossibly deeper. She could not fathom how there was any more of him to take. But more of him there was . . . and take she would. She wanted all of him and not a fraction less.

Her trembling arms stretched between them, her palms braced upon his chest, holding her up. She wiggled over him and his cock pulsed inside her.

She brought her mouth down to his again, feverish and hungry. She kissed him, tongue warring, teeth nipping until the ache grew too intense between her legs and she tore away to pant heavy breaths as she began to move, working above him, rocking and sliding him in and out of her, the friction unbearably intense.

She whimpered, moaning in a way that was not even human to her ears. Widening her legs, she ground down on his cock, sinking lower, taking him in even deeper, nudging at some before-undiscovered area inside her.

An especially sensitive little spot. His cock brushed against it and she released a sharp cry at the sensation. Moisture rushed anew between her legs. She angled her hips so that he could hit the slippery little spot again. And again. And again.

Delighted, she continued to move, using his body for her pleasure. She worked over him, increasing her tempo as desperate, dark little sounds escaped her lips amid their wild and broken kisses.

She tangled her hand in the long strands of his hair, pulling roughly, excited at his grunts.

Moaning, he buried his head in the crook of her neck as she rode him, fast and savage, pumping her body over him with unchecked ferocity.

He choked on speech. "I—I'm . . ."

He shuddered under her, reaching his climax.

That didn't stop her from claiming her own. She pounded harder over him as his cock vibrated inside her.

Tossing her head back, a scream poured from her as she shattered inside. *Again.*

Ripples of delight eddied through her. She trembled as she fell over his body, limp and completely spent.

She flexed her fingers against him, clinging to him as though he were a lifeline. Gradually, a realization came over her. She had thoroughly ravished him. And she had reveled in every wild moment of it.

"That was . . . brilliant," she gasped, shoving the hair off her forehead to meet his dark gaze.

He stared at her with wide eyes full of wonder, blinking slowly as though returning to himself, too. "Indeed. That was . . ." His voice faded as though at a loss for words. He rubbed at the top of his head, sending the dark strands flying in every direction.

"Brilliant?" she supplied.

He gulped, the tendons at his throat working as he fought to swallow. "Yes," he said in a thick voice as though that single word was difficult for him to manage. As though speech were a challenge for him.

She smiled in satisfaction and lowered her cheek to his chest, still enjoying the sensation of him inside her . . . and the fast thump of his heart against her ear.

She shifted slightly, and felt him twitch, pulse

in her channel and, incredibly, grow hard again. Fresh sparks ignited along her nerves.

"Oh," she rasped, rolling her hips, reveling in the fullness of him inside her. "Again," she commanded in a throaty whisper.

"Woman," he groaned, gripping her hips as she lifted up and slid down his cock. "You're going to kill me."

"But it will be a delightful way to perish."

Chapter Five ❧

$\mathcal{S}$ilas woke alone in a cold bed.

The fire had long since gone out, the wood in the hearth mere ash. The woman was also gone. Vanished.

Strangely, he did not know how long ago she had departed from his bed. He had fallen into a sound sleep after the third time they'd fucked and that was a rarity.

Not the fucking. Although three times was certainly a rarity. She had been insatiable and he had been more than willing. But a sound sleep was not commonplace for him.

He was especially sensitive to sounds and movements around him. How could he have not roused when she stirred and left his bed?

A few hours of sleep a night was all he could ever achieve. He would gladly sleep longer, but he was simply unable. Ever since he was a lad, when he had been too frightened to sleep. He might no longer be a frightened lad, but some habits could not be shaken.

Sleep left one vulnerable and vulnerability was not something he could tolerate in himself. His mother had been vulnerable and it had killed her, so he had purged himself of the condition lest it kill him, too.

Indeed, he was conditioned. Trained. He had thought himself constant. And yet he had broken habit last night and lowered his guard. He had fallen asleep. He had succumbed to the deepest of slumbers. He had slept in a bed with another person. He had deeply and peacefully slept alongside a stranger. He marveled at that.

What creature was she to have made him feel so totally at ease? He had not thought such a thing possible. He had not even longed for it. And yet it had happened.

He stretched an arm over the emptiness beside him, imagining he could still feel the imprint of her on the mattress. Whatever the case, she was real. She had been here.

And she was gone.

If not for her memory and the lingering whiff of oranges, it was almost as though she had never been here at all.

With a noisy yawn, he lifted himself up from the bed, striding naked across the chamber to the hearth. He added a few more logs and stirred the fire back to life. The faint purply-pink tinges of dawn pressed around the edges of the closed damask drapes. He shook his head. Remarkable. He really had slept the night away.

Too bad he knew nothing about her. Unfortunate. There would be no repeat encounters. No more nights together. No more occasions when she unreservedly and thoroughly ravished him.

Not unless she came to him again, but somehow he knew she would not. She was gone and she would not be coming back. Part of her wildness seemed to have stemmed from the awareness that this would be a onetime event. He would have to make do with the memory of it.

He moved to his wardrobe and dressed himself for the day, feeling particularly energized.

Once dressed, he rang for his morning coffee, pulled open the drapes, allowing the light of day to fill the space, and then he seated himself behind his desk, intent on getting started on the day's work.

From the start, he had been determined to know his business inside and out and never to rely on others to do things for him. In his mind that was how a man lost his fortune and he intended to keep what he had worked so hard to build. This was his empire. He alone governed it.

Clarke soon arrived with his coffee and a scone.

He set the tray on the desk and then turned to tidy the room. His valet tsked at the bits of wood and ash that Silas had carelessly spilled onto the rug before the fireplace. He seized a shovel and began sweeping up the debris.

As the two of them worked at their separate tasks, Constance arrived to clean his chamber. The maid usually followed the arrival of Clarke and his morning coffee.

Silas struggled to focus on the open ledger before him. A definite challenge. Lately he was easily distracted. So much of his business bored him these days. The hell bored him.

You were not bored last night. Not in the least. Quite the opposite.

He could still catch a whiff of her scent. Citrus. Oranges. An odd signature scent for a lady. He was accustomed to rosewater or cloying lavender. How was it she smelled so uniquely of oranges?

He gave his head a slight shake. It mattered naught. He would never know, which was just as well. It was for the best. He was not one to engage in random liaisons with strangers. And she was a stranger. Then and still. He had made certain of that by not asking her name.

The encounter was uncharacteristic of him. He was selective, often committing to one woman at a time for a prolonged period of time.

He had lived on the streets for years and observed the ravages of indiscriminate liaisons. He had seen just as many die from the effects of poverty as the pox. It had made an impression. Left its mark. He was judicious.

He had not been with a woman in nearly a year. Not since he and his last mistress had parted ways. Josephine had come to want more in their relationship than the status quo. Whereas he had been content, she no longer was.

It was fair of her to want something more after a time. People changed their minds. They were entitled to that. He did not begrudge her. He should have known the widow would eventually want something more. Another husband. Children. Last he heard, Josie was engaged to a shopkeeper.

Plenty of women attempted to seduce him since he and Josie had ended things (and before). He had resisted. He had declined. It was not a difficult thing to do. He was not a man governed by his passions. Base urges did not rule him—*usually*.

Since Josie he had not even been tempted. He had felt bored and restless . . . never enticed. He had started to wonder if he was finished with women . . . with sex. Whether perhaps that part of his life was over. Yes. At the ripe age of thirty, he had contemplated that he was done with it all. A self-decided celibate.

Except last night had happened and now he knew that part of his life was not over. Far from it. Last night he had not been a man in control. His base urges took over. It was alarming, and again, he was partly relieved his mystery woman was gone. And partly not.

He inhaled a deep breath. Again, he was beset with the aroma of oranges.

He lowered his head, determined to get some work done and forget the woman he was not going to see ever again. He focused on tallying figures.

Once he finished with the week's bookkeeping, he opened the drawer where he had stashed the vouchers from the previous week. He needed to attend to them. For these, Silas utilized agents to fetch the items acquired or visit the properties obtained, and then he would decide how they might be dispensed of for profit.

Occasionally, Silas might keep a property or item that snared his interest. He owned a flashy phaeton he had won in a game of hazard a few months ago. Although he did not recall anything from the previous week that had quite dazzled him. He doubted he would be keeping anything.

He flipped through the vouchers, thumbing over the notes and refreshing his memory on the week's winnings. Even though he owned a gaming hell, he did not frequently gamble. However, sometimes a ripe pigeon drifted in off the streets and it was simply too easy. If Silas did not take advantage of the opportunity, someone else would and he was above all a businessman at the end of the day. Very well, an opportunist. He was not ashamed to admit it. When one came from nothing—*no*. Not nothing. When one came from hell, one did whatever possible to keep from going back.

He was only partially through the small stack, already calculating which agents he would need to engage for each acquisition, when he landed on one piece of paper that was not a voucher.

He stared at the unfamiliar handwriting. The unfamiliar looping scrawl, feminine if he had to guess. It was a note. A single sentence.

I'm sorry.

He stared at it for a long moment, trying to make sense of it. What did it mean and how had it found its way amid his vouchers?

I'm sorry.

He lifted the slip of paper higher. Leaning back in his chair, he examined it for a longer spell.

Why, amid his weekly vouchers, had someone inserted an apology note? Presumably it had been left for him to find. As an amends of some kind?

Seized with a sudden thought, he dropped the note to rifle through the stack of vouchers with feverishly swift fingers, softly counting them under his breath as his unease grew. He thought there had been twelve of them. When he dropped them in the drawer a couple of days ago he had counted twelve. He was certain of it.

He went through them again, and then again, muttering the words writ upon each voucher, tracking them in his memory. He recalled his winnings . . . one was missing.

Which one?

Which one . . .

His head shot up. He stared ahead, unseeing and yet seeing. Seeing so clearly. Remembering. Remembering everything in the harsh light of day that now spilled into his chambers.

A voucher was indeed missing. The voucher for a farm somewhere in the north.

He recalled the young man from whom he had won it. He was a memorable individual. The fellow had stood out from the moment he stepped inside the house. If his bright purple jacket had not served as beacon enough, the man's manner would have proclaimed his presence.

Silas had watched from a distance as he lost everything—the money in his pockets, the signet ring on his finger, the watch dangling from his waistcoat. Everything he had on him. Gone. Gambled. Lost. Silas assumed he would leave then, take his departure at that point with his tail tucked. There was no reason for him to have remained.

But he had.

He had gone one step further. Silas had seen it before. Some fool hoping to recoup all he had lost and not walking away when he should. The man was not going to leave until he was well and fully ruined. Until he was broken and completely destroyed.

There was no saving him—not when he was so determined to defeat himself. Not that Silas was in the habit of saving foolish young bucks born into privilege but destined to throw it all away so recklessly.

So, yes. He had taken a seat at the table and in one hand won the green lad's home and lands.

He angled his head, trying to recall the details. The precise location of the property. The name of that callow gentleman.

He rubbed at the center of his forehead, urging the memory to return.

Shropshire.

That was the name of the village near the property. He could almost envision it. Some idyllic farm set in rolling hills dotted with fat sheep.

Silas had won it. It belonged to him.

Except it did not. Not anymore.

He did not possess the voucher any longer that would prove him as the rightful owner of the farm.

He quickly flipped through the vouchers again to make certain he had not missed it. No. He had not. It was not among the other vouchers. He dropped the slips of paper onto his desk. It was gone. The only thing in its place . . . an apology.

An apology left from the thief?

He nodded. It seemed the only conclusion. He stared at the words again. *I'm sorry.* Apparently the thief felt guilt over his thievery. Why?

A short gasp tore his attention from the note. Constance recoiled from his bed as though a snake lay curled up inside it.

"Constance?" He rose from his chair.

The maid flickered wide eyes his way, looking him up and down. "Are you injured, Mr. Masters?"

"Injured?" He approached the bed, a frown pulling on his lips. "No. Why do you—"

His words died abruptly as he stopped beside his bed next to Constance.

The maid looked from the bed to him and back again. She inched away from him, hugging one of his pillows close to her chest like a much-needed shield, as though she was fearful of being too close to him.

The woman had long been in his employ and

never looked at him with fear before, but now wariness radiated from her.

He followed her gaze to his bed—to his bedding. Stained with blood. The streaks of crimson were faint but no less startling, no less identifiable.

It was blood and it was not his.

"Mr. Masters?"

He looked sharply at Clarke who had come to stand beside him.

Like Constance, his valet assessed him, although his look was more curious than suspicious. He had been with Silas a long time and served him most faithfully ever since Silas had saved him from what was certain to be a tragic fate at the hands of some street ruffians who decided to beat him simply because he was smaller and vulnerable.

Silas gestured weakly to the bed and then lifted that same hand behind his head, rubbing at the back of his neck in agitation.

The blood was not his. It had to be hers. He suddenly felt ill. His stomach roiled.

Had he hurt her? Had he been too rough? He shook his head, rejecting the notion.

He was always mindful to treat the women in his life with care and respect. After what happened to his mother, how could he not?

Still, his mind tracked over the events of last night. She had voiced no complaints or objections.

Quite the opposite. If anyone could be described as the aggressor, it would be his mystery woman. She had taken the lead and he had permitted her to have her way with him.

"Constance," Clarke spoke in his ever-efficient tones, "why don't you go down and fetch fresh bedding for Mr. Masters?"

She nodded jerkily and jumped into motion, clearly eager to have the distraction of something to do and be gone from the room in that moment.

Silas could not move, however. He could only stand by and watch, a deep sinking sensation in his stomach as she removed the bedding, wadded the voluminous fabric into a ball and carried it away, holding it from her person as though it were poisonous.

His mind worked, thinking, struggling with the facts: blood on his bed. It could only be one thing. That was virgin blood. As improbable as it seemed, a virgin had seduced him with all the skill of courtesan. Unlikely and nigh on impossible . . . but true.

Why?

Why would a virgin await him in his rooms to seduce him? It was not logical. He did not consider himself such an enticement that a lass would spot him on the streets or across a room and decide to dispense with her virtue instantly and impulsively—on *him*. Oh, he knew he was attractive. He knew he possessed wealth, but they were strangers ultimately.

Unless she possessed a motive that made it a logical act.

He considered that. *What would make it logical?*

What could prompt a woman to toss aside her virtue as though it were something inconsequential? She had not been fresh out of the schoolroom. She had to be five and twenty at least. Perhaps older even. A woman in full possession of her faculties did not cling to her virginity for so long to simply give it up to a man she had known less than thirty minutes.

The answer materialized in his mind. *He had something she wanted.*

His head swiveled then in the direction of his desk. He stared in the direction of the single slip of paper on its surface. To the note. The apology. The sparse words.

I'm sorry.

He had held a deep breath that lifted his chest. *I'm sorry.* For stealing from him. For using him.

He had assumed the thief to be a man, but that was not very forward-thinking of him. The thief could have been anyone, but in this case it was a woman. A specific woman. He knew that now. He saw that. He saw everything very clearly.

I'm sorry.

She was sorry for stealing from him. For using him and sneaking off like the thief she was.

A dark tightness came over him. She would be sorry, he vowed. She would indeed be very sorry.

He was feeling . . . something. Disappointment. Betrayal. A building wrath that was steadily growing into fury. Complicated emotions—and he shied away from them all, fearful of their intensity.

He had been duped. She had tricked him.

Her weak apology did not undo that. It did not make him feel better or alleviate his determination to see her again, to find her, to make her pay.

Chapter Six ❧

$\mathcal{M}$ercy felt something different on the air.

She was home, but not home as she remembered it. Or perhaps *she* was different now. Home was the same, but perhaps she was not. Perhaps she had returned from Town as someone else entirely.

Certainly she had left London a changed person. Changed in at least one very noteworthy way. And, she suspected, in other ways, too, that had yet to fully surface.

She paused on her walk back to the house from the south field. She lifted her face to the waning afternoon. A breeze rustled the leaves on a nearby oak. The trunk of the tree stretched as wide as a carriage. There were several big oaks like these about the place. Older than the first Kittinger to live on these lands, and that was significant. Her forefather had been gifted this property by the Duke of Penning, over four generations ago.

This was why she had gone to London. To save all of this. To *keep* this.

She released a contented breath. There was no regret. She would do it all over again without another thought. A barrage of memories beset her. Her body sprawled over Silas Masters. The taste of him. The scent. The sensation of his skin under her palms, his member throbbing within her. She inhaled sharply and cast the memories away, fixing her attention on the lovely skyline.

The sun sat low, mostly obscured by clouds. The weather was mild. Mercy sniffed the air. No hint of forthcoming rain. Sometimes she could smell when a storm or rain shower was coming, but she perceived no whiff of that.

That was not the different *thing* she felt.

No. The vague thing she detected was more of a sensation. A crackle on the air. Prickles up her spine.

She peered back out at the horizon. A gentle wind ruffled the tall grass. Otherwise all was still and quiet. She knew the men would be coming up from the fields soon, but for now there was no one in sight.

Compelled, she turned and scanned her surroundings. She spotted nothing—not a single soul. But that did not mean she was alone. Someone could be out there, tucked into the deep foliage, buried in shadows. Watching.

She gave her head a swift shake. She was simply skittish. Guarded. On edge. She had committed a crime, after all.

She was a criminal. Criminals probably always felt this way—constantly looking over their shoulders, fearful of their every step.

She surveyed the line of woods one last time before turning back around. Her imagination was getting the best of her. Nothing more than that.

Readjusting her straining fingers around the handles of the two buckets she held, she continued on, stopping at the house where the workers slept and took their meals. They were all still at work in the barley fields.

Now that winter had passed, the ground was soft enough for planting. She left one of the buckets of potatoes and cabbages she had gathered beside the door, knowing the men would appreciate it for their dinner, and continued on her way.

Her home loomed ahead on top of a sloping hill. Her skirts swished at her ankles, slapping into her bucket as she cut through the verdant grass.

A white fence surrounded the house. Papa and Mama had erected the fence to keep their dog from running loose to the far corners of their property. Like her parents, the old hound dog was also gone now. Mercy had never replaced the dog with another, but they had a flock of cats that never strayed far. Not that the fence served to pen them in. The felines chose to stay near where they always had scraps and plenty of ear scratches.

Their fat tabby was more often inside the house than outside. Unlike his brethren, Whiskers preferred snuggling in an afghan by the fire and being petted rather than hunting mice out of doors.

As Mercy approached the gate, one of their many cats darted across the yard in a gray blur. Fast on its heels was yet another cat.

The area surrounding the house was otherwise free of activity. The curtains hung motionless in the windows.

Her brother was inside, likely napping. Her sister, too. Not napping though. Grace had not napped since the age of two. However, she did not busy herself about the farm as Mercy did. She kept indoors, occupying herself with the lessons Mercy had assigned to her, in addition to her needlework and practicing of the pianoforte.

She knew her sister longed for life away from the farm. Mercy did not blame her. It was natural. She was young and yearned to spread her wings. Mercy wished she could send her away to a proper school or broaden her experiences with travel outside of their little hamlet, but they lacked the funds for that. Even though Mercy had salvaged the farm, they still were decidedly short on funds. Bede had always seen to it that they *never* had a surplus.

As a lad, Papa had insisted he go to Eton and receive a gentleman's education. Papa had turned a blind eye to the truth—which was that they were reaching beyond their means. Bede's gentleman's education had only succeeded in giving him a taste for things above his station.

Papa had promised Mama that Bede would elevate the family, but he had failed to bring Bede up with the understanding that he would eventually return to the land and oversee its management and care for all those who relied on him—his sisters and nearly a dozen staff.

Mercy wondered what Papa would think now of what Bede had done.

What would he think of your actions?

Wincing, she shoved the question away and refused to consider it. She had done what needed to be done.

Passing through the gate, she rounded the house to the kitchens. At the back door, she removed her boots. She knew better than to tromp into Gladys's clean kitchen in the boots she had worn all over the farm today.

Stepping inside, she slid her stocking-clad feet

into her waiting slippers. Turning, she deposited her bucket on the work table for Cook's inspection.

"Ah." Gladys hefted a large cabbage from the bucket. "Look at the size of this marvelous thing!"

"Yes. The garden is doing brilliantly this season."

"Well, considering the bottomless stomach of that brother of yours, that is good news."

Elsie entered the room just then, catching the last bit of her aunt's remarks. "We don't have to worry about feeding him for much longer."

Mercy stilled. "What do you mean?"

Elsie spoke with a casual air as she peered inside the bucket, clearly having no idea of the implication of what she was saying. "He is packing as we speak."

"Packing?" Mercy echoed as though she did not know the meaning of the word.

"Yes. Your brother is packing." Elsie plucked one of the carrots from the bucket and brushed it off before lifting it to her mouth for a bite.

Gladys slapped her hand half-heartedly, prompting her to drop the carrot.

"My brother is packing?" Mercy demanded clarification. She *needed* clarification.

"Yes. He asked for me to launder his jacket so that he could depart with it not smelling of goats and manure."

"We don't have goats," Gladys pointed out.

Elsie shrugged. "Those were his words."

Of course he would say that. Not only did her brother eschew life in the country—he treated their way of life with disdain.

"My brother is packing to . . . depart." It bore repeating. It was too incredible. Too outrageous.

Elsie nodded again.

Good Lord. What was the fool thinking? He could not mean to leave. She had only just returned, successful from her venture.

When she had arrived home from London, Bede had swept her up into a great bear hug, treating her like a conquering hero returning home. For one rare moment, things had felt right. He was happy and relieved and grateful and she had senselessly believed everything was going to be fine whilst she had basked in his uncommon affections.

"I knew you could do it," he had exclaimed. "You never let us down, do you, you clever girl? How did you get the best of that smug bastard? Tell me everything!"

"Bede," she had chastised, disliking his ugly words about Silas Masters.

"Tell me. I must know every detail. I wish to savor his comeuppance."

"Uh." She had looked away uneasily. In no way was she going to disclose the details of her time in

London to her brother. "The only thing that matters is that we can keep our home. It's all ours and we are never going to lose it again."

Even as she had said those words, she realized it might not be so simple. Not with her brother free to go about and offer their family land as collateral yet again.

Bede had nodded in agreement as she proclaimed those words. *It's all ours and we are never going to lose it again.* But there was something vague in his eyes that should have warned her. That should have reminded her. He did not value their home, and when a person did not value something, they did not care if they lost it.

Her sister had entered the room just then and Mercy sent her brother a quelling look, conveying that they should put an end to this conversation at once.

Bede had followed her gaze to Grace and chuckled lightly. "Ah. I see you don't wish to taint tender ears."

Mercy rolled her eyes. So much for discretion.

"I am not a child and you are not my parents," Grace protested. "I have a right to be privy to family conversations."

Mercy winced. She did not wish her sister to know that she had stolen back the voucher—that she was a *thief*. She might not regret it, but it was not something she was proud of either. The specifics of what had happened at The Rogue's Den would stay in her heart and mind forever. Some things need never be shared.

"That lad. Such a shame." Gladys tsked and shook her head, yanking Mercy back to the present. "Never could stay put at home where he belongs, that one."

Mercy stared straight ahead. She willed away the sense of doom threatening to overwhelm her.

Her brother was leaving. She had hoped he would stay this time—at least for a little while. She had hoped he would learn something from his brush with ruin. That he had been rattled into changing. But now she feared that coming to his rescue had only made him *more* irresponsible. He had suffered no consequences for his actions. She had spared him from that.

And yet what choice did she have? Leaving him to face the consequences would have punished all of them: Mercy and Grace, as well as all the staff relying on them for employment.

"Excuse me," she murmured to the others in the kitchen.

Mercy left the room and hurried up the stairs to confront her brother, determined to do something, say something to get through to him. There had to be words that could reach him. Words she had never thought to use before that might work on him now.

He had no money. That had not changed. She might have reclaimed their home, but a purse full of banknotes did not come with it. Any money Bede possessed was still gone, frittered away. Until they harvested and sold the upcoming season's barley, their funds were depleted.

The bit of money Mercy earned from selling vegetables and oranges on fair and market days was safely tucked away in her room. She only went into it for absolute necessities, such as paying the staff their wages if the household funds ran short.

Her brother did not worry over such things. Only Mercy did. Only Mercy saw to it that the staff was paid and this whole place did not fall down around their ears.

She knocked lightly on her brother's slightly ajar door before pushing it open and stepping inside. To an empty bedchamber. No Bede anywhere. Just his partially packed luggage on the bed.

Well, then. He truly was leaving. No mistake about that. She should not be surprised. Irresponsible behavior was his custom in life. And yet she felt something akin to shock. She probed the sentiment cautiously. Disappointment. Outrage.

He could not go out there into the world again. Every time he did bad things happened. And the bad things never just happened to *him*. They happened to all of them.

Shaking her head, Mercy exited her brother's room and walked down the corridor to her bedchamber—where the door was also slightly ajar. She knew she had closed the door earlier. She closed it behind her every day before she headed out.

She gave the door a slight push. It swung open on silent hinges, granting her a view of her room—and her brother rifling through the drawer of her bedside table.

Outrage sizzled through her veins. She could not move. She was frozen. Rooted to the spot, her feet pinned where they stood.

Her mouth opened and closed. Words eluded her. She could only gawk as her brother stepped back from her drawers. He rubbed his chin and looked around the room in speculation, clearly evaluating the space. Clearly on the hunt for something.

Then, as though seized with a thought, he advanced on her bureau. Opening the double doors, he quickly pushed her clothes aside and searched the space, taking care to examine the floor area, too. He lifted out one of her hat boxes. Popping the lid off, he peered inside, rifling through the letters she kept there.

She had seen enough. She swallowed and recovered her voice. "Looking for something, Bede?"

He jerked with a startled grunt, dropping her hat box and scattering her letters everywhere.

"Mercy! You gave me a fright."

"Looking for something?" she asked again, feigning ignorance even though she knew the answer to her question.

She knew what he was doing in her room. He was looking for money. He was stealing from her. Or trying to at any rate. The beastly man. He was her brother. Her twin. And yet she struggled to feel any filial bond with him in this moment.

His expression was almost comical. He was horrified while trying not to look horrified. His smile was falsely bright whilst his eyes flared wide with alarm. That was a little gratifying, she supposed. That he should feel any level of panic at her displeasure with him. She had assumed he did not care one whit for what she thought of his actions. It would be the natural conclusion based on their past history.

"I don't keep it in there." She motioned mildly to her bureau.

He blinked those wide eyes as a deep red flash crept up his cheeks. Astonishing, really. She was not so certain he was capable of feeling any sense of shame. He was not without conscience then. There was that at least. One could hope. Perhaps she could get through to him yet.

"Mercy, sister, I just needed a little bit to tide me over—"

"What little I have is to pay the staff. And for necessities. Without it—" She stopped abruptly.

He should know.

He knew how desperate their situation was. He was the reason. He should understand what she was saying.

He smiled his most cajoling smile, as though that would work on her. As though they had not shared the same womb.

As though she did not thoroughly and wholly know him.

Chapter Seven ❧

Mercy and Bede were born fourteen minutes apart. Bede had pushed his way out into the world first.

Some people were born takers, and Bede was one of them. From the very beginning, he *took*, out-weighing Mercy by at least a pound. The midwife had claimed that he occupied most of the space in their mother's belly, and took more than his share of sustenance.

They had shared a crib. A large crib that the town blacksmith, Mr. Cully, made for them. Mama and Papa had laughed about the time they woke in the middle of the night to find that Bede had taken over the crib. He had turned, rotating his little body horizontally, his feet kicking up a storm all over Mercy. Their parents had to separate them into different sleeping spaces before any lasting harm came to Mercy.

Bede stayed in the crib of rich walnut with

scrolling iron hinges that Mr. Cully had made. Mercy got a wooden milk crate.

As toddlers, they were fed separately because Bede would shriek earsplitting cries each time it was Mercy's turn for a spoonful of porridge. He had no patience for anyone giving attention to another over him. He wanted everything for himself at all times. It mattered naught if it was food or a doll or a ball. If Mercy had it, he wanted it. What was his was his. And what was Mercy's was also his.

It seemed like he had been born greedy and self-serving and it had never been purged from him. He was the darling son. The firstborn. Papa had fully expected him to take over the farm after he finished at Eton, to care for his sisters as a proper patriarch ought to do. Certainly the expectation had never been for him to ruin them and yet here they were now, recovering from the near reality of that.

Perhaps if Papa had lived longer, long enough to see Bede finish his schooling, he would have seen Bede's true nature. Instead he had fallen ill when they were only seventeen, and had been gone a year later, just before Bede ventured out into the world to begin wreaking his ruin.

She inhaled a pained breath. It was as though Mercy was still inside that crib. Still getting kicked by the barrage of Bede's feet. Some things never changed.

"Come now, Mercy," Bede coaxed. "The staff is like family. They adore you. They would never leave you."

She shook her head and chuckled lightly, without mirth. Indeed, there was only discomfort in the sound for her.

"For a man of the world, how is it you know so little of the world?"

He really was a man without sense.

Bede's cajoling grin turned to a scowl. "You need not be so insulting. I am not a dimwit."

She ignored that. "The staff, as much as they may adore me, need a wage to live. If I don't pay them, they will go seek employment elsewhere as is fair and right." That went for Gladys and Elsie, too. Bede was correct to say that they were like family, but family or not, they would go. She shook her head, still grappling with the obvious . . . with the expected. "You would steal from me—"

"I am the master here," Bede inserted, tugging on his brocade vest in an effort at dignity. "I cannot steal from myself." He waved a finger about him. "This house, this land, is mine. I am master here, but I think you forget that, sister. You should turn all the money over to me as is proper. I should have control of all our finances."

She snorted. "That is not happening."

He huffed indignantly.

She moved into the room and started collecting her scattered letters from the floor. "Dinner is in an hour," she said with more calm than she felt.

"I plan to leave tomorrow," he announced, a threatening edge to his voice—as though he dared her to stop him.

"Very well." What else could she say? She could not prevent him from going.

"To do so I need funds." His tone turned petulant, the threat evaporating. "Money," he stressed. "As vulgar as it is to discuss such matters, you force me to say it. I need money."

"If funds are necessary to make your departure, then I do not know what to tell you." She shrugged. "I suppose you will have to delay your leaving."

"Where is the money? I know you have some hidden in here." Bede sent a quick glare about her bedchamber. "You might be content to remain here in this little backwater, but I am not. Papa never expected it of me. How can you? I have a life. I have friends. I have *needs*." He pointed to his chest for emphasis. "I am somebody."

On her knees, Mercy calmly and sedately tucked all her letters back into her hat box. Standing, she returned the box to the bottom of her bureau.

With a deep breath, she lifted her gaze back to her brother. "I must freshen up for dinner."

It was the only response he deserved. She would

not even acknowledge the rest of his ridiculous remarks. There was no sense arguing with him and trying to persuade him that this was *not* what Papa had in mind. No sense in pointing out that she and Grace and the rest of the staff were *somebodies*, too. If he didn't understand that, he never would.

"Mercy! Have you no heart? Please." Apparently he felt the impulse to beg now.

"Me?" She tapped her chest where her heart resided, alive and very much present.

He nodded. "Indeed. What do you think I am doing out there if not trying to uplift our family? Just as our parents wished?"

"How are you *helping* our family?" She scoffed. "By ruining us? For that is what would have happened if I had not gone to London a-and . . . salvaged things."

"I am extending my social circle with an eye to an advantageous marriage."

She blinked. "You? Marriage?"

It was the first she had heard of this from him. A wife would mean less freedom for Bede. He would have to consider someone else's welfare other than his own. It seemed highly unlikely he would do that.

"I am amenable to it. I have been navigating society of late with an eye to courting a number of heiresses."

"Yes, brother, but have these heiresses been amenable to *your* suit?"

Anger flashed across his expression. "I am doing my part, and I am considered quite the catch by many." He tugged on his waistcoat. "What of you? Why don't you marry, sister? If you had a husband, he could help ease some of the family burden. Where is your sense of duty?"

She flinched, but then recovered. With a harsh laugh, she said, "Yes, because I have suitors beating a path to my door."

Her brother looked her up and down. "A new frock might help in that endeavor. And perhaps a little rouge to liven your face. You could also stop working the farm like a regular laborer. Callused hands do not belong on a lady."

"Oh, Bede. Where do I venture where someone might see me in a new dress? Into Shropshire every other week? I know all the lads there, the eligible gentlemen. I would have none of them and none of them would have me." There was no sense even addressing her callused hands. There was no help for that.

"Beggars cannot be choosers, Mercy. Mr. Flockton is a widower with some coin to his name. At least the rumors attest to that."

"Old Man Flockton," she exclaimed, using the

less than flattering nickname. It was not compli-
mentary, but nonetheless true. Mr. Flockton was
on the far side of ninety.

Her brother flicked a piece of lint from his sleeve.
"We all make sacrifices."

He had no idea.

"Oh? Do *we* now?" She rolled her eyes at his absolute temerity.

He continued, ignoring her sarcasm, "You should
not have to suffer him for long I would imagine."

She made a choking sound. "Oh, you are a de-
spicable person."

What would Papa and Mama think of what
their precious son had become? Certainly this was
not what they had imagined.

"Merely pragmatic, sister."

Now that was a ludicrous claim. There was nothing pragmatic about her brother. Not ever on any
day of their lives would she describe him as that.

She propped her hands on her hips. "Would you
please leave me to freshen up before dinner?"

Now more than ever, she needed some space to
herself.

He stood frozen in place, glaring at her in that
petulant way of his that reminded her of when
they were children and he was denied something.
Rare occasion though that was.

Sighing, she realized what needed to be said. It was the only thing that would prompt him to leave her in peace in her room.

He had to realize his defeat.

"I am not giving you any more money. Not a penny." She crossed her arms over her chest resolutely. "You can turn this room inside and out. You won't find it."

His face burned a splotchy red. With a dramatic groan, her brother flung his hands in the air and started from her chamber, slamming the door closed behind him. Just as when they were children. Again, some things did not change. In his case, nothing changed at all.

Satisfied she was alone in her room, she moved to the window seat where she had spent many an hour of her childhood.

She lifted the seat cushion to reassure herself. With a quick glance over her shoulder, she peeled back one of the wood slats beneath the cushion, revealing the money hidden there.

Her shoulders eased at the sight of it. Still there. Still safe and secure.

There it would remain until she removed it. Bede would not get his hands on it.

This, she vowed to herself.

Chapter Eight ❧

Mercy tried to enjoy the tasty meal Gladys had prepared for the evening, but her appetite failed her. Bede sat in peevish silence, eating his food and then helping himself to seconds, piling his plate high with ham, potatoes and cabbage. Apparently his appetite was not affected by his current mood or the unpleasantness of earlier.

Grace ate sparingly, her fork toying with her perfectly buttered cabbage as she looked uncertainly between Mercy and Bede. She doubtlessly felt the tension in the room.

That tension had been present ever since Bede had arrived home. Mercy had done her best to shield her sister from it, but Grace was no fool. It had been difficult enough leaving for London with the lame explanation that she had to visit a sick relation Grace had never even heard of. It was the best excuse Mercy could come up with for her hasty departure, but Grace had looked skeptical.

Elsie entered the room then and eyed the bowls and platters arranged before them as she deposited a fresh basket of bread on the table. "Can I fetch anything else for anyone?"

"We are fine, thank you," Mercy murmured, bestowing a bright smile on the girl.

They finished the rest of the meal with stilted conversation.

Grace perked up at one point to exclaim, "Oh, the Blankenships decided to throw a grand party to welcome the new Duke of Penning to Shropshire. The invitation came while you were gone, Mercy. How lucky are we?" She clapped her hands enthusedly.

Mercy winced. The last thing she felt in the mood for was a grand party in the village. Thanks to her brother, she was not in a social disposition, even if she did enjoy seeing her friend, Imogen.

"Are they now?" Bede replied with a modicum of interest. "I suppose that is something to do around here. The Blankenships always do things in grand style."

Oh, would he give up on this notion of leaving then? At least for a spell? Mercy took a bite of potatoes and considered her brother. Perhaps some good would come of the Blankenship ball if it kept Bede here a little longer and not out in the world wreaking havoc.

"Indeed. That is something to look forward to. Especially as their annual ball is a good nine months away." Mercy hoped she conveyed proper enthusiasm.

Grace hopped slightly in her seat. "Yes! Two balls in such a short period of time. It is unprecedented and quite thrilling."

"God. You are so provincial, Grace." Bede rolled his eyes and looked in reproach at Mercy. "You really should get her to London for a season."

"Oh! I want to go to London!" Grace agreed and looked at Mercy with so much earnestness and hope that Mercy's heart ached for her.

"That would be nice, but we cannot afford it, Bede," she said between clenched teeth.

And well he knew it.

Grace's shoulders slumped in defeat. Blast the man for getting the girl's hopes up.

Bede merely shrugged, indifferent to Grace's disappointment or Mercy's frustration with him as he shoved another forkful of food into his mouth.

By the time dinner came to an end, Mercy felt as though she had just emerged from a skirmish with no clear victor. As her siblings headed off to bed, she expelled a great breath and took a bowl of scraps outside for the cats, clicking her tongue to gain their attention.

They came at her from every side, besieging her.

She spread the food out, tossing it in far-flung directions so that they did not scrabble in one giant hissing mob. They scattered after the food, going in every direction.

She gazed out into the night, breathing the sweet country air, glad to be temporarily free of the house. The windows of the laborers' house glowed with light, and she knew the men were likely finishing up their dinner, too. Otis was a wonderful cook. He was always baking bread and fabulous pies and sharing them with Mercy's family.

Her gaze flitted to the conservatory where she grew her orange trees. Setting down the empty scrap bowl, she headed that way, eager to take refuge there. It was her special place. Uncultivated and overgrown with weeds and broken pottery after her mother's death, she alone had worked to bring it to life again and make it into something for herself.

The door creaked, reminding her that she needed to oil the hinges. She closed it behind her, and sighed, feeling as though she were leaving the world behind her. Not a terrible thing. Indeed not. Sometimes one needed to escape.

She located the lantern situated on a small worktable by the door. She fumbled a little bit but managed to light the thing. A small yellow glow circled out softly from the lantern. Holding it aloft, she strolled down the rows of potted trees, all at various stages of development.

She walked directly to her newest oranges, the sweet Gargano. It was a new breed and she was keenly interested in its progress. She sent off for the seedlings a year ago. They had shipped all the way from Italy.

Stopping before the row of them, she set her lantern upon the floor and caressed one waxy green leaf, cooing to it like it was a baby. "How are you, my love?" She tested the soil in its pot for moisture. "Are you getting enough water?"

Suddenly the door creaked and thudded shut.

"Hello?" She turned around and stepped into the aisle that faced the door, the action taking her deeper into the shadows, away from her lantern.

Silence met her question.

"Hello?" she called out again, standing on her tiptoes, craning her neck in an attempt to see through the trees all around her, suspicious that there was someone else inside the conservatory with her, someone not revealing himself for whatever reason.

The same eerie sensation she had felt out walking the farm today beset her. Prickles raced up her neck. Her hands opened and flexed at her sides in readiness. For what, she did not know.

"Who is in here?"

No answer.

She swallowed nervously and stretched her fingers wide at her sides, bringing them in closer and wiping her suddenly moist palms against her skirts. She did not understand where her sense of anxiousness was coming from. *A guilty conscience perhaps?*

She shoved that notion away. No. She had done the only thing she could do to save her family home. She did not have a choice and she did not harbor any regret.

"Hello?" she called out again, disliking the tremor to her voice.

Several people lived on the farm. The orangery might be her refuge, but it was not forbidden to others. It was likely Grace playing a trick on her. Or Bede pulling a prank like when they were younger. He used to love to jump out and frighten her, delighting in making her cry out.

She started to relax in the continued silence. No one was there. It was merely her overwrought imagination. She nodded once. She must not have closed the door properly behind her. One of the cats probably pushed its way inside. They favored her. She was, after all, the one that fed them. They followed her all about the place. She would no doubt feel the little beast weaving at her ankles in a few moments.

Turning back around, a large shadow materialized before her.

She yelped, her hands flying to her mouth in alarm. She sucked in a breath, trying to slow her racing heart and telling herself that it was merely a family member or a member of the staff standing before her.

"You gave me a fright," she blurted, still unsure who she was speaking to—a man, she decided, based on his looming size.

A man who deigned not to speak apparently.

She stared, straining her eyes to peer intently through the dark, trying to acclimate to the lack of light. She wished she stood closer to the lantern she had left near her Gargano trees. She turned to retrieve it.

Even as she told herself it was obviously Bede, her heart hammered a violent drumbeat in her chest. She located the light where she had left it and spun around, lifting it high, ready to deliver a blistering tongue-lashing to her wretched brother for terrorizing her.

He might be unhappy with his current circumstances, but it was not her fault and he need not be a bully about it.

They were not children squabbling over toys anymore. They had not been that in many years. And in those days he always won, taking whatever he wanted for himself. Those days were over and he had best finally learn that fact.

She stared ahead, blinking in the sudden wash of light. It was not Bede.

No. *No. No. No.*

She staggered back a pace.

It was no one from the farm. No one it should be. No one that made sense.

"What are you doing here?" she demanded as the man stepped forward, advancing more fully into the circle of light.

Had it been only three days since she had last seen him? She gulped so loud she feared he heard the sound. Three days since she had wrapped herself around that body of his? It felt a lifetime ago.

It was beyond a strange thing, not to mention terrifying, seeing him here, in her world, away from *his* world, that domain where she had let go of herself, shed her skin and pushed herself into unfamiliar territory and permitted herself to become a creature of passion. Someone who lived only for herself. Only for pleasure.

He glanced at the orange tree nearest him, brushing a leaf with a long finger. "I see why you smell of oranges now."

Her face caught fire and suddenly she couldn't breathe. It felt like a great unrelenting weight was pressing down on her chest.

He released the leaf and looked at her again. "And taste of them."

Oh. My.

What was he doing here? He still had not answered her first question. "How did you get here?" she demanded.

"Well. I got on my horse and road north."

She flushed and snapped, "You know what I mean."

One of his dark eyebrows winged high. "Oh. You mean . . . how did I find *you*?"

She gave a jerky nod.

He continued, "Your apology note was the first clue."

She closed her eyes briefly in a hard blink. The note had been a mistake. She had left it in a moment of weakness. It had been foolish and soft of her. Not well done at all. Not smart at all.

"I went through all the vouchers and I was missing only one." He gestured around them. "It did not take me long to deduce the rest. This place. This farm." He paused. "It all belongs to me."

Hot emotion swept over her. "No," she growled in a voice that did not even sound like her own.

"I won it," he countered.

"You have no proof of that. It is not yours. This land belongs to my family."

"I won it from Bede Kittinger . . ." He hesitated, considering her. "Given the state of my bedding back in London, Kittinger is not your husband."

"No," she agreed, unsure what the reference to his bedding signified. "I am not married." She sniffed indignantly. Did he think she would have so readily shared his bed if she was married? But what did he know of her? Nothing. Nothing at all. Just as she knew very little of him. Beyond the biblical sense, of course. Her cheeks burned hot.

"Then who is Kittinger to you?"

She swallowed. Silas Masters was here. Standing before her. There was no running from him.

She supposed it did not matter to admit to her actions now—or to confess that her brother had lost their home to him. She had reclaimed her family lands. There was no existing proof to counter their claim on the home that had always belonged to them. She had made certain of that. "That fool was my brother."

He nodded as though that made sense.

"I am Mercy Kittinger. But," she continued, "he is the one with his name on the deed." She flung her arms wide. "I keep this place going whilst he plays and fritters away our money. Whilst he goes to your club and gambles away our home! As though he has ever been a skilled card player." Her chest heaved with a hard breath.

"But he has you," he smoothly inserted, "to clean up his messes and make grand sacrifices for him."

"I do my best."

"Clearly." He chuckled lightly and the deep sound rippled across her skin, leaving a wake of gooseflesh. "And your best is quite impressive, I must say, Miss Kittinger."

Her face burned hot with mortification, her body instantly humming and alive with the memory of what he referenced. Seeing him before her, hearing his voice, feeling his nearness . . . it all came crashing back. She fairly vibrated with awareness of him.

He continued, "I have to ask though. Was it your primary plan to seduce me? Or was that more of a contingency plan? In case I happened to discover you rifling through my rooms? Which I did."

"I did not go to your club with that plan at all."

Her face burned even hotter. No, but she went there determined to do whatever she had to do to get back her lands. She went there desperate. There was no denying that.

"So that was more of a spontaneous decision you arrived at when I walked in on you stealing from me. It was a ploy to distract me from realizing your true purpose."

The guilt she had been denying swamped her. It was irrefutable when faced with him and his accusations. "You could call it spontaneous, yes."

"The note was a nice touch," he complimented and yet his words did not sound like flattery in any way.

She winced. The note was not a nice touch at all. It had been weakness. Stupidity.

He added, "I doubt I would have put it all together so quickly without that courtesy from you."

Wonderful. Her flash of conscience in that moment had landed her in this trouble. Except her conscience had not been her *only* guiding impulse. She had felt a flash of tenderness as she stared at him sleeping, gloriously naked, his chest rising and falling with his deep, even breaths.

"I could not just . . . go," she admitted, her voice a grumble.

"No? You had regrets?" His lip curled in a sneer. "I have a suggestion for you then. Give me back the voucher. That might ease your guilt."

She shook her head. "It is gone."

"Gone?"

"Destroyed."

He could not have thought she would have kept the voucher. She would not be that foolish.

"Your guilt must not be too great then."

No. It was not.

"This land has been in my family a long time. Since my great-grandfather." She stabbed a finger in the direction of the ground. "You had no right to—"

"Your brother made the decision to put up your lands as collateral. Not me. It was his choice. Again, not mine. He valued your family's land so little."

There was nothing he said that she did not already know, but it was still terribly bitter to hear it pronounced out loud by another. "You do not think I know that?" she erupted. "It is not right though. It should not be his to do with as he chooses. He should not be able to gamble it all away."

"But he did." His expression turned coldly furious. "And what of you? Were you any more right to steal into my house? To seduce me as though you had no ulterior motive? As though you were no thief at all?"

"Thief?" she echoed with a hollow laugh. "Well." She squared her shoulders. "I did render a service."

She held her chin high, refusing to be daunted. Let truth prevail. As shocking as it was to admit out loud, he was not left without recompense.

"Oh." His eyes widened and then narrowed on her. "If I remember correctly I rendered *more* services than you did."

"Oh," she breathed indignantly. Her hand itched to smack the arrogance right out of him, which was so unlike her. She had never been moved to violence in the whole of her life. "I heard no complaints. You appeared quite satisfied to me. Do not act as though you were not equally pleased." She shook her head. This was a dangerous path, the two of them recounting that night. She would rather they not speak of their previous intimacy. It left her tingling in places that should not be feeling anything and filled her head with thoughts and images best left to her private reflections. Determined to steer the conversation in a different direction, she demanded, "Why are you here? Truly? I am afraid you are wasting your time. These lands are ours and no court in the land will honor your claim based on your word alone."

"That is true," he acknowledged with an evenness that felt unsettling and at odds with the dangerous glitter of his eyes. "But I am not going anywhere just yet, Miss Kittinger."

Chills started at the back of her neck and rolled over her scalp. "What do you mean? You cannot stay here."

"Oh, but I can. I am."

"No."

He nodded and his absolute confidence made her feel slightly ill. "You see, I am not in the habit of engaging in random liaisons."

She snorted at that with deeply felt skepticism. A man as rich as he? As handsome? As urbane? "Indeed?"

"Indeed," he returned.

"I find that hard to believe."

"You don't really know me at all though, do you?"

She pressed her lips together and held her tongue. He was correct, of course. What did she know of him other than her brother's descriptors? *Ruthless. Powerful. Intimidating.* Thus far, in her brief although thorough experience with him, she would not say her brother was incorrect.

She moistened her lips and adjusted her footing. "Why would you possibly wish to remain here?" He lived in grand London. He could not find this remote little corner of the country appealing.

"Let us say I have a vested interest."

"You have a vested interest here?" She pointed to the ground at her feet. "In my home?" She shook her head. "Too bad. It is not yours to concern yourself with."

"No. I am not interested in your home." He sounded disdainful at the suggestion.

"Then . . . what?"

Was it revenge? On her? On Bede? Did he have plans to exact retribution on them? Was that why he was here?

"My interest is in . . . *you.*"

"Me?" Mercy inched back a step.

"Yes. I realize now that you are not as savvy as I initially believed you to be."

Savvy?

She angled her head, his meaning lost on her. "I do not understand—"

"Your manner was quite seductive. As seductive as the most veteran courtesan. Not an untried country lass. And we both know you were untried."

She flushed. *Oh.* He was speaking of *that.* Of their . . . *time* together. Just because she wanted to avoid that topic did not mean he did.

She was not about to explain the reason for her seeming carnal knowledge. Her ripe imagination had filled in the gaps of her knowledge. Not that she had too many gaps. Her brother's lewd books were quite detailed.

"But you seemed to have failed to consider one very important matter," he added.

She stared at his handsome features blankly, waiting breathlessly, apprehensively.

The murkiness of the orangery did nothing to obscure him. He looked starkly dangerous in the shadows, reminding her that he was not a man to trifle with and yet she had done just that—and it had brought him here. To her doorstep. She was right to feel apprehensive.

She wet her suddenly dry lips. "What matter is that?"

"You could very well be carrying my child."

Chapter Nine ❧

$\mathcal{S}$ilas had never thought to sire a child. He had always been so careful when it came to such matters. But if he had, if he *did*, he would never abandon the child. Not even if the mother was as seemingly capable and intelligent as the one before him.

Silas's own mother had been lovely and intelligent. It had not saved her. Or spared him.

His father had abandoned them. Then his mother had died, but not neatly. Not an easy death that. Not a natural death that took her in her sleep. No, it had been her second husband who took her, who brutally claimed her life and snuffed it out as simply as one put out a candle.

Not that she and Harold had ever truly been married. That could not happen as long as her first husband, Silas's father, was still alive, out there in the world somewhere. And yet his mother and Harold had lived together as man and wife in a decrepit tenement in Seven Dials, pretending to be married. Harold had insisted Silas call him Papa even though the man was the furthest thing from a father to him.

Harold rained his fists down on both Silas and his mother daily until one night, one of those fists had landed one too many times, turning Mama into a broken heap, leaving Silas alone. An orphan for all purposes.

He would never leave a child of his out there to fend for himself. Children needed protectors. *He* had needed protecting.

Things had been no better after his mother's death. Silas was sent to live with her family. A proper Christian family of modest fortune who had disowned his mother when she eloped with his father.

They had a nice house in Belgrave Square. As a lad of eleven Silas had no idea nice homes like that existed. With multiple rooms and servants and fresh flowers and clean sheets that smelled of lavender. And food. Oh, the glorious endless supply of food.

He had gone from a scrawny lad whose ribs poked against his skin to a strapping well-fed lad of ten and four.

And yet his grandfather despised the sight of him.

Apparently Silas bore a striking resemblance to

his wastrel father and his grandfather could not forgive him for that. It was too great a sin.

He used the rod on Silas for any and every seeming infraction. Sometimes Silas hid. The cook had a soft spot for him. She was always plying him with food and often concealed him in her pantry behind sacks of potatoes, flour and sugar, but eventually he would have to surface. Eventually, he would have to take his due beating.

Those thrashings became predictable. He could count on them. As reliable as the daily delivery of milk at the back door. And he perhaps would have stayed with his grandfather, existing as his most contemptible relation . . . until that last thrashing.

He had been caught in his mother's bedchamber, the room she had once occupied that now stood as a shrine to her memory. Silas imagined he could still feel her presence in that space. He could see her there with all her things—the old teddy bear on the bed. A pair of ribboned slippers near the window seat. Her feet had been quite small. He remembered that. The afghan folded neatly at the base of her bed. The face cream and colorful hair ribbons on her dressing table, scattered as though she had just been there only moments before and would soon return.

His grandfather had caught him there in that

forbidden room. He had seized a thick-handled hairbrush from the dressing table and set upon Silas in a furious frenzy.

Usually he took it. Usually he endured the beatings because that man in the nice house with a kind cook who fed him gingersnaps was his mother's father, his grandfather, the only family he had left in the world, and he had felt a deep sense of loyalty to the man.

No one made him take Silas in, but he had. His grandfather *must* care for him deep down. They were blood, after all. Silas had told himself this. He had believed it. Until that day.

Something had snapped inside him that afternoon in his mother's girlhood room. As he had absorbed every painful whack, every panted curse, his eyes had finally opened to the truth. His grandfather's expletives rained down on him with every blow.

Bastard. Filthy bastard. Devil's spawn. I told you to stay out of her chamber. It should be her here. Not you. Not you! You should never have been born, you wretched cur.

If he stayed, he would die. That realization had materialized clearly in his mind. It was not a probability. It was fact.

His grandfather was not family in the true and proper sense. Family did not do the things his grandfather did. Silas had left that day, never to return. He had limped off, battered and bleeding from the house. The streets were safer for him than living under his grandfather's roof. He had made his own way. He had thrived, in fact, but he had never forgotten the lessons of his youth.

Which brought him here to this moment, to this woman—and the mistake he very well could have made.

In all his years of being cautious, it had come to this. He had been reckless, careless, and he could not leave her without knowing if their one night of indiscretion had resulted in a child.

A child he would never abandon.

He could not walk away from her until all of this was settled between them.

"I am *not* carrying your child," she choked out into the humming quiet of the orangery. And yet he did not miss how her hand went to her stomach, as though verifying for herself, as though the simple touch could confirm or deny this.

"You can't know that yet." He arched an eyebrow. "Unless in the three days since we last met, you have . . ."

"I will not discuss anything so personal with you!" She crossed her arms, folding them over her chest as though in need of the sudden barrier. She was so unlike the woman he remembered from his rooms who had pounced upon him. That woman lacked self-consciousness. There had been no modesty to her. Not like the lass before him who was all demureness and looked ready to flee.

He chuckled. "You won't discuss anything so personal with me?" He moved closer. He inhaled the sweet scent of oranges, wondering if that came from the trees or her. "And yet you would share your *person* with me."

Her hands rubbed her arms as though she were suddenly cold.

"It's simple," he continued. "When you are assured that you are not with child, I will leave. Not a moment sooner."

She shook her head in frustration. "It was just the once—"

"It's only *ever* just the once. That's the way it works."

"Of course," she snapped. "I know that. I do not need a lesson on procreation from you."

"Then you should understand this."

"I do. And you will soon see all of this is unnecessary."

"Perhaps." He angled his head. "If it's not, then . . ." He stopped himself with a single shake of his head. Time enough to talk about that later. If needed.

An air of wariness came over her. "If not then . . . what?"

"We don't need to talk about that yet."

"No," she said sharply. "I want to talk about it. Now, please."

"Well." He sighed. "If you are with child, I would be a father to that child. In every way."

She stiffened. "Could you elaborate on that? What does that mean?"

"That means that I will take care of my child. And you, of course, as the mother of my child. That is the right thing to do."

She pulled back as though he had struck her. "This is ridiculous! I will not be your mistress. We don't even know each other."

He blinked and gave a small shake of his head. "Ah. Yes. Indeed. I agree. I don't think I mentioned you being my mistress." Nor had he mentioned marriage, and that was quite deliberate. He had never seen a good marriage worth emulating. He was not about to enter into that state himself.

She sputtered. Even in the shadows he detected the deepening color in her face. Clearly he had embarrassed her.

"I do not require a mistress," he added in a gentler tone. For some reason he felt sensitive of her feelings. "Just as I do not wish for a wife." He might as well say that, too, lest there be any confusion on the matter. "But I will be in my child's life. I will be a father to him and support you both in the process."

"Him?"

"Or her," he acknowledged.

She shook her head and released a shuddery sigh rife with frustration. "I will not have you in my life, lingering about, showing up whenever you like. How shall I explain your presence—"

"And how will you explain a babe growing in your belly?" he sharply countered. "The best solution would be for you to come to London with me. I will set you up in a house and provide for you and the child and—"

"No!" she snapped with a vigorous shake of her head. "I will not leave my home and go with you to be a *kept* woman, for that is how everyone will view me."

"London is a large city. Such things are done there. No one will dare say a cross word—"

"I cannot! I have responsibilities here. People who need me!" She shook her head fiercely again, and he knew he was getting nowhere.

Her breath fell harshly. She fanned herself with a hand as though suddenly overheated. She was on the verge of panic, and he had the completely wild and unacceptable urge to take her in his arms and comfort her. *Comfort* her? *Hellfire.*

He had come here to confront her, to denounce her for the little thief she was. It should not be his impulse to comfort *her*. What was it this woman did to him? She made him forget himself.

He waved a hand in a placating gesture. "Let us just wait and see what happens. If you're correct about your . . . condition, then we have nothing to worry about. Time will tell soon enough."

She nodded jerkily in sudden agreement, taking a gulping breath. "Yes, yes. This is a moot conversation, and you shall soon see that."

Moot for now, but if she carried his child he would not abandon her.

Whether she liked it or not, whether she wished him in her life or not, she would be stuck with him. He would be there for his child in all the ways he had longed for someone to be there for him, and the only way he could guarantee that was by bringing Miss Kittinger back with him to London where he could keep her and their child close.

She looked away from him then, off in the direction of the house, as though she could see through the glass walls of the orangery—as though she yearned to be there, inside her house and away from him. Apparently the notion of them forever bound together was a misery for her.

For some reason that stung. He was not accustomed to persuading women into keeping him around. If anything, he was the one who had to persuade the fairer sex that they were better off *without* him and not *with* him.

And yet here she was, casting him most vocally from her life.

A heavy sigh expelled from her. He recognized the sound for what it was. Acceptance. She would endure his presence here, even as much as she loathed it. Her next words only confirmed that. "What will I say to my family and staff about you? How will I explain your presence here?"

He shrugged. "I am sure you will think of something. You are quite skilled at deception as I recall. A consummate actress, you are."

She made a sound: part grunt, part groan. "My brother will not be so easily fooled. He knows *you*. He knows that I . . ." She hesitated.

"He knows you stole the voucher from me?" Evidently she still had trouble admitting out loud what she had done.

She looked at him then and nodded stiffly, and suddenly he had a thought that left a sour taste in his mouth. He did not like to think that she had been *forced* into being with him, but perhaps her brother was an even bigger bastard than he thought.

"Did he put you up to the rest of it?" His voice dipped to a low growl. "Was it his idea? Does he know just *how far* you went to retrieve his voucher?"

The notion that her brother not only *knew*, but that he had sent her to Silas with the express purpose of seducing him, burned him up and had him visualizing all kinds of ways he could hurt her brother. The wretch would deserve it, of that he was convinced.

"Of course not! He doesn't know *that*. He would not have asked me to do such a thing. He's not that bad."

"Isn't he?" Nothing would convince him that Bede Kittinger was anything less than a cad who would give up his sister in just such a low manner if it gave him advantage and pushed him ahead in life. He knew greedy men, and he knew Kittinger to be one of them. He had seen plenty such men in this world. She might not yet realize her brother was one of them, but he did. It bothered him greatly that she was at his mercy.

"It was all me . . . *my* idea."

His relief was swift. Even if she had tricked him. Even if he was still angry about that. It buoyed his ego to know no one had forced her into seducing him. No. It had been all her. All *her* conniving and manipulation.

"Your idea, hmm?" he mused.

Perhaps it was not only conniving and manipulation. Perhaps a part of her had *wanted* to be with him? Wishful thinking on his part, but she had certainly seemed to enjoy their time together. She could not have faked her pleasure. He did not believe that her response had been anything other than genuine. No one could act that well. Especially someone as obviously inexperienced as she was.

He took another step that brought their bodies flush, almost touching but not quite. Still . . . he was close enough to enjoy the way her chest, so very near his own, lifted and fell with her rapid breaths.

She was not dressed as she had been that night—not that she had been dressed for very long in his presence—but the blouse and skirt she now wore were the height of modesty. The clothes did nothing to enhance her figure. *Hell.* They did not even hint that she was in possession of a figure. But he knew.

He knew what existed beneath the starched cotton and thick wool. The image of her was seared into his mind. He knew the give of her flesh. The taste and texture. The softness of her breasts and just how they filled his palms. He knew the way they quivered above him. He knew the tightness of her quim around his cock.

He knew too much, and it was a mistake remembering with her here in his presence. Once he did, he could not help himself. He reached out a hand to touch her, even if barred by a thick layer of woolen skirts. He could not resist. He squeezed a handful of fabric and met the curve of her hip.

"What are you doing?" she rasped.

"Just reacquainting myself of the way you feel, even hidden behind ugly clothes."

"My clothes are functional," she hissed. "You can't expect me to walk about the farm in what I wore in London."

He considered that for a moment, flexing his fingers on the fabric, brushing the solidness of her hip, making unsatisfactory contact. And yet he smiled. "These garments are even more enticing than that enticing ensemble . . ."

Her eyes flared. "You mock me, sirrah. You just called these garments ugly. They are in no way enticing. No one would ever say that."

His hand drifted around the voluminous fabrics of her skirts, to her backside, curving his palm over the delicious derriere he remembered with such clarity . . . and fondness.

She gasped, and then the sound turned into a breathy little moan.

"You covering up yourself like this, hiding what only *I* know is beneath . . ." He added a second hand to her backside, roughly squeezing both her cheeks until she was suddenly thrust forward against him. "It's damn arousing," he rasped over her lips, not quite making contact with her mouth but close. "It makes me want to tear these clothes off you and have at you again."

Her eyes widened and dropped to his mouth. With a whimpering cry, she lunged at him, planting her lips on his.

As unlikely as it seemed in this moment, he had not come here to do *this*—but the sweet press of her lips over his, the hot slide of her tongue entering his mouth, and he was lost.

He slid both hands into her hair and hauled her in, closer than close to him.

Her mouth mated furiously with his, her hands clawing at his arms and shoulders. Desperate little sounds escaped her around their melded lips, driving him wild.

He growled. They both had on entirely too many clothes.

He tore his hands from her hair and dragged them down the front of her chest, pulling the blouse loose from her belt and waistband. His hands went under the fabric and up her torso, seizing the breasts that were—*bloody hell!*—shielded in a corset.

"Too many clothes," he mumbled into her mouth as he cupped her through her corset and dipped his fingers inside to pinch her nipples.

She tossed back her head in a cry, and he went instantly achingly hard.

This was not the plan. He had not intended for this to happen. It had not been his intention, but their mouths stayed fused, devouring each other as though they were a pair of long-lost lovers. Her hands fumbled at his trousers.

He could not stop her.

He could not stop himself.

When her fingers wrapped around his hard cock, he was lost.

He groaned and extricated himself from her grip fleetingly to reach the hem of her skirts, dragging them up her legs, ready to take this to its most natural and obvious conclusion . . . to the reward they both so desperately craved. Whether he meant for this to happen or not, it was happening.

Dimly, he registered the creak and slam of a door.

"Mercy? You in here?"

They flew apart at the sudden voice. His body wept at the loss of her. He groaned, feeling decidedly unkind toward whoever chose this moment to interrupt them.

Her gaze collided with his. "It's my brother," she whispered.

They quickly attacked their haphazard clothing.

She stuffed her blouse back into her skirt whilst he did up his trousers.

She smoothed back her hair as though that made any difference at all in correcting the mussed strands.

"Yes," she called out in a voice that was admirably even and calm. "Back here!"

Silas erected a casual pose, and leaned a hip against a table, listening as Bede Kittinger's footsteps closed in on them. The young man emerged through the rows of trees and stopped hard at the sight of Silas.

"Masters!" he exclaimed, a shaky smile taking form on his face. His gaze darted to his sister searchingly. His bewilderment was evident. "What are you doing here?"

"Me? Oh, I thought I would take a trip to inspect the property that I won from you. Although it does not appear to be my property anymore as the voucher has gone missing. You don't have any knowledge of that, do you?"

Bede's lips worked. He looked at his sister accusingly. "Er. Mercy, I thought you—" He stopped abruptly, leaving it at that, saying nothing more, asking for no further clarification even if his eyes begged her for an explanation. Clearly he had no wish to incriminate himself in this.

Tension tightened Silas's shoulders. He did not

care for the way the blackguard was addressing his sister—as though she was at fault here.

Mercy. He let the feel of her name swim through him, flow through his veins. Her name was fitting.

Their entire interaction to this point had been a dramatic affair. Nothing mild or simple or calm about any of it. There was only one temperature between them and it was hot. Sweltering. His body still burned, aching, longing to return to her.

"Mercy?" Her brother said her name forcefully, demandingly.

"Why don't you look at *me*, Kittinger?" Silas asked tightly, his jaw aching from clenching it. "I'm the one you need to worry about."

Mercy looked back and forth between them with wild eyes and he could not help but feel a stab of pity for her. She had not asked for any of this. She had not asked for a brother to disappoint and betray her. She had merely tried to fix a bad situation.

Even if she had lied to Silas, used him and then stolen from him, his anger with her was fast fading. It was difficult to stay angry when the only thing he wanted to do was keep kissing her.

"Mr. Masters, I, ah . . ." Kittinger gulped visibly and took a hesitant step forward, offering up a hand in supplication. "Let me explain, sir."

"No need. Your sister has explained everything to me."

Kittinger looked at his sister warily. "Er. She has?"

She looked at Silas, too, in equal wariness, her deep brown eyes mirroring that question and seeming to say: *I have?*

She continued looking at him, her eyes wide and questioning, and then he heard himself saying, "She most kindly and eloquently explained how important this land is to your family, so I understand that now."

"You do?" Kittinger looked as bewildered as ever.

"You do?" she echoed.

He nodded. "Yes. I understand."

"And you are not . . ." Kittinger darted another puzzled look at his sister. "Angry?"

The fool was transparent. He wanted to know if Silas was here to punish them for stealing the voucher. The way he darted a panicky glance toward the door, he was clearly gauging the distance and debating whether or not he should make a dash for it. *Coward.*

"Your sister is very persuasive." He heard her small gasp, but did not look at her this time. Of course, only she heard the innuendo in his words. He held on to Kittinger's gaze without expression. "Let us just say she has provoked my sense of charity."

Kittinger released a great breath. "Indeed?" His

smile was one of relief. "That is very magnanimous of you."

"It is," he agreed. "I don't normally permit anyone to take back the vouchers they've handed over to me."

Kittinger shifted on his feet. "Well, er. Thank you. Thank you for being so understanding."

He nodded, looking now at Mercy. "Your sister was kind enough to offer me hospitality for the night."

Kittinger blinked. "Yes! Of course. You are welcome to stay the night with us . . . and longer if you so wish."

Silas nodded. "I will quite enjoy that. Thank you. A bit of country air is a refreshing change."

"It is?" Kittinger frowned and then blinked, chasing away the expression. "Of course, of course. Who doesn't enjoy the country?"

They stood then, frozen and silent for several moments in the fragrant space. When it became too awkward, Silas gestured for them to move ahead. "Shall we go inside?"

Kittinger readily hopped into action, preceding them out of the orangery.

Mercy wavered, not stepping forward just yet. Silas motioned for her to depart ahead of him.

Her tongue darted to moisten her lips. "Why did you say that?" she whispered.

"It seemed the easiest thing to do in the moment."

"I thought you were going to leave the explaining to me. You said *I* would think of something." A bitter edge entered her voice as she recounted their conversation. "I believe you called me an accomplished liar."

"Yes. I said something to that effect."

He had been angry. Ever since he looked down at the blood on his bedding and read her apology note, he had been angry.

The entire journey here he had felt only anger. Until he saw her again and touched her and that particular emotion inside him deflated. When confronted with her brother he had felt only pity for her.

"I changed my mind though." *I felt sorry for you.*

There was a beat of silence, and then she gave a small nod and whispered, "Thank you."

Gathering her skirts, she stepped ahead of him and followed in her brother's wake.

Chapter Ten 🦅

*P*erhaps it was foolish to hope that she would *not* have to confront the entire household this very evening. With any luck, the others had already retired for the night. Mercy would love nothing more than to put the whole uncomfortable matter off until morning.

It was not to be, however.

Of course, everyone was still awake when they entered the house. Gladys and Elsie poured out from the kitchen at the sound of their arrival into the small foyer.

"Oh! We have a guest!" Gladys's head moved up and down as she looked Silas Masters over in a thorough appraisal. Elsie watched with enormous eyes behind her aunt. Other than an occasional caller from the village, it was rare that they had a guest. And even rarer that they had an evening caller . . . much less one who would be staying overnight.

"Yes. Mr. Masters just arrived."

Grace descended the stairs then, looking bright-eyed and eager at the prospect of visitors—or in this case, one visitor.

Her sister scanned the group of them congregating in the entry hall at the bottom of the stairs. When her eyes alighted on Silas Masters, she came to a hard stop. She had only a few more steps to descend, but she froze like a hunk of marble. Her eyes flared wide and her hand flew to her hair. She patted the loosely piled plaits as though attempting to tidy the coiffure that was more than a mess after the long day.

"Gladys," Bede announced, not even acknowledging Grace on the steps yet. "Mr. Masters is a friend of mine from town who has come to visit."

Good. It was good that Bede claimed him. Even as suspicious as that was.

"Mr. Masters, welcome." Gladys nodded deferentially.

Grace darted a speculative look at Bede. The girl was far too clever. Bede had never brought any friends home before, and well she knew it. Their brother was not particularly proud of their modest country house, and he always bemoaned the lack of diversions here.

Of course, as it was such an extraordinary event, Grace could wonder, but wonder was all she would do. She would never have any notion as to why he was truly here.

She would never suspect Mercy capable of what really brought him here. In her mind, Mercy was perfectly dull and would serve as enticement to no man.

Grace would not question his presence. Indeed not. She was simply too gleeful as she drank in the appealing sight of Silas Masters. Mercy knew what her sister was seeing because she saw it, too. Just as she had seen it at the club.

Undoubtedly, Mercy would see that face and body of his for years to come; long after he was gone from here, the far too handsome man would haunt her fantasies.

"Ah, Masters. This is my other sister, Grace." Bede waved to her on the stairs, finally making the introduction.

Grace fixed a starstruck smile to her face and managed to descend the rest of the steps without tripping over her feet.

Masters stepped forward, claimed her hand and executed a very smart and gentlemanly bow over it.

Mercy gawked. He had not displayed such fine manners to her. No, they had skipped all such niceties. The sight of him doing something so ordinary to her sister, even though Mercy and Masters had done the *extraordinary*, rankled. He might have touched Mercy where no other man had, but he had not bowed over her hand.

She felt a stab of envy that she quickly shoved aside. She had no reason to feel so very proprietary toward him. And she certainly should not feel jealous of her sister. That was not right. Not right in any fashion. She had changed the girl's nappies.

At any rate, he was not *hers*. She ought not to feel anything for him.

He was an arrogant and pushy man, barging into her life without invitation and tossing his weight around and declaring that he would set her up in a house in London—of all things! As though such a fate would please her. As though she would be pleased to be a kept woman.

It's not you he wants. It's his child—if there happens to be one.

She could not wait until she had the proof that she was not expecting and he took his leave. As long as he remained, she hovered on the brink of ruin.

Clearly. She winced. She had not even been alone with him for very long in the orangery and she had succumbed to the same heat that flared between them in London. They had been seconds away from rutting like a pair of wild animals.

Her face went scalding hot at her behavior.

She'd gone at him like a woman starved and he was the last piece of bread on earth. What would have happened if her brother had not come upon them when he did? A minute later and they likely would have been well engaged and unable to dress quickly back into their clothes before being discovered.

She gave her head a small, miserable shake and pressed the backs of her fingers to an overheated cheek. This entire situation was untenable.

How could they be here, together, under the same roof, and *not* behave as though they were past intimates? As long as he remained, she toed a dangerous line. How long before her sister or brother or one of the staff looked at them together and *knew*?

Except . . . who would expect her to be so bold as to have—or *had*—a lover?

Her mind tracked over her brother, her sister, Gladys, Elsie . . . contemplating whether they would *ever* think such a thing of *her*?

No. None of them would suspect it of her. She supposed that was the only thing redeeming about being considered tediously predictable and dull.

"Pleased to make your acquaintance, Mr. Masters," Grace said in a breathy little voice, her eyes dewy and wide, like some kind of caricature and not a flesh and blood person.

"Likewise. Bede never mentioned he had such lovely sisters."

Grace's cheeks pinkened and she giggled, one of her hands flying to her chest in what seemed the move of a very practiced flirt. Only how could that be? Her sister hardly ever went anyplace where she might practice her wiles. How was it she had any wiles at all?

Mercy resisted rolling her eyes. She needed to keep up the appearance of a cordial hostess at the very least and not reveal her distaste for this entire scenario.

"How long will you be staying with us, Masters?" Bede asked, and beneath that question Mercy thought she detected a lingering thread of bewilderment.

Understandably, he still did not comprehend what the man was doing here if it was not to collect his pound of flesh. Bede more than likely struggled with the notion that this hardened and experienced man felt *charitable* toward them. Bede certainly did not possess such an altruistic streak. He would be hard-pressed to imagine a powerful man like Silas Masters being anything other than selfish and greedy and callous.

"I am not certain. Although I promise not to overstay my welcome." His gaze found hers as he uttered this, and she managed not to release a snort of derision. He was already here for too long as far as she was concerned, and well he knew it.

"Oh, that is not possible," Grace gushed.

Heaven help me.

"Indeed." Bede clapped him on the shoulder as though they were longtime friends. "That would not be possible. You may stay as long as you wish, Masters."

Mr. Masters suddenly glanced back toward the door. "Oh, I left my bags with my mount in the barn—"

Elsie hopped to action, moving toward the door. "I will be happy to fetch them for you, sir."

He called his thanks after her as she hastened from the house, and then turned back to face the rest of them.

"Shall I show you up to your room, Mr. Masters?" Gladys offered.

"I can do that," Grace quickly volunteered, her hand shooting up like she was volunteering for a game of croquet.

The girl was going to need a leash whilst Masters was here.

"We won't keep you from the rest of your evening, Gladys. I will show Mr. Masters to his room," Mercy smoothly inserted.

Grace dropped her hand, her features pulling into a clear pout.

Mercy was the mistress of the house, after all. Besides, she would not be thrusting Grace into his company. She would no sooner leave her little sister with a pack of ravenous wolves. She knew firsthand just how dangerous the man was to a woman's senses. Her sister was far too young and impressionable, her head easily turned by a handsome man.

And there was the indisputable truth: Silas Masters was not just handsome. He was sin incarnate.

"Are you hungry, sir? I can have a tray brought up to your room," Gladys offered.

"Thank you for the kind offer, but I've eaten."

"Very well. Good evening then." With a dip of her head, Gladys returned to the kitchen.

Mr. Masters faced Mercy again. He motioned to the stairs. "Shall I follow you up?"

She nodded. "Of course. I am sure you would like to settle in after your long journey."

He nodded with a vague smile and she turned, acutely conscious of him at her back as she ascended the stairs, shooing on the still gawking Grace ahead of her.

Her sister walked up the stairs ahead of her, moving, but frequently looking over her shoulder, as though verifying they were still coming behind her. To clarify, as though to verify that *Silas Masters* was still behind her and in fact real and not something imagined from fantasy. She could not care less if Mercy followed her.

Grace continued to lead the way even when they reached the second floor, forcing Mercy to take hold of her arm and stop her.

With a stern look, Mercy said, "Grace, go back to your room and ready yourself for bed, please."

Grace's presence was not needed to tuck Masters in for the night. That would establish a precedent of involvement Mercy did not want between her sister and Mr. Masters.

Grace crossed her arms over her chest in defiance.

"Grace," she said tightly.

Spinning around, Grace stalked off to her bedchamber.

Turning around, she led Masters the rest of the way.

The guest chamber was the last room at the end of the corridor, overlooking the back of the house, which boasted a profusion of flowers and a seating area for when they sometimes dined outside in temperate weather.

She opened the door, motioning him to precede her inside the room.

"I trust you can tend to your own grate while you're here."

He stood inside the chamber and rotated, surveying what would be his domain during his stay.

Although a comfortable room, the space was much smaller than what he was accustomed to. She knew that from firsthand experience. The bed was not even half the size of his back in London. "I know the accommodations are not up to your standards."

"This is perfectly adequate. I will manage."

She bristled. *Perfectly adequate.* "A fortnight will be required, at the most, for me to give you the information you wish. If you should decide to cut your stay short, I would be more than happy to send you word when—"

"I will not be departing early." His eyes glinted with resolve. "Not a day sooner than necessary."

"All of this." She motioned to him and the chamber at large. "It is not necessary. You *here* is not necessary. I can post you a letter when I have . . ." How did she delicately phrase *"when her courses arrived"*? Her cheeks warmed just at the thought of it.

"We each do what we feel we must in life, Miss Kittinger. You better than most should understand that."

She glared at him through narrowed eyes. "I understand that perfectly, Mr. Masters." She inhaled and marched to the window that overlooked one of her favorite views. "But understand me,

Mr. Masters. I will not have your undue influence on my sister whilst you are here." Unfortunately, she knew that would be a while. A fortnight with him underfoot! It was almost too much to contemplate. What would she do with him here? Staring across from her at every meal?

He looked baffled. "Your sister?"

"Yes. She is young—"

"A child." He nodded in agreement.

"And very impressionable. Gullible, if you will."

"And what is it you think I might do?" He crossed his arms, looking vaguely intimidating.

Mercy shrugged, loath to even say it, to give it utterance. "You might have noticed that she was very dazzled by you just now."

His lips twitched. "As you mentioned, she is young and I imagine . . ." He gestured around them. "Short on diversions out here in the country."

Because they were so very provincial here and lacking the amusements of London? Yes. That was what her brother constantly claimed. And yet it was difficult *not* to take offense. She loved it here and treasured her home and would not trade it for anything. What was wrong with these men who could not see that?

"Diversions do run short here." She nodded crisply. "Make certain that my sister does not become one for you during your stay."

He snorted. "You must be jesting. My taste does not run to little girls."

"You also claimed *I* did not run to your taste." What happened between them in London and just moments ago in the conservatory would prove that a lie.

"Well, you changed my mind."

His words felt like an accusation as sharp as a barbed arrow piercing her flesh. She flinched.

He looked her over almost crudely, and added, "As you so diligently intended upon our *auspicious* first meeting."

The way he emphasized *auspicious* indicated that he thought it was anything but that. *Of course.* She had most inconvenienced him. He was obviously a busy man, and she had taken him away from his busy life for the next two weeks.

He glanced around the chamber. "But it is a nice enough room and a nice house from what I've seen so far. I am sure I will enjoy my stay."

Nice enough.

"Yes. Let's be clear on that." She cleared her throat and glanced over her shoulder to make certain no one else had entered the room. Lowering her voice, she whispered hurriedly, "What just happened in the orangery cannot happen again."

He turned from his survey of the chamber to

level his intense gaze on her. "Oh, you mean when you pounced on me and kissed me?"

"Me?" Her mouth dropped open. "*Me?* You cannot remember it like that!"

"I do. You kissed me first."

"That was after y-you initiated contact, groping me through my skirts."

He angled his head as though he were not so certain of that fact. "Just admit it. Now that you've had a taste, you're hot for it, Miss Kittinger. For me."

"You're a vulgar beast!"

His eyes flashed. "That's not what you said when your little hands were diving for my cock."

She huffed in outrage even as heat flushed through her, settling and pulsing between her legs—just as he had accused. She was a hussy. This man turned her into an insatiable hussy. "You're a beastly man."

"Nah." He shook his head. "Merely an honest one."

She inhaled through her nose and fought for her composure. "Let us not debate it. Please just agree that we won't have a repeat scenario."

His expression turned into a mockery of sincerity. "Well, I certainly hope so. If you can control yourself around me, of course."

She advanced on him, her steps biting into

the wood floor. "Oh, you need not fear that." She stopped before him and delivered one poke to his chest. "At any rate, you are here to determine that I am not carrying your child. Why would you want to prolong that risk? It's counter purpose, is it not? Unless you are trying to get me pregnant?"

His face lost all softness. He nodded soberly. "I assure you that is not my goal. Fret not, Miss Kittinger. I shall keep my distance from you."

She stepped back, somewhat mollified, secretly hoping that she, too, could do the same.

Folding her hands in front of her, she glanced around the room and asked, "Well. Can I get you anything else, Mr. Masters?"

There was a knock at his door then. "Your valise, Mr. Masters." Elsie entered the room, a welcome intrusion as she deposited the bag on the floor.

"Thank you, Elsie," Mercy said.

With a nod, the girl departed.

Masters lifted his bag from the floor and carried it to the bed. "I am quite comfortable for the night. Good night, Miss Kittinger."

"Good night." She nodded briskly. "See you in the morning." Turning, she departed his chamber and escaped to her own room.

Once in the safety of her chamber, she collapsed on her bed and pressed a hand over her racing heart. It had been racing this whole time—from the moment she had turned to find him before her in the orangery. If her heart did not slow to a normal rhythm soon it might burst in her chest. How could she exist in such a state for the duration of his stay? A fortnight at least! Her heart could not take it.

None of her could take it.

She might very well perish before he took his leave.

Chapter Eleven ❧

$\mathcal{B}$y the time Silas descended the stairs the following morning and ventured to the dining room, he knew that the day was well underway in the Kittinger household.

The house was quiet. Birds chirped outside, and he marveled at that. He never heard birds in the city. They were there, he supposed, but amid all the other bustling sounds, he did not hear them.

When he entered the room, he found only Bede Kittinger at the table, slurping his coffee and eating from a plate full of eggs, sausages and potatoes.

He had just bitten off half a sausage, juice dribbling down his chin, when he spotted Silas in the room.

"Masters! Good morning to you. Have a seat," he proclaimed around a mouth full of chewed up meat. "Help yourself." He motioned to the sideboard laden with food. "Eggs, sausage, kippers.

The sticky rolls are marvelous. Better than anything you will find in Town."

Nodding, Silas helped himself to a plate before sitting himself across from Kittinger and snapping his napkin onto his lap, deliberately not remarking on the absence of Mercy Kittinger, difficult though it was to refrain from inquiring about her whereabouts.

Kittinger tapped the paper sitting on the table beside his plate. "The Moscow circus is in London. I imagine there is much fanfare. Can't believe you're here instead of there."

"I was compelled to leave the city," Silas reminded him.

Kittinger shot him an uneasy glance, clearly still distrusting the extent of Silas's forgiveness.

"How long might you be staying with us?" The question was posed mildly enough. Kittinger did not even look at him as he voiced it.

Silas shrugged. "For a little while. The country air is a nice change."

Kittinger focused on his food, piling his eggs atop a slice of toast and then taking a messy bite. Chewing, he spoke around his food. "I appreciate you being so understanding about this situation. Your . . . forgiveness in this matter is most admirable."

"Situation," Silas mused. "That is one way to

describe it. Not how I would describe it, but certainly it is a way."

"How would you describe it?" he asked casually, clearly fishing for a glimpse into Silas's motivations and whether Silas might still thrash him to a pulp for sending his sister to steal back the voucher from him.

"Theft. Plain and simple. I would describe it as that."

Kittinger chuckled uneasily. "No, no. I would not say that."

"Would you not? That is precisely what happened, and the only reason you're sitting here leisurely eating your breakfast and not somewhere else in a great deal of pain, is because of your sister."

"My sister," Kittinger echoed with a curling lip as though the notion of his sister doing anything beneficial astounded him.

"Indeed. You can thank her."

"Thank her?" Kittinger still looked bewildered. Shaking his head, he suddenly stopped the motion and said, "Oh. Wait. You . . . *like* her." He spoke slowly, as though this realization was just dawning on him.

Silas tensed, not enjoying Kittinger's incredulous and faintly insulting manner.

Kittinger grinned and continued. "You *like* my

sister. That is where this magnanimity springs from. Not a sense of charity and compassion at all. Oh, this *is* rich!" Instead of becoming outraged or even adopting an air of concern he looked vaguely . . . calculating. He immediately appeared to be plotting how such a thing might work to his advantage. *Of course.*

His objective was not to protect his sister from the likes of Silas Masters—as a good brother ought to do, as one would expect a good brother to do. *No.* Bede Kittinger was looking out for himself.

Silas chose not to even acknowledge the allegation. To deny it would only make him look exactly as Kittinger insisted—enamored of his sister. Whether he was in fact enamored . . . and that was nonsense.

So instead of denial he went with intimidation. It felt like the right tactic in dealing with a coward like Kittinger. "Do you know what happens to people who cheat me?" he asked in a low voice, his finger tapping the edge of his fork. "Or steal from me?"

Kittinger's smile slipped. He shook his head emphatically, his eyes as round as the buttered potatoes on his plate.

Silas drank deeply from his coffee cup, taking his time replying. "No one has done so in years. Not since I was a lad in Seven Dials, surviving day to day with my wits . . . and fists." He turned his attention to a sausage on his plate, cutting it in half. "Do you know what that's like?" He looked up at Kittinger, noticing that he had not even dressed for the day yet. The man still wore his silk dressing robe. Silas laughed lightly and shook his head. "Of course, you don't know."

Kittinger had no response for that.

Silas glanced around the table with its vacant seats. "Everyone else has already breakfasted?" he asked mildly.

"People here rouse themselves at an unholy hour," Kittinger chattered, appearing happy for the change in subject. "They eat and then they're out the door to their tasks."

"Your sisters . . ."

"Yes, even them. Well, mostly Mercy. Grace busies herself with the pianoforte and whatever lessons Mercy has assigned to her. She rarely has chores outside of the house."

Silas nodded slowly. That already fit with what he knew about Mercy Kittinger. She herself would work the land while she assigned the lofty, high-brow tasks to young Grace for what she viewed as the betterment of her sister. She was selfless that way.

Is that what I was to her? A mission of grand self-sacrifice?

He scowled as he buttered his toast with vigor. He did not like that thought. Not at all. Mercy had seemed genuinely to enjoy their night together. She had even seemed amenable for a repeat of it in the orangery—even if she had said otherwise in his chamber last night. He did not—*could not*—think it had all been a miserable sacrifice on her part that she had to endure. He took a bite of toast, hoping to cover the sudden sour taste coating his mouth.

"I do not know what your plans are for the rest of the day, but I thought to take a ride. Would you care to join me? It looks to be a fine day. There is little else to do here."

Silas looked up from his plate. "That would be acceptable." He would like to observe this land that meant so much to Mercy Kittinger in daylight hours and see all there was to it. It had to be beautiful country indeed to make her risk herself and resort to crime and seduction to get it back.

He told himself he was riding with Kittinger *not* because he hoped to come across Mercy again. He was not here to rekindle what they had started in London, contrary to what had happened last night.

She was a respectable country lady. That was not the type of woman he chose for dalliances. His purpose here was to establish that they had no ties binding them. He was not here to *create* ties that *would* bind them.

She said it would take a fortnight to determine that.

Over the coming days, he would not forget that. He would remember his purpose here and that it was not to get beneath her skirts again.

THE SUN SHONE brightly, warding off the day's chill as Silas settled atop his mount and nudged the beast forward, following Kittinger out of the yard.

Silas glanced at the house, spotting the housekeeper, Gladys, cleaning the front windows. They passed the girl, Elsie, carrying eggs in her apron toward the house. She nodded them a greeting.

It was lush green everywhere. So much so that it blinded the eyes. Spring was here and the countryside was humming with life and vitality. It was a gloriously bucolic scene.

As someone who spent the whole of his life in London, Silas could appreciate it. He could see why Mercy loved this land so much.

Kittinger was dressed to the nines as though he was going for a ride in Hyde Park and not out and about on his country farm.

Silas shook his head and looked out at the countryside. It really was beautiful land. Technically it was *his* land—or should have been. He had won it fairly from the dolt riding beside him.

It should not astonish Silas that people would gamble with their lives and homes so easily. As though homes were easy to come by. He had seen it time and time again. And yet it filled him with wonder and no small amount of disgust. It was usually this very disgust that made it palatable for him to collect his winnings. If reckless gamblers did not appreciate what they had, then they deserved to lose it. At least that was what he had always told himself. Until now.

Until he met Mercy Kittinger he had never come face-to-face with family members of those he had ruined. Now he felt differently. Now doing what he did . . . felt different.

The Rogue's Den felt just a little more dirty, a little more disreputable in his mind. He had always told himself he provided services that people needed. Now he was not so sure what he did was a necessary service. Certainly it was wanted, craved even. But was it essential? Were the diversions he provided, in fact . . . healthy? What good did it serve?

Gah. He was letting Mercy affect him. These were not his thoughts.

Silas had ruined no one. That had all been her brother. Kittinger had been destined to gamble away his home that night. If not to Silas, then to someone else.

If that had happened, what would Mercy Kittinger have done then? Seduce some other man?

The very idea left a bad taste in his mouth. He shook off the notion and swallowed against the taste. Such speculation was not here nor there. Because she had seduced *him*. He was here now . . . and that fact should not have gratified him so greatly.

They trotted up a rise of rolling green and Kittinger stopped at the crest. The view was lovely. The valley below revealed a freshly tilled field. *Mostly* tilled. There was a plow at one end of the field that was stuck and appeared to have halted all progress. The recent rain had done no favors for the laborers.

Silas and Kittinger continued down the hill at an easy pace.

Kittinger paid no heed to the workers or their obvious plight. And they did indeed have a plight. Three men and a mule struggled to get the plow free, and it seemed a hopeless task.

Silas peered across the distance at the men, slowing as he watched their efforts even as Kittinger rode ahead unaware or indifferent.

The men themselves were covered in mud. The smallest one, almost knee-deep in muck, pulled at the mule by its bridle. He strained and leaned backward as he worked. The mule brayed in protest, sinking its backside deeper into the mud, settling in and clearly giving up whilst the men had not.

"Masters?" Kittinger called out. The younger man glanced back impatiently to where Silas had stopped his mount. "You coming?"

With a distracted shake of his head, Silas urged his own mount down the hill to the field. It looked like they could use a helping hand to—

He stopped hard, pulling on his reins and halting his horse in his tracks. He stared, gaping at the trio working so diligently to dislodge the plow.

The smaller man of the three was not a man at all. Indeed not. It was Mercy, clad in work boots and trousers.

Her brother rode up beside him. "Come. There's a lovely view a few miles from here that I was eager to show you. It borders the Duke of Penning's lands. I wager you did not know we share the border with a bona fide duke."

Silas did not know that and he did not care.

He felt Kittinger's stare on the side of his face, awaiting his reaction, clearly expecting him to be impressed.

"It appears they could use some help." Silas nodded toward the stuck plow.

Kittinger followed his gaze and gave a mild shrug.

Silas gestured toward the trio. "That is your sister," he stated, as though that might have some impact on Kittinger's unwillingness to lend aid.

Kittinger squinted across the distance. "Oh, I say. It *is* Mercy." He sniffed. "In trousers. Our mother must be rolling over in her grave. Mercy has always been a rather untraditional female."

For some reason, Silas bristled at the criticism. Even though it was not directed at himself it felt rather personal. Almost like a poke at him. "She appears to be quite industrious. I am sure your mother would applaud her work ethic."

Kittinger shrugged as though he could not care either way and Silas realized that was about the right of it. Her brother did not care for this place or the people here, including his own family. Obviously that was the situation or he would not have so carelessly gambled it all away.

And what was to keep him from doing that again? At some other place? Some other time? Would Mercy attempt to steal the voucher again?

The very notion had him fighting back a shudder. She would end up in prison next time. Or perhaps worse. Perhaps she would face the barrel end of a pistol. The next man she stole from might not be so understanding.

It was a dreadful possibility and one he did not

want to give any more thought to. Without further comment, Silas swung down from his mount, his boots sinking into the moist earth.

"Masters! Where are you going?" Kittinger blustered.

Ignoring the man, he started across the field. Most of it was freshly plowed, and his boots sank ankle deep into the tilled soil.

They were so busy at work they did not notice his approach until he was upon them. He clasped the mule by his bridal. The beast eyed him distrustfully.

"Mr. Masters," Mercy exclaimed, looking up at him with astonishment. "What are you doing here?"

"Thought I might add my weight to the task here."

Her cheeks flushed pink and he suspected it had nothing to do with her exertions and more to do with his arrival at her side. "That is not necessary."

He shook his head. She frequently said that.

"Gor, miss! Another strong body would be appreciated before I break my back," one of the men standing beside the plow complained, his gaze looking Silas over approvingly.

She frowned, but held her tongue.

Another lad added, "Hank does have a point,

miss. No sense in us getting injured. Then we won't be any good to anyone."

"Oh, very well." She cast Silas a cross look as though he were here to deliver poisoned fruit and not an offer of help. His lips twitched.

With a huff of breath, she made a move to resume her thus far futile efforts to free the plow. Silas held up a hand, halting their labors.

"Give me a moment, would you?"

The men stopped. Mercy stared at him with speculation. Resentment for his involvement still glimmered in her eyes, but he had clearly piqued her curiosity. She blew at a dark strand of hair that had fallen loose and dangled before her nose. Stepping back, her boots made a great sucking sound as she lifted them out from the muck.

Silas resumed his focus on the obstinate animal. He dropped his forehead against the side of the beast's face, stroking his muzzle.

"There now," he whispered. "You're having a difficult day, are you not, my friend?" He clicked his tongue and continued in a low, hushed voice, cooing and petting the beast until the mule started huffing and blustering a little less.

Silas did not know much about animals, but he knew something about weary souls that felt browbeaten and bullied.

Silas felt the others waiting, watching him. He

sent a quick glance Mercy's way, noting the pretty pink flush creeping back up her cheeks as he continued to murmur nonsense to the mule.

Her deep brown eyes were wide and luminescent as she surveyed him with the animal. She was fetching. Deceptively innocent—especially as he knew there was another side to her. A decidedly *not* innocent side—and that was fine by him. Innocence was overvalued. Better reserved for childhood, he had always thought. Not that he had had much of an innocent childhood himself. His early years could be characterized as many things, but never that. And yet he did not want a woman who was as innocent as a child. He wanted a woman. Not a child.

He wanted someone who knew what she wanted and was not afraid to go after it. *Like the woman he had met in London.*

That version of Mercy had been waiting for him in his rooms that night. Well, not waiting for him precisely. She had been stealing from him and ready to seduce him to accomplish it. Waiting like a jungle cat, ready to pounce. As furious as he had been, as he *still* was when he thought about it, he was more in awe of her than angered. Intrigued. Fascinated. Impressed.

He gave the mule a few more leisurely strokes from his forehead down to his muzzle. The animal grew calmer, leaning forward into Silas's ministrations.

"You have mesmerized him," she whispered.

"Just settled his nerves with a bit of love." He gave a few more tender pats and then moved along the length of the mule's body, keeping a hand on the beast at all times, letting him know that he had not left him, that he was still there for him.

His gaze met Mercy's over the mule's back. She watched him with slightly parted lips, as though mesmerized by him herself. "You're very good . . . at that."

Why did it suddenly feel like she wasn't talking about the mule any longer? Her gaze flitted back and forth from his face to his hand on the animal.

"Now I will help by pulling on the plow." He nodded once to the nearby men. "You two as well. Join me." He looked at Mercy. "You take the mule's halter."

She sent him a dubious look, but obliged, taking her place beside the mule's head.

Silas gave an encouraging pat to the mule's rump and then moved into position, seizing hold of the bridle.

With a nod to the two men and then to Mercy, he declared, "Ready? Go."

He strained with every bit of his strength, feeling his boots sinking deep, burrowing, but then the plow suddenly shifted, surged, and he took full advantage of the momentum, moving his feet, first one step, then another and another.

Soon they were all moving right along with the plow. They broke free of the mud pit that had trapped them. One of the men took control of the handles and steered the plow the rest of the way, finishing the row.

Mercy came to stand beside him, slightly out of breath. "That was brilliant. Thank you," she murmured. "You did not have to do that."

He shrugged. "Should I just have stood by and watched you struggle?"

She cast him a curious look. "Why would I expect differently? Not many people would get down in the mud to lend a helping hand." As if to prove her point, her gaze drifted, landing on her brother still astride his mount at the top of the hillside.

It was bewildering how siblings could be so far apart—twins, no less. Mercy and Bede Kittinger might have grown up together and come from the same people and place, but they bore no similarities otherwise.

Her brother lacked integrity and loyalty. He possessed no work ethic. Whereas, he suspected, those three traits were the core of her.

Silas looked at her and heard the words emerging from him as though someone else was saying them. "No man worth anything permits the women in his life to labor without pitching in alongside them. That's not who I am."

As unplanned and unexpected as the words, they were the truth.

She blinked. Her mouth sagged open. It took her a moment to recover her voice.

"And *I* am a woman in your life? That's who I am then? Someone you feel is . . . part of your life?"

Hearing her say that out loud was a bit startling. He studied her a moment. The tender line of her throat worked as she swallowed. "It's not what you are *not*," he admitted.

Silas knew his answer was evasive, but he did not know how else to respond. He could scarcely credit the words he had said. He had *claimed* her as a woman in his life. Incredibly. But yes. She was that.

His woman.

He squeezed his eyes hard in a long blink. *Bloody hell.* Where had that thought come from?

Thankfully he did not utter those shocking words out loud, however true they felt to him. He would sound like a veritable caveman. So primitive and proprietary. He had never felt that way toward any of the women in his life before.

Whenever a relationship ended it ended. As simple as that. He never mourned it. He simply let it go with well wishes and a farewell. Never had he felt grief over the parting. Never had he felt possessive toward the woman.

"Ohhh," she said slowly, dragging out the word as though she had reached some sudden conclusion. "This goes back to why you are here."

She glanced around, making certain the other men were nowhere close to them. She leaned in and he was awarded—or punished—with the scent of sweet oranges again. He would never be able to eat or smell the fruit again without thinking of her. Without remembering and aching . . .

Shaking his head, he focused on what she was saying.

She continued in an aggrieved whisper, "This is about your notion that I could be carrying *your* child. You think this connects us. You feel obligated toward me because you think I carry precious cargo. Nothing more."

He blinked. He had not thought that at all.

Her voice turned slightly scornful as she pressed the point. "That is it, is it not? You saw me working in the field like a common laborer and you wanted to stop me from overtaxing myself for fear that I could harm *your* child. It has naught to do with me personally."

He had not even considered what she was suggesting. He should have thought of his possible child in her womb as she exerted herself—but he had not. He had thought only of her.

"Could I simply not wish to help you?" he asked.

"You need not be so concerned with my welfare, Mr. Masters. Even if I do turn out to be in a family way . . . doubtful, of course, but if I *am*, I am no delicate flower. I am healthy and strong. I have been working this land since I was a young girl. Also, women are a lot heartier than given credit for. We can manage to work *and* bring children into the world."

He considered her words and then glanced around. This felt like a dangerous conversation. Especially with witnesses so very close. "Very well. What is next?"

"Next?" She looked puzzled at his sudden change of subject.

"On your agenda for the day? If you mean to work the land as you put it, then I will be right beside you."

"You?" she asked as though struggling to understand his meaning. "You want to help? Me? Around the farm?"

He nodded. "What else do I have to do whilst I stay here?"

She shrugged and her glance slid to where her brother waited on the hillside. "I don't know. Occupy yourself with gentlemanly tasks like riding or . . ."

"You mean spend the day with your brother?" he finished for her.

She winced. "Well. Yes. You could ride and hunt and . . . play cards."

"I've played cards with your brother before, if you recall? There is no fun in it without a challenge."

She fought back a laugh and tucked a loose strand of hair behind her ear. "Yes. I suppose we have indisputable proof that he is not a skilled player."

He chuckled, and her gaze fixed on his face in fascination, as though just now seeing him for the first time. He sobered, feeling unusually self-conscious under her rapt regard.

"You have a nice laugh. You should do it more often," she murmured, and then blinked, fresh color staining her cheeks. With a small shake of her head, as though dismissing such a fanciful thought, she shrugged. "You could always take a nap. My brother usually naps in the afternoon."

"I don't think I've napped since I wore nappies. And do I remind you of your brother?"

"No," she allowed, her lips twitching. "Not in any way."

"Then I suggest you do not assume that his pastimes are the same as mine. Now." He clapped his hands together and rubbed them briskly. They'd conversed long enough. Flirted, really. If he was to keep his vow and keep his hands off her, then he needed to put an end to that. He looked away from her face, scanning the landscape. "Where are we off to next?"

Chapter Twelve ✧

A week into Silas Masters's stay with them, Gwen Cully arrived early one morning.

"You are just in time to join us for breakfast," Mercy declared from the front door with a wave and a smile.

Gwen clambered down from her wagon with practiced ease and hopped to the ground. "I will never turn down a meal, especially prepared by a cook as marvelous as yours."

Mercy smiled as Gwen tied off the big bay and moved into the house, her steps as solid as a man's on the entryway floor.

Everything about Gwen Cully was solid.

Standing nearly six feet tall, she was stronger than the average man. Even without her unique size, as Shropshire's blacksmith, she was made strong from laboring hours a day with a hammer and anvil.

Mercy took her hat and gloves and set them on

a side table. Gwen wore trousers as she always did. Ever since she was a girl working in her family's smithy, she had eschewed the normal trappings of womanhood. No one in town ever gave her a second glance, so accustomed to the sight were they. It was normal. More uncharacteristic was the sight of her in a dress or skirts, although that did happen occasionally. For church or one of the Blankenship balls she would break routine and don a dress.

"My apologies on taking so long to deliver your order. Since the Duke of Penning took residence I have been inundated with work. The new duke is making a great many improvements at the hall. Too many for his staff alone to manage and he has commissioned me for several projects."

"I am happy to hear your business is flourishing."

"It is at that." Gwen nodded, but there was an edge of weariness to her voice. "More than I alone can manage. If only I could find reliable help. My last apprentice ran off with a troupe of musicians passing through town. And the one before that decided he could do better for himself in a bigger city and left me for Yorkshire."

They entered the dining room where everyone was gathered.

Silas pushed up from the table at their arrival. Bede followed suit with much slower progress, only halfway rising from his chair and then dropping back into his seat gracelessly to then continue shoveling sausages into his mouth.

"Gwen, er—Miss Cully," Mercy corrected herself as she motioned to Silas. "This is our guest, Mr. Masters. He is an . . . acquaintance of my brother, from London." Mercy winced at that mangled introduction.

"Miss Cully." Silas inclined his head and, unlike her brother, remained standing until Gwen took her seat, eagerly accepting the platter of sweet buns and crumpets Gladys passed to her.

"Funny how you always arrive at mealtime."

"Nothing funny about it, Miss Gladys," Gwen declared with no remorse. "It is quite deliberate as I am a great admirer of your cooking. I have a woman help with my uncle a few hours a day. She is not very handy in the kitchen though. My uncle and I must endure my lackluster culinary efforts when I come in from work at the end of the day."

Gladys shook her head in sympathy. "I will have to send a basket home with you."

"You are too kind, Miss Gladys. My uncle will enjoy that greatly."

"The least we can do. You do such fine work for us."

"Indeed." Mercy nodded.

"What is it you do, Miss Cully?" Silas asked.

Gwen stared at him levelly, almost coldly, as though braced for his censure. Mercy supposed she was accustomed to that from strangers—from people outside of Shropshire who did not accept or embrace the notion of a female blacksmith.

There would always be people afraid of those who were different, of those who went against their concept of what was normal. Mercy understood that. She had her own experience with that kind of narrow-mindedness.

Papa had known how capable she was at running the farm and the household. She might have been young at the time, just seventeen when he fell ill, but she took over managing everything. Bede stayed away at school whilst she supervised all matters with skill and competence. Papa witnessed that. He knew. He saw, even from his sickbed— and he'd still left everything to Bede. Because that was what people did. That was tradition. That was *normal*.

If Papa had been more open to the idea of pushing beyond typical expectations, of going against custom, he might have left the farm to Mercy and not Bede.

Everything would be different then. They would not suffer as they did. She would not live in a perpetual state of worry.

You would never have met Silas Masters. Silas Masters would not be sitting at her table this very moment. Inexplicably, she frowned. Bowing her head, she focused her attention on her plate.

"I am a blacksmith," Gwen finally answered. "I brought some tools for Mercy. A new set of scythes she requested and I repaired some other tools in need of attention."

"Oh." Silas blinked and it was the extent of his reaction. His surprise was mild, but no less apparent. Gwen Cully could well be the only female blacksmith in all of England. Of course he was surprised, but he did well to temper his reaction. Not everyone was so polite. At least his lip did not curl in distaste.

Bede, however, did not moderate his reaction. Even though he already knew that she was Shropshire's blacksmith, his nostrils flared with disdain and he made a grunt of disapproval.

"And what is your business, Mr. Masters?" Gwen returned the question. "Or are you a gentleman of leisure?" Gwen sent a pointed stare Bede's way, clearly implying: *like this worthless sot.*

"I wish I was a gentleman of leisure." Silas bestowed a dazzling smile on Gwen, and Mercy felt an unfamiliar stab of jealousy. This was different than how she felt when Grace had flirted with him. Grace was a child and her sister and he professed to be uninterested in her.

In contrast, Gwen Cully was a beautiful and complex woman. Definitely not a child.

Was she to his taste?

He had claimed Mercy was not to his taste. Was Gwen Cully then? With her lovely golden hair and endless legs and generous breasts that pressed against her blouse and leather vest in the most enticing fashion? Her well-shaped derriere was also gloriously and amply displayed in her trousers.

Grace propped her elbow on the table and rested her chin in the palm of her hand, locking her gaze on Silas dreamily. "What occupies your days? And nights, Mr. Masters?"

The brazen chit! Where did she learn such flirtatious tactics?

"I own a gaming hell in Town. It occupies much of my time."

"Ah." Gwen glanced in the direction of Bede again. "That makes sense."

Even the residents of Shropshire knew how her brother lived his life . . . or rather how he wasted it. He did not put himself to any honest enterprise. It would indeed fit with their notions of him that he should spend his time at a gaming hell.

"I am certain that is quite a lucrative career for you."

Silas gave a modest incline of his head.

"Lucrative," Bede snorted. "That is putting it mildly. The Rogue's Den is the most popular hell in Town. Some nights it is so crowded they turn people away at the doors."

"My, my, my," Grace murmured. "I should like to go."

Gladys clucked. "Ladies do not patronize gaming hells."

Silas looked at Mercy across the table. A small secret smile played about his lips and a rush of warmth swept over her face.

Ladies do not patronize gaming hells.

She had spent the night under the roof of The Rogue's Den engaged in activities that were decidedly outside the boundaries of what was considered ladylike. Mercy supposed the argument could be made that she was not a lady then.

She averted her face and willed her cheeks to cool, concentrating as she did so upon slathering blackberry jam on a still warm from the oven crumpet.

Suddenly a knock sounded on the door.

"Another guest?" Gladys remarked, blinking in surprise.

It must be a guest. The staff never knocked on the front door. They simply used the back door or came in through the kitchen.

Mercy started to lift up from her chair, but

Gladys beat her, launching to her feet. "You stay put. I will see to the door."

She departed the room, but her voice carried from the entry hall, mingling with the voice of a man. Soon after, she arrived with a gentleman behind her. "Mr. Masters. You have a visitor."

He had a visitor? He had been here a little over a week and he was receiving callers? Her stomach squeezed. It was as though he had moved in and was a permanent resident now.

The well-dressed man lingered in the threshold, his gaze seeking Silas. "Forgive the intrusion, Mr. Masters." He patted the leather satchel at his side. "I have some pressing matters that require your attention."

Silas's expression turned grim as he stood. "If you will excuse me."

"You can use the parlor," Mercy offered. "We won't disturb you."

"Thank you."

The two gentlemen departed the room and for several moments there was only the clink of cutlery and dishes and the sound of Bede slurping his coffee and munching his breakfast with gluttonous abandon.

"Well." Gwen wrapped her fingers around her teacup and brought it close to her lips. "You have quite the busy household this morning."

"Yes. It is usually much quieter than this."

"I, for one, am glad for the activity. It is not so dreadfully boring for a change," Grace said as she stirred her tea.

"Still *dreadfully* boring," Bede mumbled around a mouthful of sausage. Grease dribbled down his chin, which he did not bother to catch with his napkin.

Mercy took a deep breath, reaching for patience. They finished their meal and then Mercy led Gwen from the room, deliberately not glancing at the closed parlor doors where Silas tended to his business. Whatever they discussed was none of her affair. Just as Silas Masters was none of her affair. As difficult as it was for her to accept, especially after this last week with him working by her side about the place, he was not her affair.

Outside, Mercy helped Gwen unload the tools she had brought from her wagon, admiring her craftsmanship. She had repaired at least half a dozen tools and made three more scythes they would need for the forthcoming harvest. "Fine work," Mercy praised.

"Again, my apologies for how long it took. I am hoping to find a new apprentice to help me soon. I have given up hope of finding anyone in Shropshire. I've placed advertisements. I'm spreading out my search into other towns and villages."

"Best of luck with that," Mercy murmured. "I know from the days when I nursed my father, it is not easy to care for an ailing family member, in addition to all your other duties."

"No, it is not." Gwen squinted and peered toward the house. "How long is your brother staying? I do not imagine he does much to ease your burdens here," she said bluntly. "I used to wish for a brother or brothers . . . someone to help me when I lost my father and my uncle became too ill to do much of anything."

Mercy laughed lightly and shook her head. "Be careful what you wish for." Her brother had been more detriment than benefit. "Mr. Masters has been more helpful about the place in the span of a week than Bede has been in the entirety of his life."

She winced. It was a rather ghastly thing to admit, but she and Gwen had often confided in each other. As two women in the unique position of overseeing their families and all the responsibilities thereof, they had often commiserated together.

"Mr. Masters?"

Mercy nodded.

Gwen pointed to the house. *That* Mr. Masters?"

Mercy nodded and shrugged. "I know. I know. It was unexpected. I did not anticipate he would be so . . . helpful." *That he would even care.*

"For a rich city swell to be laboring alongside of you? Yes, I would say so." Gwen propped her elbows on the side of her wagon, her gaze fixed on the parlor window in a thoughtful manner.

Mercy suddenly felt a wave of nervousness, wondering what Gwen was pondering.

After a moment, she sent a searching glance in Mercy's direction. "He is a friend of your brother, you say?"

"Er. Yes."

"Curious."

"What is so curious about that?"

"How Bede Kittinger could have a friend so very unlike himself." Gwen paused and then began listing, counting on each of her fingers. "Wealthy, handsome, enterprising, ambitious . . . Not afraid to get his hands dirty. A curious thing, indeed."

For some reason the mention of Silas's hands had her envisioning them: slightly callused, broad palmed, long tapering fingers. She could see them. She could still feel them as they had been, touching her, skimming over her skin.

Her throat tightened uncomfortably. Speech, the simple flow of air—suddenly it all became a challenge. Too much for her.

Of course, she was not certain what to say in response. Were words even necessary? It appeared

Gwen still had plenty to say on the subject of Silas Masters.

"Perhaps when he is finished here, you could send him my way. I could always use a houseguest who is willing to pitch in with free labor." Gwen sent her a teasing smile. "And not to mention . . . he's a pretty man. I would not mind looking at him every morning across the breakfast table."

Jealousy returned with a quick stab. Mercy laughed shakily, hoping she did not reveal how possessive she suddenly felt. "Well. He is not mine to dispense."

"Pity." Gwen's long legs took her around the wagon to embrace Mercy. "Shall I see you at the Blankenship fete in a few days?"

Mercy could not hide her grimace. "Grace and Bede are both looking forward to it. We would not miss it."

"Well, I shall only make an appearance. I can't leave my uncle alone for long and I have no one to look in on him in the evenings. Everyone in Shropshire will be at the party."

"Oh, be truthful now. You don't regret needing to duck out early."

Like Mercy, Gwen never danced. Half the time, she stood along the back walls, a tall form nestled among the potted ferns, talking to Mercy and the other spinsters and widows. The other half of the time she spent with the men: farmers and yeomen and laborers who talked on the topics that were of more interest to a blacksmith.

Grace lifted one shoulder in an unassuming shrug. "Will your houseguest be accompanying you?"

"I imagine he will. Yes." Thankfully, her voice reflected nothing but equanimity. No jealousy. No sudden irrational urge to pull the hair of her life-long friend.

Gwen's smile widened. "Staying for a while then, is he?"

What could she say to that? Certainly not the truth. *Until it's proven I am not increasing with child.*

Gwen clambered up to the seat and picked up the reins without, evidently, needing a response from Mercy. "Thank you for breakfast. I will see you very soon."

Mercy waved a hand. "See you soon."

She watched her friend drive out of the yard before turning back to stare pensively at the house where Silas was in private conference with his man.

A part of her longed to go back inside and linger near the parlor door where she might overhear the happenings in that room. The *nosy* part. The part of her that longed to be near Silas Masters and know everything about him. To unravel the fascinating man and see to the core of him.

Thankfully, there was the other part of her.

The sensible part ruled by logic that was not persuaded by his handsome face or his proximity. The part of her that refused to allow his nearness during this last week to turn her head or heart—no matter how nice it was to have someone to share in the work, to be a companion, to . . .

She stopped herself before she got carried away with weak and needy thoughts.

Turning away from the house and the unmistakably seductive pull of the man inside, she headed for the stables and the work that awaited her.

Chapter Thirteen ❧

"And our last matter of business." Clarke stuffed the final document bearing Silas's signature in the satchel and leveled his gaze on Silas. "Albert Gordon requested I speak with you on his behalf."

Silas leaned back in his seat with an aggrieved sigh. "I have given my answer once already. There is no further negotiation to be had."

"He thought you might reconsider if he offered you a greater percentage of the profits."

"The man is a pimp. I will take no profits from the selling of flesh. The Den is not a brothel and I will not have Gordon step foot in my establishment." His lip curled faintly over his teeth. "He's not allowed through the door again. No more audiences with him. Are we understood?"

"Yes, sir. I will inform him."

Silas shrugged. He cared not if Gordon was warned. The man was a purveyor of human flesh. Boys. Girls. Men. Women. He sold them all, abusing them terribly, withholding their wages and giving them little protection in turn for their services.

Silas tapped the desk. "The next time Gordon steps inside my place, he will end up in the Thames. You can tell him that."

Clarke inclined his head in acknowledgment, well aware that Silas meant what he said. He made no idle threats. He learned early on in the streets to carry through and never suffer bullies or abusers lest he wanted to be a victim himself.

They both stood and moved toward the parlor doors. Clarke cleared his throat. "How much longer do you think you will be here?"

A fair question and yet Silas was reluctant to give an answer. He was here until he had an answer regarding Mercy's condition and he was not about to volunteer that very private information.

Instead of answering, he instructed, "Collect the rents due next week."

In addition to The Den, Silas owned various properties throughout Town.

He had started acquiring them once his business at the hell took off. He rationalized that it would behoove him not to have all his money and assets tied into one enterprise.

He owned a tenement, along with a few shops and a warehouse along the docks. He was a fair landlord, listening to his tenants and never forgetting where he came from and what it was like to have nothing and have to fight for a foothold in the world.

"Of course." Clarke nodded deferentially. "I will see it done."

"If you need anything else you know where to find me. I appreciate you manning the helm in my absence."

He walked Clarke to the door. Silas could tell he was curious at what he was doing there, but he would not ask.

As much as he relied on Clarke to assist him in matters of business when needed, Silas's private affairs were his own concern. He did not invite judgment or the opinions of others. He was the arbiter of his own life and he had been ever since he walked out the door of his grandfather's home. He had been alone then and alone ever since. And nothing had changed. He was alone now. Still.

Following Clarke's departure, he advanced to the stables, intending to saddle his mount and find Mercy and see how he could help her today.

As soon as he entered the confines of the stable, he heard a rhythmic scraping sound. He followed the noise past several stalls holding horses, including his own mount.

He found Mercy mucking a stall at the end of the row, filling a wheelbarrow full of manure.

It was grueling work and she wiped at her brow as she toiled, unaware that he was there, unaware that she was being watched.

"Here." He stepped forward and attempted to take the shovel from her.

"I can do it," she protested.

"You take the wheelbarrow and angle it closer. We will work faster together this way."

She relented, releasing the shovel to him. "It is messy work," she warned him.

He grinned as he bent over the shovel and set to work. "You think I'm afraid of messy work?"

"No," she murmured. "I suppose this past week has shown me that you are not."

"Even if I was, do you think I would stand by . . . watching you do all the *messy* work and not lend a hand? That's not who I am."

"Yes. You mentioned that before."

"It bears repeating when you continue to attempt to dissuade me from helping you."

A playful smile curved her pretty lips. "Very well. Thank you for your help." She released a breath. "Did your friend leave?"

"Yes. And I assume Miss Cully took her leave as well?"

"Yes."

"And I would not call Clarke my friend." Come to think of it, he did not have many of those. Although Clarke was probably the closest one he did have.

"He works for you." She nodded. "And did you conclude your business satisfactorily?"

"We did."

"I hope your business is not suffering from your prolonged absence."

He paused amid shoveling and rested his elbow on the end of the handle. "The world will not stop because I am here for a little while."

"I know you are an important man. I hate to keep you from—"

"Is this your way of chasing me off? A new tactic? Compliment me? Stroke my ego?"

"No! Not at all. Bede merely explained to me that you are a person of some importance in London."

He laughed harshly. "And believing that, he sent you to steal from me?" He shook his head in disgust. "You are going to have to do something about him."

"What can I do?" she asked sharply, shooting up straight in obvious indignation. "All of this belongs to him." She waved a hand around them. "Papa left it all to him. His name is on the deed. The law does not recognize my sister and me as anything more than chattel. That is what I have to contend with." Her cheeks flushed with angry color.

"There must be some way—"

"Oh? Indeed. You think I have not considered every possibility? That I am not clever enough? Pray, enlighten me on what I am missing."

"No," he said slowly, carefully, reconsidering his perhaps brash and insensitive words. "I think you are very clever. You have been managing this place all by yourself for years and I think your father would be very proud of you."

She stilled. "My father?" She stared at him in wide-eyed bewilderment. "What do you know of what he would think? He left all of this to Bede."

"Only because he expected that your brother would be an honorable man, that he would step up and do what is right by you and your sister. That is what any father would expect."

"Yes. Well. He was wrong, was he not?"

"Yes. He made a mistake. That does not mean he did not love you. I am certain he would be proud of you . . . and if he could, if he were still here, he would do things differently and place more trust in you over Bede."

Her eyes gleamed with moisture, and he was not certain if he had overstepped himself. Had he upset her?

She sniffed and nodded jerkily. "Thank you. Thank you for that."

His chest loosened a bit at the realization that he

had not upset her. She seemed almost . . . moved. Relieved from his words. As though he had said something she desperately needed to hear.

They returned to work in companionable silence. As messy as the task of shoveling horse shit was, he could not help but think it was one of the most pleasant mornings he had spent in a long while.

Chapter Fourteen ❧

Mercy had not expected to be back at the Blankenships' ballroom so soon. It seemed she was here just a short time ago. Of course, she had been a different person then.

She felt like another woman now as she stood in the glittering ballroom, staring out at a sea of familiar faces—residents of Shropshire she had known all her life. Of course, no one knew of the change in her. No one was aware. They still saw the plain spinster, Mercy Kittinger, wearing the same tired gown she wore to all these events.

The well-to-do Blankenship family had always included everyone when they hosted these affairs. All the denizens of the village and surrounding countryside in every varying level of rank were present. It really was quite egalitarian of them.

Mercy and her family never missed a Blankenship ball. Grace would be beside herself if such a thing happened. These balls were a long-standing tradition in the area, but, thankfully, they usually only occurred once a year. It was not such a great commitment to attend once a year.

Once a year Mercy could tolerate it. Once a year she would don her best gown—and a smile—and ride the hour and a half to Shropshire and the Blankenship estate that sat outside of town. For her sister it was a small sacrifice.

It was the highlight of Grace's year. It made her happy. Even if in the weeks following she moped about, depressed to be back in her quiet life in the countryside, removed from all of society and its diversions. That was the drawback to these events. Contending with Grace afterward.

Mercy craned her neck, searching for her sister among the crowd. She had seen her with friends earlier, near the refreshment table. Mercy's brother was out there, too, doing what he loved most. Socializing. Hopefully not gambling in one of the card rooms. He had nothing left to gamble, after all. No money, certainly.

But Bede still has possession of the farm.

Unfortunate, that. A familiar hopelessness rose up inside her chest. There was nothing she could do about the situation. That would forever and always be the case.

He might not make the mistake of gambling away their family home *here*, in Shropshire . . . or perhaps this soon after the last time, but how could she trust that he never would again? Later, in another place, another time, he might be so reckless. She swallowed thickly. It only felt like a matter of time. Inevitable.

Then what would she do?

"Someone does not look like she's enjoying herself. What is such a scowl doing on your face?"

Mercy spun around at the sound of the much-loved voice. "Imogen!" She stepped forward and happily embraced her lifelong friend, Imogen Bates.

Well, she would not be Bates for much longer. She was soon to be married. They would no longer be the two spinsters huddled together near the potted ferns at these events. Those days had come to an end. At least for Imogen.

Mercy fought down the twinge of sadness that realization brought forth. Her friend had fallen in love and she was happy for her. True, it was unexpected. She would never have guessed Imogen the type to have her head or heart turned—especially not by the likes of her soon-to-be husband, the erstwhile Duke of Penning. And yet it had happened.

Imogen was set to wed Peregrine Butler, a *former* duke. He had been stripped of his title and lands, naturally, once it was learned he was the *illegitimate* son of his father. None of that seemed to matter to either Imogen or Perry though. They appeared blissfully content with each other and their lives and his lack of a title did not seem to signify.

"I did not think we would be back here so soon." Imogen waved to the ballroom at large.

"No," Mercy agreed, "I suppose we have to owe our thanks to the new Duke of Penning for bringing us together again tonight."

"Indeed. Have you met the man?"

"No. Have you? What is he like?"

"Yes. He invited us to tea shortly after his arrival. Most hospitable of him. He is a bit of an eccentric, but perfectly pleasant. I suppose that is to be expected. He was not born a duke nor brought up to be one, after all."

He was not a pompous blue blood then. "That is to his credit, I imagine." Mercy had scarce to no interaction with nobility, but she had oft heard they were quite high in the instep. Peregrine had fit that mold in the days whilst he was still the duke. Now, of course, he was of humble and modest character. She much preferred him as he was now in his present role.

"There he is. That is the duke." Imogen nodded to a man of middle years with a florid complexion. He was imposing. Easily the tallest man in the room. Mr. Blankenship stood near him, naturally. The two of them were the most important men in the room, after all.

One was a duke and the other was the wealthi-est gentleman in Shropshire. Even so, Mercy knew for a fact that no previous Duke of Penning had ever demeaned himself to attend a fete in the village. Not even Peregrine Butler, when he had been the duke.

"He seems nice." It was the truth. The man smiled widely and seemed interested in those around him, speaking not only to Mr. Blanken-ship, but others that approached, no matter their rank.

"And he has a son," Imogen volunteered.

Mercy felt her eyes widen. She waggled her eyebrows. "A son? Goodness."

"Indeed. A *bachelor* son," Imogen said with heavy emphasis.

"A bachelor? As in unmarried? Dare I say it? Not for long."

Imogen laughed delightedly. "He has been deemed the most eligible man in the area and he has not even arrived in Shropshire yet."

"But of course!"

"Can you imagine when he actually arrives here?"

"The Blankenship sisters will camp out on the grand lawn at Penning Hall." Mercy laughed.

"It won't even matter if he looks like a frog."

"He need not even speak English . . . or any language, for that matter!"

"So long as he has a pulse," Imogen agreed jovially. "That would be the only requirement for Penning's son."

Their joint laughter faded into contented sighs. Imogen held her side as though her ribs ached.

Oh, it was good to see her friend. It felt nice to laugh with her again. Living so far outside of the village could be rather isolating at times.

Mercy certainly did not long for city life, but it would be lovely to have a friend in close proximity to talk to when life became stressful. When she was forced to contend with Bede and Grace, which was often. More than often. Mercy on her own. Coping on her own. It was the way of things. All the time.

Except recently.

Recently she had not been on her own. For over a week she'd had Silas at her side, and it had been nice. *Nice.* She winced. It was a weak and insignificant word, but accurate.

"Do you recall the last time we were here? A few months ago?" Imogen asked, intruding on her thoughts.

"Mm-hmm."

"It feels like a lifetime since then," Imogen

mused. "I was quite at odds with Peregrine Butler then."

Mercy nodded. "Oh, yes. You wanted to claw his eyes out that night as I recall. The things you were saying! I worried for you."

Imogen glanced around rather surreptitiously, and then said, "But that also happened to be the night we first kissed." Her cheeks pinkened at the admission. "You must take me for a perfect scandal to confess such a thing."

Mercy did not immediately reply. Her own thoughts went to Silas.

Heat crept over her as she recalled all the things they had done. It had been more than kissing. She tugged at her modest neckline, feeling suddenly constrained, her clothes too tight, too restrictive chafing against her.

Imogen's face blanched at her prolonged silence. "Oh, my! You do! You think me shameful."

"No!" Mercy shook her head. "I was not thinking that at all," Mercy assured her, wondering what Imogen would say or think of *her* if she knew the extent of *her* wicked actions in London not so very long ago. "I think that you and Mr. Butler were clearly meant to be together and you are very much in love." She shrugged as if the matter were as simple as that.

It *always* seemed that simple for others. For everyone else. Others could fall in love. Marry. Live among their family with trust and love. It always looked so very easy from the outside looking in, but Mercy was not so naive to believe others did not have their hardships, too. People were complicated. Lives complicated. Everyone had their trials. Nothing was simple for anyone.

"When did your brother arrive home? He has not been here in a while. And he brought a friend with him, I see."

"Hmm," Mercy murmured noncommittally, hoping she looked casual at the mention of Silas. Even as close a friend as she considered Imogen to be, Mercy was not about to confess the entire sordid debacle to her. "He's been home close to a fortnight now. His friend arrived . . . a little behind him." Again, she hoped she gave nothing away to her friend that alerted her to the fact that there was something more between Silas and her.

"A handsome man," Imogen remarked in such a way that Mercy felt certain her friend was looking at him at that very moment.

Mercy followed her gaze, searching over the many faces until she landed on Silas Masters so at ease among a group of ladies. *Of course.*

They surrounded him like a flock of pecking hens. He was a young and handsome finely attired stranger, dropped into their midst—at a ball no less. Naturally he would not be spared from their attention.

They would eat him alive.

He would be lucky if he was still standing at the end of the night.

As though he felt her stare, his eyes lifted and locked on her.

She smiled and gave him a small, unassuming wave.

"Uh-oh," Imogen murmured.

"What?" Mercy asked quickly, anxiously, immediately worried her friend detected something in that small wave to Silas.

"Would you look at that? Both Blankenship girls and the Widow Berrycloth are closing in on him fast. Should we rescue him? He is looking rather desperately at you."

Mercy's lips twitched. "He is, isn't he?"

Imogen giggled.

Mercy continued, "He is a grown man who is accustomed to life in London. No doubt he can cope with a few admiring country ladies."

"I don't know," Imogen said, "these are Shropshire ladies. They're cut from a different cloth and not to be underestimated."

Mercy nodded in agreement. Whatever she intended to say next flew from her mind as she caught a flash of pink skirts. Her sister. *Grace.*

Grace dancing in the arms of one Amos Blankenship to be exact.

Grace tossed back her head and laughed with an abandon. Mercy winced. Such behavior would have tongues wagging, to be sure.

"Oh. Your sister looks lovely tonight. So very grown-up."

"Yes," Mercy grudgingly agreed. Unfortunately. Things were so much simpler when Grace was nine years old.

So *very* grown-up indeed. Seventeen years old but she could not be led or directed or—heaven forbid—told what to do. Grace knew what was best for herself, and Mercy should simply keep her opinions to herself. As her sister frequently reminded her: they were *sisters*. Not mother and daughter.

Amos Blankenship swirled Grace around the dance floor, holding her closely. Too closely in Mercy's estimation. He leaned close and spoke into her little sister's ear in a far too familiar manner. Whatever he said made Grace's face burn bright red.

Cad.

Mercy had to fight back the urge to storm across the room and yank Grace free of him. What reason did she have to react so emotionally? Only that Amos Blankenship possessed a reputation of being a spoiled and lecherous libertine and he danced with her sister. She would look like a madwoman if she reacted that way though. It would serve no one to cause a scene. Grace would be mortified. Mercy would never hear the end of it. And Amos Blankenship was the son of their most lauded host. She dared not give offense.

She took a measured breath, reaching deep for her composure.

"Unfortunately Amos Blankenship noticed how lovely she is, too," Imogen muttered. "He really is a cad, you know?"

"Oh, yes. I know."

Mercy and Imogen had grown up with Amos Blankenship. They knew precisely the manner of man he was. They were united in this opinion.

"Grace is a clever girl," Imogen added encouragingly. "She will see through him."

"Did you already forget? She is seventeen. Do you not remember being seventeen? No one at seventeen is *that* clever. It is not possible. Your emotions are in control of you."

Imogen laughed. "True."

Mercy looked out over the crowd. Frowning, she took a few steps forward and craned her neck, searching with renewed focus. "Um. Do you see Grace anywhere?"

"Ahh." Imogen joined Mercy in her efforts and scanned the dance floor. "I am certain . . . well, she was just here. Perhaps she went to the ladies' retiring room."

"I don't see Amos either." And that made her stomach cramp uncomfortably.

Imogen clearly agreed. She nodded swiftly. "You go search the gardens. I will check the ladies' room."

They parted and went their separate directions even as Mercy told herself she was being silly and overly suspicious. Grace would not be so foolish as to be lured outside by a gentleman. True—Amos Blankenship might be young and mildly handsome and perceived to be the biggest catch in all of Shropshire—at least before the duke's son arrived in town—but Grace would not be so reckless and throw caution to the wind in such a manner.

Mercy exited the crowded ballroom through one of the French balcony doors. A few people lingered on the expansive veranda, but none were Grace or Amos Blankenship.

Grimacing, Mercy held up her skirts and descended the curving steps that led down into the lush gardens. The darkened parkland was an ideal location for assignations. The grounds were extensive and there was many a dark corner or hedge or cluster of trees to offer cover for romantic liaisons.

She walked slowly, cautiously, peering into the shadows, not wanting to overlook anyone. Nor did she want to startle anyone either. Inconspicuous was the goal. It would not do to attract attention. No one need be alerted that she was out here searching for her rogue sister.

A hand clamped on her shoulder and the beginning of a scream escaped her before she had the sense to cut it off and kill the sound in her throat.

Chapter Fifteen ❧

*M*ercy pressed a hand to her pounding heart to keep it from escaping from her chest and spun around to face Silas Masters.

"Mr. Masters," she exhaled heavily.

"Silas," he corrected.

"You gave me a fright."

He gave a nod that could be construed as an apology, and then dove into: "What are you doing out here?"

"Just taking some fresh air. It was a bit crowded inside."

He nodded slowly. "Yes. It was."

She looked back out at the garden, anxious to continue her search.

"Are you . . . looking for someone?" he asked.

She snapped her gaze back to him, wondering how he knew. Was she so obvious? What had she given away in deed or expression?

Rather than answer him, she turned a question of her own on him. "What are you doing out here?"

"Following you," he replied without shame or pretense.

She blinked. "Oh." That was disconcerting. Had he been watching her that closely? She thought she had been the only one doing the watching. If she had not been so distracted tracking him and his movements through the packed ballroom, she might have not lost sight of her sister.

"You do realize that people out here are engaged in trysts of an intimate nature?"

That was the entire issue. Her total concern. The reason she was out here at all. "I realize that, yes."

He nodded in the gloom. "Is that why you are out here then?" A beat of silence followed the question. "Have you a rendezvous planned with a gentleman?"

She pointed at herself. "Me?" Her voice squeaked out the question, her astonishment undeniable.

"Yes. *You.* This is your home. Your familiars are here. Your neighbors. It is not so unbelievable to consider there might be someone in your life here. For you. Someone you wish to meet out here."

Is that what he thought? That she would jump from him to someone else so soon? Absurd. She laughed. "Don't be ridiculous."

"How am I ridiculous? I can attest firsthand to your significant wiles."

That only made her laugh harder. *Her wiles?* "Well, I assure you. No one else can. Not here or anywhere else."

Did he not see her relegated to the far walls with the rest of the unmarriageables? Ancient widows and spinsters. She was the consummate wallflower. Wiles, indeed!

Even in the gloom, she noted the easing of his shoulders at her words. His body relaxed as though he had been holding his breath. He had been tense. Because of her? *Why?* Because she had potentially been meeting someone out—

She sucked in a sharp breath. *No.* Certainly not. He could not be . . .

"Are you . . . jealous?" She sounded just as she felt—incredulous.

The question rang out absurdly on the air between them. *Astonishingly* absurd.

No one had ever felt such a sentiment on her behalf. Naturally. She was a spinster. She would have had to have a romantic attachment or entanglement and there had been nothing—er, no one—like that in her life.

"Me? Jealous?" He scoffed. "Now who is being ridiculous?"

"Oh. Forgive me. I did not mean to offend." Mirth still pushed at the edges of her voice though. She took a sobering breath. "If you would excuse me. I was only . . ." Her voice faded as she remembered her task. He had distracted her. His presence always had a way of doing that, but she felt a jolt of shame at being distracted from being a good sister and locating Grace.

"What were you saying?" he pressed. "Why are you out here?"

"If you must know—" She sighed. "I was looking for my sister. I thought she might have stepped outside." She supposed she could trust him with one more of her family's indignities. He knew most of their secrets by now. What was another one to keep?

"She is out here?" He looked around and even though she could not read his expression in the shadows, she perfectly gathered his thoughts. She easily detected the judgment in his voice. He, too, thought it was highly suspect and ill-advised for Grace to be out in this garden. "Well. We shall locate her."

We?

She put the thought into words. "We?"

He continued in the direction she had been walking when he had first startled her. Walking ahead of her, he nodded. "Yes. I will accompany you."

"I do not think that is necessary—"

He glanced back at her and she heard a smile in his voice as he called over his shoulder, "You say that often, you know? Now come along. Let us find that sister of yours so we can feel better and enjoy the rest of the evening. That is *necessary*, is it not?"

His usage of "we" this time gave her pause.

So we can feel better . . .

Did that mean he cared about her sister? Was he also worried? She stared thoughtfully at the dark shape of his back before moving to catch up with him.

They proceeded side by side, the sounds of the house party a distant buzz on the air.

"Are you enjoying the party then?" she queried.

It felt like someone should speak into the silence.

"It is a pleasant affair."

A pleasant affair. A perfectly polite response.

"A little different from your London parties, I imagine."

"Yes and no." He paused a beat. "No matter the event, a country soirée or raucous night at the gaming hell . . . everyone is playing a part at these things."

She had been an observer at enough of these Blankenship balls to understand what he was saying. The antics she observed always felt like a game being played out.

"All the world's a stage, and all the men and women merely players . . ." she recited.

He nodded in agreement. "The bard was not wrong."

Soft tinkling laughter suddenly floated in the air and Mercy froze.

Silas stilled beside her, too.

They stood together, listening, identifying the general whereabouts of those giggles. The sound subsided and then there were whispers. Rushed intimate whispers. But even the low pitch could not disguise that one of the voices was female and recognizable.

"Grace," Mercy breathed. Lifting her skirts, she took off in that direction at full speed.

"Mercy, wait!"

She did not wait.

Ignoring Silas calling after her, she veered off the row onto one of the smaller intersecting paths. Silas's footsteps sounded behind her, so she knew he was close on her heels. The pebble path curved and descended a few steps to abut a tall hedge. Mercy paused, looking the wall of greenery up and down.

Silas arrived at her side. With a light touch on her elbow, he turned her around to face her left—and the couple tucked away there, blending into the hedge, almost hidden if not for the familiar pink skirts peeking out of the foliage. Grace was wedged between the hedge and Amos Blankenship.

"Grace!"

The couple sprang apart guiltily.

Before she could caution herself to adopt a calm air, Mercy charged forward in full quivering outrage. "Grace Kittinger, what are you doing?"

Grace nervously grasped and fidgeted with one of the plump sausage curls draped over her shoulder. "Mercy, did you follow me?"

"That is not the question to ask me." She eyed her sister up and down, relieved to see she was still quite fully attired. It appeared no garments had been discarded. Evidently there had only been kissing and petting. Not that such activity wasn't ruinous enough if they were discovered. Grace flirted with serious danger here.

Determined to save her before irreparable harm was done, she seized Grace by the wrist and pulled her to her side, leveling her glare rightfully so upon Amos Blankenship. "You, sirrah. Have you nothing to say for yourself?"

Blankenship tugged on his waistcoat. "No damage done here."

"I will not have you dally with my sister's reputation or affection, sirrah. She is but seventeen."

"Mercy! I am not a child!"

"Indeed, she is not," Blankenship agreed rather lecherously.

Before Mercy could properly express her indignation at that, Silas grabbed Blankenship by his jacket and gave him a fierce shake. "You will keep your hands to yourself and off Miss Kittinger."

Blankenship's face puffed up and his voice blustered out, "How dare you? Who are you? Do you even know who I am? This is my house, my party—"

"Then why don't you take yourself back to *your* party inside *your* house and forget about young girls who are unavailable to you?"

"Unavailable," he sputtered as though the very notion that any female could be unavailable to him was preposterous.

Grace stomped her foot in childlike pique. "Please, stop! You are both embarrassing me!"

"Enough, Grace," Mercy hissed. "This is a serious matter. You are in no position to wage a protest right now."

Without waiting to hear anything else from Amos Blankenship—really, who wanted to hear him bluster further?—she guided Grace out from her little trysting spot against the hedge, leaving the gentlemen behind.

When her sister was at a more appropriate age to be considering suitors, she would do far better than the likes of Amos Blankenship. There was more to a man than the plumpness of his pocketbook—or rather, his father's pocketbook.

Mercy walked a brisk pace. Her sister did not resist, more or less. She was deadweight that Mercy pulled after her.

"I know you are angry, but someday you will realize the error of your ways tonight and be grateful it did not go any further."

As she heard the words she uttered, she felt a colossal hypocrite. She herself had been less than discreet with a man.

Recently, too.

But you are not seventeen and you did it for a reason. A good reason . . . even if you did enjoy it.

Grace uncharacteristically held her tongue.

Mercy stopped with her just outside the doors leading back into the ballroom. "Are you well enough to rejoin the party or—"

"I was never *un*well!" Her sister at last found her voice. "And I am perfectly capable of returning inside." Grace lifted her chin with a sniff. "In fact, that sounds perfectly delightful compared to staying out here in *your* wretched company one moment more." With that said, Grace preceded Mercy into the ballroom with a swish of her pink skirts.

Mercy took a step, on the verge of following, when Blankenship and Silas approached.

She turned as they emerged from the shadows, Blankenship walking at the front. He walked straight inside and past her without even a cursory glance. As though she was beneath his notice.

She crossed her arms and stared after him as he plunged back into the crowd.

Silas stopped beside her. "Well, we briefly spoke. I would *like* to tell you he is well dissuaded from pursuing your sister."

Mercy shook her head, knowing that had not happened. "But he is a jackanapes chock-full of arrogance and he made no such promise."

"Precisely. He did not express an ounce of shame or regret for his actions. He did not seem to even care that he had been caught with your sister, which does not bode well for her. He cares naught for her reputation at all."

Nodding, she mused, "An honorable gentleman would have offered marriage." He made a sound of assent, and she continued on, in full indignant rant now, "Or at least declared his intention to a proper courtship." Not that she wanted her sister bound for eternity to Amos Blankenship.

Silas went still and silent beside her. She stopped and looked at him . . . and then felt a sudden warm flush of embarrassment as her own ill-chosen words played back in her head, echoing in her ears. *An honorable gentleman would have offered marriage.*

And yet Silas had not.

Awareness passed between them. Words neither would say, but the knowledge was there between them, a living, pulsing thing. Mercy had done everything and more than what her sister had done with Amos Blankenship. *Much more.* She, however, could muster no shame. She knew she should, but she could not.

Staring at Silas, she did not sense regret from him either.

They were quite a pair. Both shameless and both against the notion of marriage to each other. He had not offered, and she would not accept if he had.

She had more than compromised herself by society's standards, and she harbored no expectation of marriage from him. Not on that night. Not now. Not ever.

If she was with child, he had vowed that their futures would be entwined, but that was not the same thing as marriage. It was not even close. He had offered her support and a roof over her head but not a ring. Not respectability.

Time, however, would soon reveal that she was not carrying his child and then he would go on his way. Return to his life in Town and forget all about her.

He would no longer be a familiar sight at her home. He would no longer spend his days at her side, or sitting at her dining table, or sleeping down the hall from her bedchamber. He would no longer occupy himself with her family or on her land as though it were his home, too.

As though he cared about her home, about her family, about *her*.

He motioned to the door. "Shall we?"

She nodded. "Yes. I should locate Grace and make certain she is not near Amos Blankenship again." She winced, her confidence of that was not very high. In her present mood, Grace might do that very thing simply to thwart Mercy.

Silas followed her inside the crowded house. No one gave her a second glance, but she noticed plenty of people looking past her to Silas Masters.

Silas stayed close as she navigated the ballroom. Eventually she found Grace standing with some girls her age, the baroness's young daughter among them. Annis and Grace had their heads close together in conversation.

Mercy stopped searching at the sight of her, some of the tension easing from her.

"She's not with him," Silas murmured beside her. "There is that at least."

She nodded as she watched her sister. Grace's gaze landed on her then across the distance. Mercy's stomach rolled over at the sudden expression of animosity on her face. It was immediate and vicious. She did not even resemble the Grace she knew in that moment.

"Oh, my." She breathed heavily. "She is not happy with me."

"She will forget and forgive," Silas reassured her.

Mercy appreciated him saying that and she hoped he was right, but as she stared at her sister's face she was not so certain. She feared that her relationship with her sister might never be repaired. At least it felt that way.

Hopefully, she was wrong. Only time would tell.

Chapter Sixteen ❦

The ride back home was a quiet affair. They traveled in two conveyances, Otis driving the carriage Mercy, Grace, Bede and Silas occupied while Gladys, Elsie and the other farm workers followed in the wagon.

Mercy studied her sister discreetly in the shadowed interior. Grace stared out the window into the dark night with a sullen air, ignoring everyone inside the carriage.

The hour was late. They could not reach the house soon enough. The sentiment was not expressly stated, but it felt shared by everyone.

As soon as they stopped, Grace was flying out the door. She did not wait for anyone to help her down. She vanished in a flurry of pale pink inside the house.

Mercy met Silas's gaze and felt a little comforted at the empathy there. It was nice to feel like she had an ally in the world. Usually she was on her own coping with her sister. Not that she and her sister had ever been *this* at odds before.

Once inside the small foyer, Bede yawned. Mercy covered her nose with her gloved hand. The whiff of spirits from him was strong.

"Well, good night, everyone." He scratched his stomach through his vibrant yellow and purple waistcoat. "I will see you all in the morning."

More like afternoon, she suspected. She did not expect him to rise early, especially not after their late night. Mercy watched her brother ascend the stairs, his tread heavy on the steps.

Silas lingered at the bottom of the steps with her. He nodded up to the second floor. "I am certain things will be better in the morning."

He, of course, meant things with her sister.

She nodded brusquely. "I am sure you are right. Thank you. For tonight. You were really . . . a good friend."

He blinked as though surprised by her words. A small part of her felt that same surprise resonate within her.

She had never thought to see Silas Masters again after she left him in London. She had resigned herself to that. She certainly had not thought to consider him a friend at any point in the future. And yet she did. He *was*. He had become her friend.

He recovered from his obvious surprise and

held her gaze steadily, peering at her with those much too keen eyes of his, dark and intense and impossibly deep. "Of course," he murmured.

She glanced around the small space, marveling that it felt smaller than ever before. Almost as though the walls were closing in around the two of them, trapping them, pushing them together.

"Good night, Silas."

She moved past him up the steps and into her own chamber. Closing the door, she leaned against it for a moment with a heavy exhalation.

She was coming to enjoy his presence here in her home, in her life, far too much. With him here, she did not feel so alone, and apparently that was a condition in her life she suddenly found less than pleasing. She had not realized that about herself. Until now.

She had not realized companionship of a romantic nature was something she might even want for herself. It was getting more difficult to maintain her equanimity when she wanted to pounce on him—to be with him as she had been before. To taste passion again.

It would be over soon. She would have the proof to send him on his way. But she feared it would not be soon enough for her heart.

She should not become so attached. She should

not rely on him. That was foolish of her. He would be gone in a matter of days, if her calculations were correct, and she was rarely wrong. Her courses always arrived in a prompt and predictable manner.

Then she would be alone again.

Shoving that less than exciting notion aside, she changed out of her gown and into her nightgown—a modest confection of wool that buttoned up to her neck.

She knew she should probably climb into her bed. After the long day, she should sleep the night away. And yet going to bed so at odds with her sister didn't feel right. Not without at least saying good-night.

She departed her room and knocked softly on her sister's bedchamber door. After a few moments of no response, Mercy pushed open the door and entered the room.

Grace was sitting at her dressing table, her back to Mercy, but her reflection was visible in the mirror and it was instantly apparent that she was crying. She wiped roughly at her splotchy cheeks.

"Grace?" The sight of her sister in such a state immediately brought forth a pang in her heart.

"What are you doing in here? I didn't say to enter."

"I thought—"

"No," she broke in, her voice shaky with emotion. "Have I lost all rights to privacy in this house? I don't want you in here. Go away."

"Please, let me—"

"No! I hate you."

The words were flung out like a wet rag hitting the ground with a hard splat. Mercy fought back a flinch. She was proud of that. Proud that she did not show a reaction. She was the adult here. The responsible person. Essentially, the parent. She had to be above hurt feelings. Unbreakable. Strong. Immune to barbed words.

Still, it was difficult maintaining her composure and calm facade when her sister stared at her like a stranger. There was no regret in her face or eyes over her harsh words. She looked cold, and that was frightening. Grace had never looked like that . . . never so far away from Mercy. As though Mercy could not reach her no matter what was said or done.

She looked like she meant those cruel words and that scared the devil out of Mercy. Who was this girl who could loathe her so much? It made Mercy feel like she had lost her forever.

The pain of that prospect was intense, but she held herself steady in the face of it.

If she lost her poise and reacted dramatically it really would be all over.

She had never forgotten her mother's words. They had been the last ever spoken to Mercy, uttered on her deathbed, hours before she took her final breath.

It's all on you, Mercy. You have to be brave. You have to be everything to everyone now. The family needs you.

A bit much, perhaps, to rest at the feet of a ten-year-old. She recognized that now in a way she had not as a child. But there was no promise of fairness in life. Her mother had never planned to expire before the age of thirty but that had been her fate nonetheless. Fairness did not apply. Not then. Not now.

Before Mama had died, she had exacted Mercy's vow. Perhaps her mother had known even then that Bede would be useless when it came to matters of responsibility. He was no Papa, to be sure. No mind for farming or business and no heart for it either.

"We will talk tomorrow. When tempers have cooled."

"No!" Grace sliced a finger through the air like a sword. "Don't do that. My temper is perfectly cool," she said calmly, her eyes still flat and distant. Not at all like the little girl who had once picked flowers and been full of giggles and basked in Mercy's love. Where had that girl gone? Was she lost forever? Would Mercy ever see her again?

She realized with some wonder that Grace did not recall that girl either. Of course. All those good memories of cheerful days were too far past. She had been too young then. Just a child. Only Mercy remembered those days. Grace would remember *this* though. These days of strife and discontent. Only the bad. Not the good.

It broke Mercy's heart. She moistened her lips. "Grace. Let us not argue—"

"But we do it so very well," she snapped with a bitter edge.

"Aren't you weary of it? Don't you want it to stop?"

Grace shrugged, petulant and indifferent. "I don't see how. It will never change. Not as you are."

Mercy's chest clenched. Please, God. *It has to change.* She wanted her sister back. She wanted an end to the discord. "Of course, it can. Things can always get better—"

"As long as I fall in line like a good little soldier, you mean? Allow me to enlighten you. I don't want to end up like you—a dried-up spinster wasting my life in this place, worrying about crop rotations and if my orange trees are getting enough sun."

Mercy flinched anew and inhaled thinly through her nostrils. They might not get along as well as they once did, but this was even too cruel for Grace.

Mercy should not have come here tonight. She should have allowed them both a good night's sleep before trying to talk. She should take her leave now before worse things were said.

"Good night, Grace. I will see you in the morning." At the door, she hesitated and looked back over her shoulder, latching onto her sister's gaze. "I love you, Gracie."

It seemed the thing to say. The thing to hold on to, to cling to in these most turbulent times. What else could she say?

Grace stared hard at her, unblinking. She was the embodiment of stone, unrecognizable as the girl Mercy knew her to be.

Mercy held her breath, waiting, watching, hoping to hear her say those words back. That could not be so hard.

It *should not* be.

The words never came though, and that perhaps hurt the most. The absolute silence was deafening . . . and it stung.

Mercy turned and left the room, without ever hearing them.

Chapter Seventeen ❧

*O*nce back in the refuge of her room, Mercy stared at herself in the mirror positioned above her dressing table for a long while. She stared so long and so hard, that her likeness started to blur, but perhaps that was the right of it. It made sense that she was unrecognizable. She did not feel as though she knew herself these days.

She blinked her eyes several times until her vision corrected itself. It had indeed been a long night. The woman with tired eyes, dark hair tamed and pinned atop her head very properly, looked like a worn and faded version of herself. As worn and faded as the wool nightgown she now wore.

Shabby and faded felt like a wholly appropriate description for herself.

She was like an old rug with frayed edges that needed repairing and sprucing up—or perhaps needed to be retired and replaced altogether. However accurate, it was a sobering thought. Presently she was so tired. She felt beaten. Certainly she was too young to feel this way.

Too young to be feeling old.

"How am I going to do this?" she whispered to her reflection staring back at her, as though the answer would return to her.

She was not a mother. Obviously.

Grace had made that abundantly clear. She was not a mother, merely an unwanted and interfering older sister.

Mercy unpinned her hair and let it fall loose down her back. Reaching for her hairbrush, she began dragging it through the long dark strands, sighing from the pleasure of it.

She couldn't sit in one place. She was too agitated for that. She rose and strolled the space of her bedchamber as she brushed her hair out.

Hopefully Grace would be calmer tomorrow. After a good night's sleep. Less overwrought. Less hateful. She was young. She always had a flair for the dramatics.

Time.

People said that time was the healer of all. Mercy hoped so.

She and her sister both needed some time. Time for Grace to see reason. Time for Mercy not to feel so hurt. Time for Grace to forgive Mercy for protecting her and realize that her life here was not so very terrible. She simply had to be patient until then.

Too fidgety to fall asleep, Mercy decided to take herself downstairs for a glass of milk and a bite to eat. Despite the abundance of tasty fare provided at the Blankenship ball, Mercy had scarcely eaten. She had been too preoccupied watching after Grace—for all the good that had done.

Except she was not the only one with the inclination to eat. Someone else shared her impulse and he was already in the kitchen, sitting at the table, leaning over a plate of food when Mercy entered the dimly lit room.

"Mr. Masters," she said, momentarily stopping at the unexpected sight of him as she entered the room.

He looked up from the pie he was enjoying. He quickly worked to swallow a mouthful of the tasty dessert, circling his fork in the air as he did so. "I think we are well past the use of surnames, Mercy."

It was not the first time he had suggested they use each other's Christian names, but she had clung to formality, telling herself it was a necessary barrier even if she thought of him as *Silas* in her mind.

"Yes," she agreed, inclining her head in acknowledgment as she moved to retrieve a fork. "Of course we are. Silas."

They definitely could be classified as *intimates*, and as she felt so very alone in the world right now that did not feel like such a terrible thing. She needed to feel kinship to another soul. Especially beneath her roof. Especially in her own home where she felt estranged from her own family. She felt that need strongly and Silas Masters was here to fulfill it.

She would not examine the wrongness of that too closely. There were things far more wrong in her life at the moment—at least it felt that way.

She settled down at the table beside him and dug a fork into the large wedge of blackberry pie on his plate as only an intimate would do. As *friends*. He was that. She had told him that tonight, and she had meant it.

He watched her wide-eyed as she carried a heaping bite to her lips.

"Hmm." She closed her eyes in a long blink of pleasure. "I'm glad Gladys made pie. She must have sensed I was going to need it." She nodded in approval and went in for another bite. "Some people go for spirits. I go for pie."

He chuckled. "Help yourself."

She grinned at him from around a mouthful of pie. "I know this pie. We are old friends. There is no resisting it. Or *any* of Gladys's pies, for that matter. You should taste her apricot pie. It's divine."

His gaze scanned her face closely. "You seem to be feeling better about tonight."

"Do I?" Interesting. Especially since she only felt worse after her encounter with Grace.

He nodded. "Yes. Did you and your sister make amends?"

Mercy snorted. "Certainly not. Quite the opposite. She is not in a talking mood. At least not with me. It will be some time before I am forgiven, I fear."

He nodded in sympathy. "Hard decisions are never met with gratitude."

"Hard decisions are never met with gratitude," she echoed, rolling that around in her mind. She angled her head, absorbing that . . . and concluding it felt accurate. "No, they are not. That is very true and very wise. Hard decisions are indeed *not* met with gratitude or understanding." She took another bite of pie. "Tonight she claimed to hate me."

He made a hissing sound. "She is young. She doesn't mean it. Whatever she's feeling right now, this very night, will change. Like a puff of smoke, it will fade away. Your sister will feel and think entirely differently in a fortnight from now. Hell, a year from now she won't even remember any of this."

Mercy hoped fervently that was true.

"Have many sisters, do you?"

"No. Not a one, but I do know what it is like to be young and an idiot. Or is it . . . a young idiot?" He shrugged as though they were one and the same.

Her lips twitched.

He continued, "Someday your sister will look back on all of this and shake her head . . . *if* she even remembers it with any great amount of detail."

She released a breath. "I am not so certain, but I will take heart in your words and try to believe that."

"It's true. You shall see in time."

She lowered her fork to the plate, idly squishing the tines against a blackberry until the fruit burst in an explosion of dark juice.

"I hope so," she whispered and the words suddenly felt too thick in her mouth. A lump formed in her throat and her next breath was suddenly choking her. She dropped the fork with a clatter. Her cheeks burned hot as a sob broke loose from her lips. Her sister was there, in her mind's eye, her voice as sharp and cutting as it had been in her bedchamber. *I hate you.* Mercy had held herself together before, in the face of that, but now it seemed she had no control over herself.

"Oh, no," he murmured beside her, one of his big hands coming down on her shoulder. "Don't do that. Everything will be well. You will see."

His comforting words were almost too much. They were kind and tender and they undid her.

She twisted around in her seat and fell against him, her arms reaching up to loop around his neck.

He folded her into his arms and pulled her in close. She went willingly, settling into him, fitting against him and sighing in delight at the warm wall of his chest against her.

It was just a hug. An embrace. She told herself the lie.

"There, there," he soothed rather expertly, looking down at her intently. She felt stripped bare under his scrutiny and the sensation was not entirely unwelcome.

She felt the moisture on her face then. The hot glide of her tears. Oh, no. *Blast it.* She hated that she was crying in front of him. It was so mortifying that he should see her like this . . . so vulnerable and weak.

His arms relaxed around her without entirely releasing her, which was a relief. She did not want him to let her go. She wanted his arms to stay caged around her, as troubling and impractical as that was. She did not want practicality. She wanted this. She wanted to stay put, right here, right now, feeling good in his arms forever. *Forever.* The word jarred her. That was a bold and unrealistic wish. As bold and unrealistic as the *other* things she wanted.

She wanted searing kisses and the heavy press of his body over hers and the slick glide of skin against skin . . . and his hardness. His hardness filling her again.

She wanted *him*.

She released a breathy sigh and snuggled in closer to him.

His big hands slid over her tear-coated cheeks, holding her face tenderly up to his. He spoke her name, a dark little whisper flowing over her parted mouth.

His hands moved down her shoulders and around to her back, brushing up and down her spine in rhythmic strokes that she tried to pretend did not affect her—did not awaken those feelings inside her that she had been trying to bury ever since she left him in London, ever since they had gone at each other in the orangery.

Perhaps such a thing was impossible? Perhaps when you spent the night with someone—in that person's bed, in that person's arms—it was impossible to ever pretend otherwise? Impossible to feign indifference to the eddying tremors of sensation running through your body.

A dried-up spinster, Grace had called her.

There was some truth in that, Mercy realized. That was why she had been so susceptible, so willing to engage in a dalliance when she was in London. She was hungry for intimacy of the physical variety with another person.

Not just any dalliance either. A dalliance with Silas Masters. If one was to dally, it should be with someone like him. Someone extraordinary. Someone whose big callused hands spanned her back now, singeing her through the fabric of her dress. Someone whose butterfly gusts of breath felt warm and arousing on the side of her face, so close to her ear that she heard the cadence of his breathing like the rush of a second heartbeat, working in rhythm with her own.

She did not know the precise moment the air shifted. The precise moment that hand felt less comforting and more sensual in nature.

His hand traveled up her back, reaching her nape beneath the heavy fall of her hair. His fingers curled around her neck, his palm pressing flush against the bump of her vertebra, exerting more pressure as his fingertips played at the skin on the side of her throat.

She could summon no words to speak. She knew she should disengage. He had kindly offered his solace, obligingly held her when she flung herself against him, but she could not continue to do this. This was something more than comfort. Something she was not entitled to have. He was not hers. This could not last.

Pull away.

She moistened her lips, her eyes fluttering shut as the velvety pads of his fingers started a rhythmic stroking.

Easier said than done.

She relaxed, arching her throat to the side to grant him better access. Another inhale and she had the full fragrance of him. The rich aroma of his masculine scent: freshly laundered garments, leather and a whiff of something else. Whiskey from earlier tonight perhaps.

His arms around her felt so strong and enveloping—as though he could hold and keep all of her burdens, as though he could carry the entire weight of the world in their breadth.

For so long she had carried the bulk of it all, held her family up—admittedly not successfully at times. Especially recently. Recently she felt she was failing.

It felt nice. *This* felt nice.

It was a real indulgence to be able to lower her guard and lean on someone else for a change.

She exhaled, her whole body easing, a bow released, a line let go.

Mercy slumped, fell heavier against him, letting his bigger, stronger body prop her up. She couldn't move. Couldn't tear herself away from this—she didn't want to.

The mad impulse to scoot from her seat and crawl atop him where he sat and press her mouth anywhere his skin was exposed seized her. She remembered his skin. The warmth and give of it, the tempting texture slightly rougher than her own.

The *taste*.

She was bolder around him. Wanton. Not herself . . . or perhaps this was who she really was. Could that be possible? Was this who Mercy was? Who she was meant to be? Could she be more of her true self with him?

She lifted her gaze to find him considering her with his deep brown eyes. She went all soft and fuzzy beneath that gleaming, bottomless gaze. She lowered her head, dropping her forehead to his shoulder as though not looking at him might give her the strength to resist him.

She took several breaths. "I really should go upstairs," she murmured into the warm and tempting buffer of his shoulder.

His thumb swept over her nape. Goose bumps sprang up all over her skin. "Then go, if you like."

She did not like.

She closed her eyes against him, against the very reasonable words he presented to her.

She should take his advice, his invitation for her to go, but she did not wish to leave the security of his arms. And yet it was more than that. She was making excuses. Lying to herself even . . . telling herself this was only about comfort and friendship. How pathetic was that?

She wanted to be with him as she had been before. She ached for him. She wanted to kiss him again and do *all* the things with him again. And again.

Quite simply . . . *she wanted.*

She was no girl who had to invent reasons to be with a lad she fancied. She was well past such girlhood modesty. She had never been that girl at *any* age. And she could not claim shyness either. Of course she had never been interested in a specific lad—or *man*—before. Until now.

That had changed.

He had changed her.

She pulled back and looked into his eyes, wondering if there was anything in those depths and within him that echoed even a fraction of the longing tremoring through her.

He was no stranger to this—to desire. If he was even feeling that. It was rather arrogant of her to assume, but assume she did. Or rather she hoped.

He was not like her. She was not his first liaison. Perhaps he was fine with just the once between them. Perhaps he did not crave more.

He was here for one reason, after all, and it was *not* to bed her. It was not to be a shoulder to cry on either. He had made it clear upon his arrival that he was here to verify whether or not she was with child. For no other reason than that. He was not here for any repeat dalliances.

She could read nothing in his eyes. He was not holding her hostage. By word and deed, he was permitting her to go. Permitting? More like encouraging.

Then go, if you like.

"It is late," she murmured by way of agreement, giving a single jerky nod.

"It is," he agreed. "And you wake early," he reminded her.

"I do. I am a perpetual early riser. There is always so much to do . . . but you've been getting up early, too." She was rambling and could not seem to stop herself. "You don't have to do that, you know. You're a guest. You should not be laboring like a farmhand. I feel as though I am taking advantage of you. Perhaps tomorrow you could sleep at least until sunrise," she suggested.

"Doubtful, and I don't mind. I don't spend much time sleeping."

"Why is that?"

He shrugged. "I have never been one to sleep well."

She shook her head. "That is a shame. And it can't be good for you. My father always said a soul needs a minimum of eight hours of sleep at night to repair itself and ready for the next day."

"Eight hours? That would be decadent."

She frowned, not liking that he should not have the rest he deserved—and not liking that she should care so much. But she did. "There has to be a reason you sleep so little."

"Your concern is touching. You needn't fret, however. I have subsisted on very little sleep ever since I can remember and I am no worse for wear."

She felt her frown deepen. She did not approve. He needed healing rest as did everyone.

"Perhaps if you discovered *why* you cannot sleep, you could work on that and then sleep better. Longer."

He smiled. "Knowing your problems does not make them go away. It is not that simple. *Life* is not so simple as that."

She felt those words keenly. She knew about a complicated life. About a life riddled with problems. He was one such problem. *Her* problem, she supposed.

He'd become her problem the moment Bede arrived home to tell her that he had lost their home to him. He had continued to be her problem after that, too. In London. And now here.

He was her problem and he was not going away. At least not anytime soon. Not until her menses arrived and she said the words that would send him away.

She moistened her lips.

Perhaps you will never have them to say.

The thought slipped into her mind like an intruder, quickly and unexpected.

She gave her head a swift shake. She did not mean that. She could not wish herself the scandal of being unwed and with child. To what purpose? To push him into marriage? He had not promised that.

Did she think he would change his mind? Would the bond of a child be enough to keep him with her?

She did not want that. She did not want him compelled—no, *forced*—to be in her life.

"What is going through that mind of yours?" His voice dragged over her skin like a physical caress.

She looked into his discerning gaze, and then deliberately looked at his mouth, letting her eyes settle there, letting him see and feel her attention there.

Letting him *know* her mind since he had asked.

His head dipped, almost tentatively, giving her plenty of time to pull away. She did not.

His warm mouth came down on hers, sending a jolt of heat through her that shot to all her aching places—her squeezing belly, her suddenly heavy and tingling breasts, her throbbing sex. She could not pull back. She could not say no, could not reject this. This was what she wanted, after all.

There was only one thing left to do. The thing she wanted. *All* the things she wanted.

She kissed him back.

Chapter Eighteen ❧

*M*ercy's mouth moved against Silas's, and what should not happen did. Her brain shut down. *Broke.* This man and his delicious mouth had broken her brain.

The kiss swelled between them, melting her bones and turning her to pudding. Their tongues met and a dazed fog rolled over her, eradicating all thoughts, all logic. There were only feelings. Sensation.

Her arms coiled around his neck. He leaned forward just as she did, their two bodies merging, fusing, becoming one.

His lips ate hungrily from hers as though she was his first meal after a long famine. His hands found her breasts, cupping them over the rough scratch of her wool nightgown.

Heat coursed through her as he massaged the mounds. Everything inside her turned melty and so achy it almost hurt. She fidgeted, eager to part her legs and welcome him inside her.

His erection rose hard and prodding against her hip, pushing, seeking. The pressure of him there was unsatisfactory. He was in the wrong place. She wanted him between her thighs. Hard and deep and fast.

It was both too much and not enough.

His name tore from her throat, spilling into his mouth, into his kiss.

His hands went everywhere. Her face. The line of her throat. They came down over her shoulders, over her breasts, her sides, sliding to her hips, clutching the fabric of her nightgown in his fists.

He dragged his mouth down her throat and she saw flashing spots. The room spun as his hot lips worked over her, and she closed her eyes. Her muscles dissolved. Her head fell back and she went as limp as a rag doll as he feasted on her. She smiled, floating in a heady state of pleasure.

She had to taste him, too.

She lifted her head and brought her face back to his neck, breathing in the delicious smell of him. She nuzzled his throat, kissing him with her open mouth, licking him, savoring his warm, slightly salty skin with a satisfied growl.

His breath snagged just above her ear, ruffling

her hair. She felt him swallow, his throat working against her exploring tongue.

She pressed her body against his until she could feel every part of him: all the familiar lines and slopes and hollows. All of his hardness that she had been dreaming about since the last time she felt him. The last time they had been together. Her stomach tightened, and the low deep ache between her thighs throbbed.

She had done this before. With him. Once should be enough—at the time she had said it would be enough to last her forever—but it was not. Dimly, she wondered how many times it would take to get this man out of her mind . . . out of her blood.

Need gripped her. She reached her hand between them, seeking and finding the hard bulge of him pushing into her hip, and squeezed him.

"I remember this," she rasped against his throat.

"It remembers you, too," he growled as one of his hands burrowed between the many folds of her nightgown to cup her woman's mound with his big hand. He flexed his hand, squeezing her sex. She cried out, arching under him. "My cock aches for this sweet quim."

She shuddered at his naughty speech, thrilling at it, reveling in it . . . wanting more of such shameless talk. More of his hands on her combined with such talk.

She lifted her head to gaze into his eyes, her hand holding his face, cupping his cheek, her thumb stroking, grazing that soft pelt of his beard, longing to feel it against her skin, rubbing over her breasts, chafing the insides of her thighs.

With a desperate little cry, she dove for his lips and renewed their kiss. He met her directly, plunging into the kiss with equal fervor. Their tongues tangled. Teeth clanged. The fiercer the better. She didn't care.

A screech shattered the cloud of desire enfolding her. "Mercy! What are you—"

Mercy wrenched away, tearing her lips free with a gasp, her gaze flying to her sister standing in the doorway.

"Grace!" Mercy climbed off Silas's lap gracelessly, nearly tripping and landing on her face, but catching herself in time. Once on her feet, she staggered a few steps clear of Silas.

He rose and stood beside her, reaching out a hand to help steady her. She slapped the hand away. Heat scored her face. The last thing she wanted was to appear in need of his support right now. However fruitless the effort might be—she had just been caught kissing and groping their houseguest, after all—she did not wish to appear in alliance with him.

She held out a hand toward her sister in supplication and released a nervous little laugh. "Grace, it is not what it—"

"Is this where you tell me I did not just see what I *saw*!" She waved wildly at both of them. "Please do not insult me with that lie."

Mercy sent a guilty glance Silas's way. She need not see her own face to know she looked guilty. Because she felt guilty. She *was* guilty.

Where she had not felt shame before, she did now. Now reality was encroaching all around her, and for whatever reason, Silas did not look guilty at all.

He looked . . . unruffled and relaxed. The nerve!

"I don't know how you can explain this." Grace gestured wildly to the both of them. "You are such a fraud! How dare you try to stop me from being with Amos when you're down here getting . . . *shagged* by Bede's friend!"

She flinched. "Grace! Your language—"

"Don't 'Grace' me or reprimand my language! *Shagging* is the proper description for what I walked in on. Shag! Shag! *Shagging!*" She stomped her foot several times for emphasis.

Mercy winced. Her sister was right, of course. It was an apt word even if hearing it out loud made the situation all the more sordid. And what could Mercy say? That she and Silas were *not* lovers? That was not precisely the truth. They had been together before, and she and Silas had been heatedly *engaging* when Grace walked in on them.

"Now," she began, "Grace, I am older than you." Apparently, she would *try* to explain it, however. Try and *fail*.

Grace let loose a hard bark of laughter. "Oh, that is rich. So *your* reputation and virtue are somehow expendable and less valuable than mine? Is that what you tell yourself?"

Yes. Perhaps so. She winced at the obvious fault in that logic. She knew that was wrong, but, of course, she applied different rules to her sister.

Grace looked her up and down in scathing perusal. "You disgust me."

"Now there," Silas cut in, stepping forward, clearly ready to defend Mercy. Or even worse . . . intervene and admonish her sister. Grace swung a scowl on him, ready to eviscerate him if he so much as dared to get involved in this. It was not his place. Mercy put a subduing hand on his arm and shook her head in silent message.

"Oh, that is sweet. He is your great defender, is he?" Grace snorted. "Well, I am so glad *you* have found someone, Mercy, buried out here in the country. How brilliant for you! I am so glad *you* can be happy."

"No, Grace. It is not like . . ."

Her sister did not stick around to hear the rest of

her words. She whirled on her heels and marched from the kitchen. Mercy stared after her even when she was gone. Even when there was no sight of her. Even when her steps were distant creaks on the stairs.

She crossed her arms, hugging herself. "I suppose we weren't very discreet." She looked at Silas.

"No," he agreed. "We weren't."

His hand landed on her shoulder, feather light. She sidled away, ducking out from under his touch, putting proper distance between them. She did not deserve his comfort in this. At any rate, comfort from him always led to other things. She did not deserve those things either.

Without looking at him, she inched back, ready to escape the kitchen. Her sister interrupting them had been a good thing.

Well, it had *not* been good to be discovered and earn her sister's eternal wrath, but stopping Mercy before she did something really foolish with Silas (*again*) had been a good thing.

"I'm going to bed." She permitted herself to look at him then. "Before anything more calamitous happens tonight."

His expression was mild as he stared at her across the distance of the room. Inscrutable. "Good night, Mercy."

"I'll see you in the morning." Turning, she took

to the stairs, wondering fleetingly, longingly, what would have happened if her sister had not interrupted them.

Would she even be heading to her bedchamber alone?

Chapter Nineteen ❧

The following morning it was as though nothing untoward had occurred at all. Mercy and Silas faced each other with total equanimity, taking their breakfast with Gladys and Elsie in the warm and cozy kitchen where so much wicked behavior had transpired the night before.

Of course that could change once Grace joined them. The calm could shatter. Mercy eyed the door uneasily, braced for her arrival. Hopefully she would not reveal Mercy and Silas's indiscretion to all and sundry. She had been angry enough to perhaps do that very thing. Hopefully, she exhibited more discretion and would not punish Mercy by doing that.

Silas held up a thick slice of fresh bread and patted his flat stomach. "This bread is delicious, Miss Gladys. That hint of sweetness to it." He adopted an expression of rapture. "I'm going to have to bring you back to London with me. I can't live without this bread . . . or any of your cooking, for that matter."

"Oh, go on with you." Gladys blushed, clearly reveling in the kind attention.

Back to London.

Of course he was going *back* to London. Why would he not? That was his home. She knew that and yet it was a useful reminder to hear this out of his lips.

Their gazes locked across the table, and Mercy pasted a smile on her face as she stirred honey into her porridge. The last thing she wanted him to think was that she was affected or troubled by the prospect of his departure from her life.

He smiled in turn, but his deep brown eyes were the slightest bit inquiring, and she worried that he read something in her expression. At least he wouldn't ask about that here. That would be too personal and they had witnesses. Mercy was grateful for Gladys and Elsie as a buffer. Clearly, after last night, she had no business being alone with Silas anymore. She could not trust herself.

She was finishing her last bite of toast when she glanced up at the clock. Grace was usually up by now.

Mercy frowned. Her sister was not especially a morning person, and she loved her sleep, but it was still not like her to sleep this late. Did she intend to stay in her rooms all day? Was this in protest of last night's activities? It felt like a definite result of the previous evening. She was obviously still upset with Mercy and meant to avoid her.

Well, Grace had pouted long enough. She could return to the world and the life she had waiting, whether she liked that world and life or not. She had lessons to complete, not to mention chores that needed tending. No one would be doing her work for her merely because she'd had a bad night. She could be mad and loathe Mercy, but she would fulfill her responsibilities.

Resolved, Mercy marched from the kitchen and up the stairs toward her sister's room. She knocked briskly on her bedchamber door.

Nothing.

No response.

"Grace," she called out with forced cheer. "Time to rise."

Mercy waited a few more moments before turning the latch and entering the room—only to find her sister's room empty. No sign of Grace anywhere. The bed was neatly made.

Mercy frowned. Had Grace slipped past her and headed outside already for the day without Mercy noticing? It seemed unlikely. The steps in this house creaked. Mercy would have heard her descent. Unless she had crept down the stairs while everyone was asleep.

Mercy stared ahead blindly as that thought penetrated, sinking in deeply.

Oh. No.

No no no no.

She blinked and examined Grace's bed with fresh eyes. Had the bed not been slept in at all?

Mercy muttered beneath her breath, panic rising high in her chest. She strode into the room and flung open the bureau. Bending, she rummaged at the bottom, searching for her sister's valise. Not finding it.

It was gone.

The valise was gone and so was her sister.

Mercy straightened and dragged both hands over her face, as though attempting to wake from a horrible dream. This could not be happening. Her sister was gone. Left, presumably, in the middle of the night.

Mercy rotated in a swift circle, uncertain what to do, where to begin, where to go from here.

Where could Grace have gone? She had no money. She could not take a carriage out by herself. Especially at night. She was a passable horsewoman, but not proficient enough to ride very far in the dark.

Mercy stopped hard, reaching for the chair before her sister's dressing table to quell her sudden surge of dizziness, and that was when she caught sight of the folded piece of paper with her name boldly scrolled across the surface.

With a sharp gasp, she snatched up the note and unfolded it to read the words. The unbelievable words.

Then she read them again just to be certain. Just to make certain she was not mistaken and this nightmare had, in fact, just gotten terribly, dreadfully, worse.

A SCREAM YANKED Silas from the pleasure of his morning coffee.

Gladys looked up from her bowl of porridge with wide eyes. "What in heavens is that racket about? I hope it's not another mouse. We had a mouse last winter and oh! Grace caterwauled to high heaven over that."

Silas dropped his napkin on the table and rose from his chair, intending to see for himself what distress might have befallen one of the ladies of the house. Hopefully the younger Kittinger sister was not maiming the older one. After last night, that was a very real possibility.

"Your breakfast will get cold, Mr. Masters," Elsie called after him as he hastened from the dining room and took the stairs two at a time.

The screaming stopped, an eerie silence left in its wake.

The house was not overly large. It did not take him long to locate the source of the scream. The door to young Miss Kittinger's bedchamber loomed wide open, and he easily spotted Mercy standing before her sister's dressing table. She stood as still as a marble pillar.

He stepped into the room and spoke her name hesitantly. There was no sight of her younger sister anywhere. "Mercy?"

She turned slowly, blinking as though emerging from a dream. "She is gone. She has gone to Gretna Green." She choked on this last bit. "If that is to be believed or trusted."

He shook his head, stepping closer, noticing then that she held something in her shaking hand. It appeared to be a note.

He motioned to the paper. "What does it say?"

She looked down at it, gazing at the paper as though it were living thing that might turn on her at any moment.

At her lack of response, he reached for the note. "May I?"

She nodded jerkily, her wide, wounded eyes alarming him. He took the paper, but did not even have a chance to read it before she was speaking in a rush. "She is gone. She left. Gretna Green," she said again, clearly the point that most stuck in her mind.

His gaze flew to the paper then. He read the words and erupted with a curse.

She blinked slowly. "She is ruined." Shaking her head, she added, "Or as good as is. I know Amos Blankenship. He will not do right by her. He does not intend to marry her. He has duped her. I doubt he is even taking her to Gretna Green. Most likely just a nearby inn. He will use and discard her. There will be no marriage. Only heartbreak and disgrace."

Silas crumpled the note in his hand. "It is not too late. Do not despair."

She fixed her wide eyes on him. "I beg your pardon?"

"They can't have gotten far."

"You mean we should give pursuit? Bede . . ." Her voice faded at the mention of her brother and she shook her head as though coming to terms with something.

It was clearly Bede Kittinger's place, his role to give pursuit and seek honor for his younger sister. Of course, Silas could not envision that happening. Kittinger was not a man who got things done.

Silas nodded. "No one need know. I will give pursuit." He briefly considered bringing her brother, as might seem right and proper, but dismissed it. Kittinger would only be a hindrance and slow him down.

She blinked. "You?"

"Yes. I will bring her back safely. This I vow to you."

"What of Amos Blankenship?" She gestured weakly with a hand and released a choked, humorless laugh. "He will carry tales. He will not keep this to himself. Indeed not. He will—"

"Oh, he will not talk. I will see to that personally." Nodding with renewed determination, he turned, marching for the door, hoping that she took solace in his assertion of that. Hopefully, she believed him.

"Wait."

He turned back around. Mercy was gazing at him resolutely, a fiery light in her eyes. "I am going with you."

"I will be riding hard—"

"And I will ride hard alongside you. I can keep up. I am accustomed to long hours in the saddle. I won't be a burden."

He shook his head, frowning. "You don't understand."

"No. *You* do not understand." She pressed a hand to her chest, over her heart. "She is my sister. I am going."

He held that determined stare of hers and recognized at once that she would not be swayed on the matter. "Very well. I will meet you downstairs in ten minutes."

"I will meet you downstairs in five minutes," she countered.

That said, she turned and hastened from the room in a whisper of swishing skirts. He followed on her heels, continuing on and venturing to his own bedchamber and packing a few items should they have to stay the night on the road, as he suspected they would.

He didn't tell her, but he doubted he would catch up with Grace and Blankenship in time to save Grace *entirely* from the clutches of Amos Blankenship. There would be no undoing that. Mercy likely already knew that. She was an intelligent woman. The couple would have had plenty of time alone and opportunity for all manner of vice.

Silas's greatest challenge would be not thrashing the man on sight. He would have to work hard to crush that impulse when they came face-to-face.

Grace Kittinger was a child in every sense. Certainly he had seen girls younger than her lost to the hardships of the streets, but Grace had a loving home and family. She had a sister like Mercy. She should be safe from the likes of Blankenship and all manner of men like him. She should have been safe . . . and he knew it was going to wreck Mercy that she had not fully shielded her.

Sighing, he shut his bag and lifted it from his bed, determined to not keep Mercy waiting.

Chapter Twenty ❦

$\mathcal{D}$usk tinged the sky as they reached the fifth village of the day. Silas could not precisely recall what number inn this would make. The last village of Clembury had boasted no less than four inns and it had taken some time to visit each one of them.

He tossed a coin for the lad to take both their horses and together he and Mercy strode inside.

"Do you think this is the one?" Her voice was still anxious, even after a long day of riding—and searching. She had not given up.

"Let us hope," he murmured.

The hour was growing late. It would soon be too dark to continue much farther, and if they did not quickly locate Grace and Blankenship that meant the two of them were holed up in some little love nest for the night. There would be no coming back from that. Once that happened, Grace would be well and truly lost.

She would have no hope except marriage to

Blankenship. With any luck the fellow meant to offer for her, but Silas had his doubts. He knew men like Blankenship, and they rarely acted with honor. On second thought, marriage to Blankenship might not be the hoped-for outcome. It would only lead, ultimately, to misery for young Grace. He would not wish that on her.

With a hand at the small of her back, he guided Mercy toward the front desk. Raucous sounds spilled from the taproom to the right. Silas rapped the bell at the desk and a man soon emerged to greet them.

"Good evening," the gentleman said, eyeing them, no doubt assessing their worth based upon the richness of their garments and appearance.

Mercy tucked a bit of hair that had fallen loose back up inside her bonnet in obvious self-consciousness. The day had been long. Even as comfortable and accomplished as she was upon a horse, they had not gone a slow pace. Urgency had pushed them. She was exhausted and looked every inch of it.

"A room for you and the missus?" He reached for a ledger.

"Ah. Perhaps. That is, I hope so. This is rather complicated. Allow me to explain." Silas scratched his head as though struggling for thought—as though he had not performed this very little drama at each of the previous inns they had visited today. "We are attempting to locate another couple, but you see we do not know their names. We saw the pair earlier this morning. Presumably they were on their way north as are we. I confess I overheard them speaking to the innkeeper over their breakfast. They were seated at the table beside ours. I did not notice until they had departed from the inn, unfortunately, but the gentleman left this on his seat where he was dining."

Silas pulled from his pocket his very own watch piece dangling from a gold chain, displaying it to the innkeeper as he continued, "It looks to be a fine piece, excellent craftsmanship, and I was hoping to return it to the gentleman. I am certain he will miss it. Might he be staying here?"

The innkeeper's eyes rounded. "Gah. That is a fancy bit of a gewgaw there." Now it was the proprietor's turn to look as though he were in serious contemplation. "Well. Could you describe the gentleman and his lady to me?" he asked slowly, as though the idea was slow to seize him.

Silas snapped his fingers as though this were a brilliant and not obvious suggestion. "Right. Yes. Splendid idea. The gentleman was perhaps of my age." He looked to Mercy as though for confirmation.

"Yes, some might consider him a handsome

fellow. Light brown hair." She held up her hand a few inches above herself. "About this tall. He cuts a rather dashing figure in fashionable attire."

Silas nodded in agreement.

The innkeeper canted his head thoughtfully. "Perhaps, perhaps." He stroked his furry chin. "What did the lady in question look like?"

Mercy took a careful breath. "Quite pretty. Young. Dark haired. About my height."

They looked quite alike, the two sisters. Grace was merely a younger version of Mercy. He knew Mercy must be thinking that, too. She had to have been told that throughout her life. Of course, she could not simply say *she looks like me*.

The innkeeper smiled. "Yes. Yes! You are in luck. Or rather your gentleman is in luck for you have found him. They are here."

"They are?" he asked excitedly, not even having to feign his enthusiasm at this news.

Mercy grasped his arm in eagerness, delighted color brightening her face. "Oh, praise be."

The innkeeper sent her a curious look at her high-spirited reaction, but continued on, "Yes. The young couple checked in earlier this evening. They requested dinner be served in their room."

Mercy's fingers on his arm turned to claws at these words. *Dinner in their room.* There was no unhearing that.

"I see," Silas murmured.

"They're up the stairs, second room to the right. The room directly next door to theirs is our remaining vacant room for the night. All the others are taken." The man slid the ledger toward Silas on the counter. "Shall you and the missus be taking it for the night? I recommend you do so. You don't want to risk being left without accommodations."

"Yes. Of course. We will take the room." Silas signed the ledger and then dipped into his pocketbook to pay the man.

The innkeeper brandished their room key. "I'll show you the way, sir."

Silas turned to take Mercy's arm, quelling the impulse to rush past the man and up the stairs to the door that barred Blankenship and young Grace from the rest of the world. If that was his impulse he knew it must be amplified for her.

They both followed the proprietor up the narrow staircase, moving in single file as that was all the tight space would allow.

He took them first to their room, stopping before the door and unlocking it for them. "This is your chamber for the night."

Silas glanced at Mercy. Her eyes went wide as they traveled the room and fell upon the single bed that dominated the small space.

He swallowed thickly. Of course they would

not be sharing that bed. No matter how much he would like to spend the night in the same bed with Mercy. No matter how desperately he craved that very thing.

If all went as planned, they would be extricating her sister from the room next door, from the *bed* next door, and the two ladies could have *this* bed in *this* room for the night. Whilst Silas took the room next door. Of course that would be *after* he gave Amos Blankenship the solidly sound thrashing he so deserved and tossed him to the streets. That bastard could sleep outside with the horses for all he cared.

"Thank you very much," he told the innkeeper, wishing the man would take himself off. Silas imagined the upcoming scene would be a bit of a spectacle, and he did not wish to have the innkeeper present as a witness.

The man still lingered, nodding most genially. "Let me know if I can be of any other service to you during your stay. Would you care for any refreshments? Dinner? I can have one of the lasses bring up a tray for you both."

"Ah." Silas looked at Mercy questioningly, and then answered for them, "If we need anything I will just come down myself to request it. Thank you."

He knew without being told that Mercy wanted

nothing more than to be rid of the man so that she could go rescue her sister next door.

With a cursory bow to each of them, the innkeeper at long last took his leave, shutting the door behind him.

Silas and Mercy faced each other. For all the hard riding today and searching every inn on the road north, neither one had discussed what to specifically *do* in this moment.

Neither one knew exactly what they were going to find on the other side of that door, but Silas assumed her imagination was overflowing with worst-case scenarios.

She took a breath and blinked eyes that had suddenly gone bright with emotion, and gave a single hard nod as though preparing to march into battle. "Let us do this then."

He nodded and proceeded to open the door of their room, holding it wide for her. She hurried ahead into the corridor and took the few steps necessary to reach the door next to their room. Mercy knocked briskly upon it.

There was a slight stirring on the other side of the door. No one answered, however. Mercy knocked again. More sounds emanated from the other side. Mercy cut him a quick glance and then knocked a third time, this time more insistent and louder yet.

A voice at last carried from inside the room,

a shrill, trembling thread on the air. "Go away, Amos! Leave me alone. You are not stepping foot inside this room. Be gone from here!"

Mercy lifted wide eyes to Silas, her expression full of bewilderment. Her gaze shot back to the door. "Gracie!" She slapped her palm against the door for emphasis, leaning closer to the panel of wood. "It's me! Your sister! Open the door!"

There was a strangled sob from the other side of the door, and suddenly it was open, flung wide, and Grace was there, her face a pale smudge. The usual pink of her cheeks was nowhere in evidence, and she looked far younger than her seventeen years.

"Oh, Mercy!" The girl lunged forward and flung herself into her sister's arms. Sobs burst from her lips amid an angry spill of words. "I am so sorry! So dreadfully sorry! You were right. You were right about everything. Please forgive me for being such a brat. I just want to go home! Please! Take me home!"

Mercy wrapped her arms around her sister and held her close as her slight body shuddered with tears. "You're safe now, Gracie. Everything will be fine now. We will go home."

Grace hiccupped through her sobs as she lifted her tear-streaked face to gaze at her older sister. "He said we were going to be married. He said we were traveling north, to Gretna Green, and we would be married there. He . . . *promised*." This last word faded in a choked breath.

"We assumed as much. That's why we're here. We followed you. Thankfully our hunch was correct. We are so lucky we found you." Mercy plucked a strand of hair back from where it stuck to her sister's wet cheek.

Grace shook her head vehemently. "No. You don't understand. He was lying to me. As soon as we checked into the room, he was upon me like a beast."

A rare surge of rage took hold of Silas. "What did he do to you? Are you hurt?" He looked her up and down, assessing for injury.

Grace darted a tremulous glance his way. Her cheeks burned fire as she answered him. "I am unharmed. I struck him in the head with a vase . . . and pushed him out of the room, throwing his things with him. I locked him out."

"Clever girl." He nodded approvingly even as he knew this story could have ended terribly different. It could have ended simply . . . *terribly*.

His gaze met Mercy's and he knew she was thinking the same thing. She was thinking how very lucky her sister was that no worse fate had befallen her.

"Where is he now?" he asked.

Grace shrugged. "I assume he left. I have not

heard from him in hours, and the last time he was pounding on the door he called me a brat and said I could find my own way home."

Bastard.

"The wretch," Mercy growled. "Hopefully some highwaymen will come upon him and make short work of him."

"T-thank you for coming after me," Grace whispered, resting her head on her sister's shoulder and looking every bit the young girl she was. "I did not think anyone would come. I was so wretched to you." Her gaze flitted to Silas. "To you both."

"Of course, I would come after you. I'll always come for you when you need me, Gracie."

"Even when I'm a wretched little beast to you."

"Especially then. That's when you need me the most."

Silas stood there for some moments, uncertain what to do as the two sisters moved to sit on the bed. "Are you ladies hungry? Shall I fetch us some food?"

Mercy looked up from where she stroked her sister's hair. "That would be much appreciated, Mr. Masters."

"Mister?" Grace lifted her head and looked between the both of them. "Don't cling to formality on my account. I am obviously aware that the two of you are more than friends."

Hot color flooded Mercy's cheeks.

More than friends.

"Grace," she softly chastised.

"What?" Grace blinked wide eyes. "Just because I made the mistake of choosing the wrong man, doesn't mean you have done the same thing." Grace settled eyes on him that suddenly possessed all the maturity and wisdom of someone twice her age. "Clearly you've chosen well, Mercy."

"G-Grace," she stammered, the color only deepening in her cheeks. "Please. It is not like that between Mr. Masters and myself—"

"Rubbish." Grace shook her head in dismissal of her sister's objections, still holding Silas's gaze. "I know you will do right by my sister. Won't you, Mr. Masters?"

They stared at each other, ignoring the embarrassed sputterings coming from Mercy.

"Yes," he answered, meaning every bit of what he was saying.

It was not so different from what he had said from the start to Mercy—when he had first arrived at her home. "I will do only right by your sister, Miss Kittinger."

That had always been the plan. To do right by Mercy Kittinger and any offspring that might result from their indiscretion. Or rather, indiscretions. Because the more time he spent with her, it was clear that the two of them were destined for future indiscretions with each other.

Currently, Mercy stared at him in wide-eyed dismay, but she knew it, too. She felt it just as he did. The pull. She had remarked on it before. *The heat between them,* she had called it. If anything, it had only gotten hotter.

Of course, Grace thought he was an honorable man. In her mind, "doing right" meant marriage. He had not offered marriage to Mercy Kittinger, but perhaps he should.

Perhaps. He. Should.

He marveled that the thought had even entered his mind. He had never considered matrimony. In fact, he had eschewed it. He had never witnessed a happy union in his life, and he did not intend to inflict that unhappiness on himself or any woman. Except here he was considering that very thing with Mercy Kittinger. A woman who had duped him, seduced him and stolen from him.

And yet he liked her. He wanted her. He *craved* her.

Grace nodded in satisfaction at his promise, a contented smile on her face. "I thought as much." Her composure regained, she continued, "Now. How about that dinner? Let us order a feast. I am famished."

Chapter Twenty-One ❧

*Th*e three of them took a surprisingly delicious and hearty dinner of roasted pheasant, freshly baked bread and an array of vegetables in front of a low crackling fire in the room's hearth. Only a day's ride north from Shropshire, but it was decidedly chillier—especially now that the sun had gone down. For dessert, they all enjoyed an apricot pudding in relative silence, the pop and crumble of burning wood and the howl of the wind outside the only noise.

"What now?" Grace asked as she licked the last bit of pudding from her spoon. "When we get back? Will I be . . . ruined?" She lowered her spoon to her bowl with a careful, bracing breath, as though preparing for the worst of news.

"I will get to Blankenship first," Silas vowed, the words emerging tightly from his throat. He would have to call upon every bit of his restraint when dealing with that bastard. "As long as he does not carry tales, and I shall see that he does not, no one should know of your little . . . misadventure."

Grace considered this for a moment and then seemed to accept what he said as true. "Thank you."

"My pleasure."

"Thank you," Mercy added, her gaze peering deeply at him, her brown eyes bright with an excess of unspoken words. She settled for: "Thank you for everything."

Silas nodded, uncomfortable under her grateful regard. She was looking at him like he was a saint—a magnanimous prince. He was not that, and no one would ever hold that opinion. At least no one back in London. No one in the life he led separate from this one. The life he needed to get back to because this was clearly not real. He was playing house with Mercy Kittinger. No more than that. This was simply a game. Reality waited him.

He stood to take his leave, announcing that he would let them know downstairs to come and collect their trays. "Do you need anything else for the evening, ladies?"

"No, thank you," Mercy murmured.

"It's been a long day." Grace sighed and rubbed at her forehead tiredly. "I can hardly keep my eyes open."

"Well, get your rest. I'll see you in the morning."

He spoke to both of them, but his gaze was trained on Mercy. Just as everything in him was fixed on Mercy.

She sat in her chair, her hands neatly folded in her lap—the very vision of demure womanhood, and he wanted to wreck that image. He wanted her without the trappings of modesty. He wanted her naked and writhing under him. Or as she was in London, wild and unrestrained, riding atop him, taking her pleasure for herself.

The chit was in his blood. He wanted her. It was a disconcerting truth.

With a slow blink, he managed to tear himself away and depart the room. He lingered outside the door for a moment, waiting for the sound of the bolt to drop into place, sealing them in. It fell with a clank.

Satisfied that they were safe and settled for the night, he descended the steps to ask the staff to come and fetch their plates.

GRACE HAD NOT been exaggerating. She fell asleep almost the instant her head hit the pillow, her soft snores a gentle cadence on the air.

For Mercy, sleep was not so simple. She lay on her side, her hand tucked beneath her cheek, staring at the door. They'd bolted it after Silas left them for the night, but she was well aware that he was only feet away, just on the other side of their room in his own room. A mere wall separated them.

She forced her gaze off the door onto her slumbering sister. She was glad she could sleep. She needed the rest. Tomorrow would be another taxing day in the saddle.

Mercy, however, needed something else besides sleep. Time was running out. Silas would not be with them much longer. There would not be many opportunities left.

She flung back the counterpane and slipped from the bed. Turning, she made certain that her sister was still snug beneath the covers, snoring gently, and then located the key to the room. She had no intention of leaving her sister vulnerable in an unlocked room. What if that blackguard, Blankenship, returned? Or some other stranger?

She quietly locked their room, and then moved to stand before Silas's door. Mercy lifted her hand to knock, and then paused, her fist poised midair. She bit her lip, debating whether or not to go ahead and do this. There would be no coming back if she did.

What had happened in London had been necessary. If it happened again when it was not necessary. Then that meant she was well and truly infatuated. Perhaps even more. Perhaps this went deeper than that.

Even though her mind shied from thinking it, it was there already. The glaring truth. She was in love with the man, and if she went to him tonight she would be lost.

Shaking her head, she lowered her hand and started turning away. She couldn't . . .

It might be your last chance.

She stopped. Squaring her shoulders, Mercy turned back to face the door and lifted her hand once more, but she did *not* knock. It felt too . . . *too.*

Shaking her head yet again, she dropped her hand to her side and inched back several steps from the temptation of that door—and the man she knew to be on the other side of it.

A sudden burst of raucous laughter from a few rooms down startled her and had her looking in that direction. Returning her gaze to Silas's door again, sanity had reasserted itself.

What was she doing? This could go nowhere. And what if her sister woke in the middle of the night looking for her?

It was an altogether bad idea.

With an agonized sigh, she turned around again, determined to put this longing behind her and stay in her room all night like a proper young woman, a proper spinster who would live out the rest of her days in her family home, a caregiver to the nieces and nephews her siblings would one day give her.

Oh, stuff proper.

She whirled back around, seized with the determination to have a very *im*proper night. One more time.

One final time.

She lifted her hand to knock, ready to let it fall—only to have the door suddenly yanked open.

Silas stood there. Staring at her.

She stared back, fist still poised, ready to fall in the vicinity of his shoulder. His very *bare* shoulder. He was shirtless.

"Mercy."

Numerous words rose up, ready to trip off her tongue as the sound of her name in his deep voice vibrated through her.

Were they linked together by some invisible string? Because it certainly felt that way as they stared at each other in strained silence, their breaths the only sound—raspy torment-laden scratches on the air.

Why did you open your door? Did you know I was standing out here? Could you feel me? Hear my heartbeat?

She voiced none of those things, however.

They did not need words. There was enough being said without them.

They came together in a mad collision. Bodies

fitting as one, like two slices of bread reunited, longing to be rejoined.

Lips locked. Hands everywhere, touching, grasping, roaming over bodies, diving into hair.

There was no patience from either one of them. No leisurely pace.

The fleeting thought flashed through her that they could have been doing this all along. For over a week they had been denying themselves this. Such a waste.

Silas fumbled for the still open door, grasping the edge of it and shutting it with a resounding slam.

They both fell against its length. She was glad for the support at her back, the solid hardness that kept her from sliding into a boneless puddle on the floor . . . so that she could enjoy the solid hardness of the man in front of her.

"What are you doing here?" he rasped against her throat, his lips a burning singe on her skin.

"Aren't you glad I am?" she returned, seizing his head in both her hands and feasting on his mouth, giving him no chance to reply.

His tongue met hers as her hands feverishly tugged on his hair, controlling the angle of his head, maneuvering him to her liking.

He grasped impatiently at her nightgown, at the fabric barring them from skin-to-skin contact.

His hands seized fistfuls of her nightgown at her hips, yanking and pulling until he had the fabric bunched around her hips and she was exposed from the waist down. Shockingly exposed. Her naked skin was bare to the air and to his hands, which wasted no time running a burning trail up her naked thighs.

His fingers slid under her knees. She didn't need to be told or guided. He lifted her up and she went willingly, hopping slightly to wrap her legs around him. The crush of him wedged tightly between her splayed thighs felt like bliss. He was where he belonged.

She moaned into his mouth, the kiss a clumsy wild thing now, but it was still thrilling and erotic and perfect and right.

His chest pressed against her own, mashing into her breasts. Breasts shielded by an ugly wool nightgown she longed to tear from her body—almost as much as she longed to rid him of his trousers.

He grabbed her bottom, squeezing her with two big hands. The pressure of those hands on her tightened everything inside her. The heat between them burned to a fevered pitch.

She pushed her pelvis forward, digging her aching core into the bulge of his cock.

He groaned against her lips. "There's that sweet

quim. So demanding. So hungry for my cock." He reached between them, cupping her womanhood and giving it a firm squeeze that nearly undid her right then. She bucked against his hand, despising the trousers he wore that impeded them from contact. "Ah, so impatient," he growled.

"Then stop delaying," she panted, bucking into the palm of his hand again.

His eyes darkened at her command. He pulled back slightly and swatted her sex.

She hissed at the delicious sting she felt through the fabric of her nightgown. "Silas," she begged.

"Have you missed me here, Mercy?" He brushed the back of his fingers gently over her sex. Too gently. Too softly. It was agony. She wanted him hard and fast inside her.

She nodded jerkily.

"Then say it, Mercy. Say how much you have missed me."

He gave her another swat that brought forth a sharp joyous cry, her nether lips vibrating from the erotic slap.

"I've missed you," she sobbed.

He smacked her sex again, and followed up by rubbing and stroking firmly and swiftly, expertly and unerringly locating the tight little button at the top of her sex. She shuddered as a climax washed over her, her body clenching and then finally snapping, releasing, going limp as waves of sensation eddied through her.

Her vision blurred. She clung to his shoulders, dimly processing the way his muscles bunched under her fingers. He shifted a bit whilst still holding her up, keeping her pinned to the door. A good thing because she was useless, boneless, and desperate for the support.

With one hand gripping her bottom, his other hand fumbled between them, opening his trousers. Shoving them down. Not all the way, but enough.

His cock prodded at her core, at the soft give of her flesh. Nothing was between them there, nothing to keep him from entering her. She barely had time to take a breath before he was sliding inside her, slamming her back harder against the door.

She cried out, exulted, delighting in the fullness of him buried inside her. Her thighs quivered, clenching around his hips. Her fingers dug into his warm skin, her nails scoring his smooth, delicious skin.

His breath crashed against her lips. His intense brown gaze held hers, drowning her in its depth as he began moving again, thrusting into her over and over, and then she could no longer focus on anything as she bounced between his strong body and the door, riding his rod as a barrage of sensations overwhelmed her.

She simply let herself be carried away on the wave, crying out as his cock continued to pound into her, the friction only increasing, becoming unbearable until she came apart again. With her legs still wrapped around him, she hugged him close, clinging to his shoulders as she convulsed, spasms eddying throughout her whilst he finished, driving into her several more times and reaching his own end with an exultant shout.

He stilled then. His head pulled back to look at her. He pushed the strands of hair that clung to her face free from her cheeks. "Are you weeping?"

There was indeed moisture on her cheeks. She reached a hand for her face, feeling for herself. Tears had leaked from her eyes unbidden amid their tryst.

"It was so good," she whispered thickly.

"I know. I'm glad you came to my door. It saved me the trouble of coming to get you."

"You were going to come for me tonight?"

"I don't think I could have stayed away another moment."

She smiled tremulously, gulping back a breath. Stepping back from the door, he lifted her up in his arms and carried her to the bed, setting her gently down upon it.

In one smooth move, he pulled her nightgown off her, tossing it through the air. She watched him as he stood beside the bed and stripped off his gaping trousers, baring his beautiful form deliciously for her eyes.

Then he was beside her in the bed, kissing her deep and long, his bigger body stretching out sinuously next to hers. These kisses were different. Slow and drugging. Not as wild and desperate as before. These kisses were leisurely. As though they had endless time. As though it were only the two of them in the whole of the world. As though they would never have to leave this room.

It was a lovely feeling.

Chapter Twenty-Two ❧

$\mathcal{M}$ercy woke before Silas and slipped silently from their bed. Er, *his* bed. *Dash it all*—the bed belonged to neither one of them, but they had both enjoyed it together last night . . . and into the wee hours of the morn.

Her cheeks stung as she quietly dressed herself, pulling her hopelessly wrinkled nightgown on over her head. She did not know why her cheeks warmed. She did not think there could be anything left to embarrass her. Not after what had passed between them.

The barest purple tinges of dawn pressed around the edges of the drapes as she crept from his room and returned to the room she shared with her sister. Or rather, the room she *should* have shared with her sister.

She slipped back into bed with Grace without a sound. It was early yet. She could probably sleep for another hour, but she doubted that was possible. She felt too awake, too alert, her senses still too heightened, her body too alive, her mind too busy with thoughts and questions—the images from last night looping through her head.

She was wrong, however. Within moments of rejoining her sister, she was dead to the world in a dreamless sleep.

She was jarred awake much too soon though.

In no time at all, her sister was shaking her.

"Come, Mercy. We must be on our way. Mr. Masters has already knocked at our door and is downstairs readying our horses. He said he will have the innkeeper pack us some food to eat for the road."

Groaning, Mercy sat up, rubbing her achy eyes.

"Goodness, you were snoring."

"I don't snore," Mercy denied.

"Oh, yes. You do," Grace insisted, looking her over critically. "Perhaps you're ill and that accounts for your snoring. You don't look well."

"Thank you," she replied mockingly, wincing as she adjusted herself on the bed, feeling rather sore. She supposed last night's activities had been vigorous, but she did not recall feeling this sore the first time they were together.

Grace continued to survey her. "Are you certain you are well?"

Mercy wished they did not have to rush home and they could take their time, but she knew they were under a cloud of urgency. They needed to catch up to Blankenship.

"I am well," she muttered, scooting from the bed even though she did not feel like freeing herself from its cozy warmth. By some miracle, Silas could manage to be up and about on much too little sleep—perpetually, it seemed. She could manage, too.

She got to her feet and staggered behind the screen to the chamber pot to relieve herself, marveling how she could have gone to feeling so poorly so suddenly. She had felt splendid only hours before.

The answer presented itself instantly. She gasped before she could catch and contain the sound.

"Mercy," Grace called, her steps drawing nearer to the curtain. "Is everything—oh," her voice faded as she peeked around the curtain and looked down to where Mercy crouched.

They both stared at the nightgown Mercy had just removed, the fabric wadded in her hands, the blood stains standing out in stark relief against the cream-colored fabric.

"Well, that explains why you look so poorly. Your menses arrived."

Nodding, Mercy stepped forward and reached for her dressing robe. "It appears that way," she said tightly, the words thick and heavy in her mouth. She rolled her soiled nightgown into a ball and set it aside.

"Do you need me to fetch you anything?" Grace asked.

"Would you bring me my valise, please?"

Nodding, Grace disappeared, granting her some much-desired privacy.

Mercy swallowed against the sudden lump in her throat, gripping the table upon which a fresh pitcher of water and basin sat.

She was not with child.

She had predicted as much. She had told Silas there would be no baby. And there was not. There was no baby. No tangible bond between them.

Her sister returned, passing her valise to her. Mercy accepted it with a murmur of thanks and quickly set about putting herself to rights.

She was not with child. Silas could leave. He could go. Return to his life.

She would not be forced into an untenable situation as a kept woman, ruined for good society. She could go about life with no threat of scandal hanging over her head.

So why did it feel like her heart was breaking?

Chapter Twenty-Three ❧

$\mathcal{I}$t was dark when they arrived home.

Mercy did not think she had seen a sweeter sight than the whitewashed walls of her house in the moonlight, the smoke curling softly from its chimney, a white plume against the night sky. The home fires burned and she had never felt so welcomed. No matter what happened, she would always find comfort here.

Grace slid off her mount and leaned against the horse for a long moment as though her legs needed the support.

Silas dismounted and grasped her sister's reins, nodding toward the house. "I'll take care of the horses. Why don't you go inside and get something to eat?" His gaze shifted to Mercy. "You, too."

She descended to the ground, watching as her sister made for the house.

Silas reached for her reins and she shook her head. "I have this."

He held her gaze a moment and then shrugged. Turning, he led his and Grace's mounts toward the stables. Mercy followed.

The stables smelled of fresh hay and horses. He deposited both horses in empty stalls and then reached for Mercy's reins, leading her docile mare to a stall as well.

"I'll rub them down and give them feed. Then I'll take a fresh mount to Shropshire to speak with Blankenship."

"This late?" she inquired. "Won't you come inside and get something to eat first?"

"I would rather see to this. The sooner this is done, the better. I can eat when I get back."

She nodded, appreciating his dedication to righting things for her family—and yet she had the sense that he wanted to be gone . . . that he was using the trip into Shropshire so that he could be free of her company. Not that he needed that as an excuse anymore. He was free. Free to go forever and never look back. The thing keeping him here was no longer a factor anymore. Only he did not know that. Yet.

"You think I should leave the task until morning?" he asked, clearly sensing her thoughts on the matter of him riding to Shropshire right now.

She winced. "No. I suppose not." He was right.

The quicker he got hold of Blankenship the better, and they both knew that.

She watched him for some moments as he worked on the horses, mesmerized by the play of his strong hands moving and gliding over the horses, remembering how they had felt moving over her only the night before.

She knew what she had to do. She had been thinking about it all day. It had to be done, of course.

She moistened her lips. "I have some news."

He arched an eyebrow. Doubtlessly, he wondered what news she could have. They had been together all day and the day before.

"Do tell," he prompted.

She took a deep breath, knowing once the words were uttered, once they were out there, there would be nothing keeping him here. He would go. She would never see him again.

Lifting her chin, she commanded herself not to look as miserable as she felt. Because she ought not to feel this way. She had no right or claim on him . . . on this, whatever it was between them.

She had to let him go.

SILAS RAN THE brush over his mount in steady strokes and tried to pretend he did not long to drop the brush and haul Mercy Kittinger into his arms. He wanted to back her against the stall wall and lift her skirts.

He wanted her. Last night only confirmed that. He wanted to keep her. He wanted her in his bed where he had miraculously slept . . . *peacefully* and *soundly* with her beside him.

For the first time in his life, he had slept long and deep and hard. He could only conclude Mercy was the reason for that.

Mercy brought him peace. At least ultimately. She fired his blood and thrilled him and made his heart race and thump so hard he was certain it would break loose from his chest, but then, ultimately, he felt only relaxed and at peace beside her.

They were alone in the stables right now. He could reach for her. And yet it felt unwise. Unsafe to touch her. If he touched her, he would not be able to stop. There would only be more. More touching. More of that and more other things.

And that could not happen until he decided what it was he wanted . . . until he knew what *she* wanted. Perhaps that was the most frightening thing of all. Discovering what it was she wanted. Because he already knew what he wanted.

He wanted her. What if she did not want him?

"What of your news?" he asked more brusquely than he intended.

She blinked, and rested her hand on the outside wall of the stall. "You can set your mind at ease, Mr. Masters."

He paused amid brushing, wariness creeping over him. And why was she addressing him so formally again? Especially now. Were they not well past that?

"Mr. Masters," he echoed, gazing at her and feeling anything but at ease.

"Yes. I had a bit of . . . news this morning."

This morning? What could she be talking about? They had traveled together. He had not seen her speak to anyone since they left the inn. What news could she possibly have to share that he would not also be privy to?

"Indeed." Her chest rose high on a breath. "I am not with child. You are no longer obligated to remain here for another moment. I am certain that is a great relief to you."

He could not make sense of her words at first. They were the last thing he was expecting to hear, although they should not have been. It was what had brought him here, after all. It was the news he had been waiting for, and he had known it was coming.

A great relief . . .

Of course, he should have expected something in the vein of this. Of course—and yet he felt as though he had just received a blow to the face. There was no relief. Just jarring . . . disappointment.

"Oh." He straightened. "Well. That is very good news."

Good news. Yes. It should have felt that way.

"I thought you would appreciate it," she said, looking as starchy as a schoolmistress—and he could admit that he did not like that. He did not like that at all. "You can leave in the morning. You no doubt have much to attend to back in Town. I know you have been neglecting your life."

He did not like the solemn look of her. Or the news she was imparting. He wanted her to look as she had the night before. Not this creature so very eager to push him out the door and out of her life.

Of course, what he wanted did not signify. He supposed he had his answer. He supposed he knew what she wanted now and what she wanted was not him.

This was what she ought to be doing and saying. It was the agreement between them, after all. He had no reason to remain.

It dawned on him that he had been hoping, just perhaps, that she was in the family way. That she would present him with a reason, a sound excuse to stay in her life. The decision would have been made. They would have been stuck with each other.

But now there was no reason. No excuse to stay whatsoever.

"Thank you for telling me." He nodded, his throat closing in, making the words difficult to get out. "It is . . . good news."

He nodded in the direction of another stall, where her brother's horse was lazily munching hay. "I'll take a fresh mount into town and see to our remaining business with Blankenship."

"That is very generous of you. You don't have to do that."

"I promised as much. To you and Grace."

"Yes, you did. You are a man of your word, Mr. Masters." She smiled tightly. "Commendable."

Commendable? Rot it all. He did not want to be commendable in her eyes. He wanted to be a man she could not live without, but she clearly did not see him that way, and he felt like a fool.

He moved away, fetching a saddle and hefting it on the back of Kittinger's horse. As soon as he completed this errand, he would be on his way.

"Good night, Mercy."

He heard her behind him, the rustling of her dress, the scuff of her riding boots on the ground. "Good night." She paused a beat. "Mr. Masters."

They were back to being strangers.

He finished saddling his mount, tightening the cinch and not looking behind him as she departed the stables.

MERCY RUSHED FROM the stables in a blind run, eager to be away from this cold stranger that Silas had become. She held up her skirts from her shoes to avoid tripping, blinking rapidly against the sting of tears.

She should not feel like this.

She should not feel as though she were coming apart at the seams . . . as though when he left a part of her would go with him.

She did not know where this barrage of emotion was coming from. Things were resolving in the best outcome possible for the both of them.

She had not planned for any of this—she had not planned for *him*. It was all for the best. Certainly she did not long for scandal and ruin. She should not feel this crushed.

She stopped for a moment before the front door of her house, taking a few careful sips of air and regaining her composure. She moved her hands down the front of her riding habit, attempting to smooth out the wrinkles.

All would be well.

With a less than decisive nod, she turned the

latch and entered her house. Instantly the sound of deep male voices carried from the parlor to her ears.

Ignoring her hungry stomach that prompted her to join her sister in the kitchen and the food doubtlessly awaiting her there, she turned toward the parlor.

The double doors were slightly ajar, and she pushed one of them fully open to find her brother ensconced in Papa's comfortable old wingback chair, a glass of brandy loosely gripped in his hand.

He knew she and Silas had left in pursuit of Grace. She had apprised him before they departed—not that he had seemed to care one way or another. His reaction had been an eye roll.

Presently, he was the vision of a gentleman at leisure. Across from him in the parlor sat an older gentleman whom she had never met.

Her brother's gaze landed on her. He gave his head a swift little shake, as though conveying to her that he wished for her to disappear from the room.

Frowning, she paused, uncertain what to do, but suspecting that doing anything her brother wanted was likely not the best course.

The decision was made for her when the other man spotted her hovering in the threshold. He shifted his large girth slightly in his seat to better survey her, sending the sofa springs squeaking in protest. "Oh, my," he exclaimed. "What do we have here? Is this, perchance, your lovely sister?"

Mercy opened her mouth. "Ah," she said, uncertain how to respond to that.

Her brother was now looking at her as though he wished for the earth to open up and swallow them both. Not a good omen. Not at all.

The older gentleman did not even rise to his feet. He merely continued to look her over in a bold and rather offensive manner. She looked down her nose at him, returning his rude scrutiny. Standing, she had a perfect view of his head, of his white hair so thin and wispy his bone-white scalp was visible through the strands.

"Come, lass. Speak up. Which one are you?"

She shook her head. "Which one . . . What?" She looked pointedly to Bede, ready for an explanation.

The older gentleman turned his sharp stare on her brother. "Kittinger, do you want to properly introduce me?"

Bede tugged on his collar and cleared his throat. "Yes, of course. Mercy, this is Mr. Hinton, an acquaintance of mine from Town."

Another acquaintance from Town? What were the odds of that? It could not bode well. She shifted on her feet uneasily. This could not be good. No one ever called here on Bede—other than Silas, if he was to be counted. And truthfully . . . he had come here for her.

Indeed, this did not bode well at all. Her mind immediately leapt to the reason for Silas's visit here, and she shuddered to think what reason could have brought this man here. Did Bede owe him money? That was her immediate suspicion . . . and fear.

She inclined her head slightly. "Mr. Hinton. A pleasure to meet you. What brings you to our home?" Rather direct, but she felt the need to get to the heart of this visit. Something was afoot, and she wanted to know what.

"A pleasure indeed," he said, his rather swollen-looking lips savoring and hugging each word in a manner that made her skin crawl. "And how old would you be, my lovely?"

She flinched at the overly familiar manner in which he spoke to her. Not to mention his ill-mannered *and* prying question. A gentleman did not ask a lady's age upon their first meeting.

Again, her gaze drifted to her brother. An explanation was well past due, and yet he was not volunteering any information. Instead he continued to look back and forth between Mercy and Mr. Hinton, as though unable to formulate words.

"Bede?" she prompted, an edge to her voice.

Her brother shrugged rather helplessly.

At that moment her sister came up behind her, bringing with her the most delightful aroma of cinnamon. "Mercy, Gladys made your favorite crumpets." Grace took a crunchy bite of the cake in her hand. "Help yourself while they are still hot from the oven."

Mr. Hinton perked up at the arrival of Grace.

Her sister came to an abrupt stop, peering inside the parlor around Mercy. "Oh." Grace's eyes widened. "I did not realize we had a guest."

At the arrival of a *second* lady in their midst, the older gentleman finally labored to his feet with several pained pants of breath, as though the exertion fatigued him. "What delight is this? Now we have the pleasure of *another* lovely little bird. What is your name, my dear?"

Mercy flinched, disliking this man completely and quite past the point of tolerating him with any level of civility.

"Bede!" she snapped. "Who is this man?" She gestured at him impatiently.

She could not even bring herself to call him a gentleman anymore. Not the way he was ogling both her and Grace.

Hinton looked askance at Bede. "Well, go on with you, Kittinger. Tell your sister who I am." He sent Mercy a bold, exaggerated wink. "I have been most eager to meet you, my dear."

She pointed a finger at herself as though to say, *Me?*—but could manage no words. She was quite astounded by the man's temerity.

Bede cleared his throat, tugging at that infernal collar of his again as though it were choking him. "Ah, Mr. Hinton. These are my sisters, Mercy and Grace."

Mr. Hinton clapped his hands together and then rubbed them as though he were about to devour a particularly tasty morsel. "You made no mention of *two* sisters. Such bounty! I thought there was just one. Which one is mine?"

Grace gasped beside Mercy.

Which one is mine?

Mercy could only gawk, convinced she had misunderstood the man. Certainly he had not said—

"Well. Which one is mine, Kittinger?" Hinton repeated, a hard edge entering his voice. "I came all the way from London to get what is mine, and I am not leaving empty-handed."

Her brother's face had gone white. Bloodless.

Mercy took an instinctive step in front of her sister. "What is he talking about, Bede?" Her gaze split between both of the men, uncertain which one posed a greater danger, but certain that they both did.

Mr. Hinton sighed and lumbered back toward the sofa where his coat was tossed. He searched through the pockets whilst her brother buried his head into his hands and mumbled, "I'm so sorry. I was trying to get it back, Mercy."

"Get *what* back?" she demanded, even as a dark suspicion took root inside her.

His hands gripped his hair, tugging on the ends as though he would like to rip them from his skull. "I was desperate."

"Oh, no." *No no no no.* She shook her head, unaware of what it was she was precisely dreading, but she knew it was bad. If he was reacting like this, then it was bad. Very bad.

"Mercy?" Grace whispered nervously beside her.

"Here it is!" Mr. Hinton brandished a paper in the air. "I have it right here. Feast your eyes!"

"What is that?" She nodded toward the paper in his hand and then turned a hot glare on her brother, still hoping for some explanation from him. "Bede!"

"This is a contract your brother signed." The man waved the paper rather loftily, the gesture menacing even in his old gnarled hand.

The sinking sensation in her stomach only worsened. She feared she was going to be ill.

"What kind of contract?" she asked forcefully, her hand tightening around her sister's hand.

Bede had been here for weeks. He had to have negotiated whatever was in that contract previous to venturing here. What could he have done? And how could he not have warned her that this, whatever *this* happened to be, was coming for them?

Mr. Hinton unfolded the paper and read with great flourish. "Permit me to paraphrase. This here is a contract promising one Miss Kittinger, sister to Bede Kittinger of Shropshire, in marriage to me."

"What?" Grace choked out. Grace went limp beside Mercy, and she had to loop her arm around her waist to help hold herself up.

"What nonsense is this?" she asked with an impressive amount of aplomb. She could not fall apart now. She needed her wits and composure even if she wanted to shriek and take a fist to her brother.

Bede finally lifted his head up from his hands. "I am sorry! I am so bloody sorry. I had just lost everything to Masters, and I was desperate. I was hoping I could win it all back and then return to Masters for another go. I was trying to set things right."

"By gambling away your sister? Your own flesh and blood? Like we are nothing more than property to you! Something to be leveraged?"

Once again, he had failed them. Once again, they were victims of Bede's poor choices whilst she had no choices. Her brother had all the power and the injustice of it enraged her.

"Begging your pardon, I am sorry to interrupt

this little family squabble, but I am still here," Hinton interrupted. "And I want to know which one of you gels is my future wife."

Mercy allowed herself to freely evaluate Mr. Hinton. He had to be close to seventy . . . older than her own father if he was still alive. He had lips that looked like they had just been stung by bees. To say nothing of his large bulbous nose that was riddled with unfortunate sores—and he was presently treating Grace and Mercy like they were a pair of mares for sale. She had a feeling that he might request to examine her teeth next.

One of them . . .

"How could you?" she demanded of Bede. After he had gambled and lost her home, she had told herself nothing he did would surprise her. But this? This astonished her. She had not thought him capable of such a thing.

Grace stepped closer, averting her face as though she could not stomach the sight of him. She hissed into Mercy's ear. "Does one of us have to marry him? Truly?"

For however old he might be, Mr. Hinton's hearing was perfectly intact. "That's what this contract says. One of you is mine!" The old man rattled the paper in the air.

Mercy glared with accusation at her brother. "Say something."

He shrugged helplessly. "I gave him Gracie."

Oh, no. That was not what she was expecting him to say.

Grace started wailing at once.

Mercy turned and faced her and took hold of her shoulders for a little shake to get her to stop. "We will straighten this out. You are not marrying this man. I promise you that, Gracie." Somehow she would make certain of that.

"That is not what is set forth in this contract," Mr. Hinton volunteered with a wheezing chuckle, still waving that infernal paper.

"You do not have her consent. I know that much is necessary. I don't care what that contract says, without her consent it is not legally binding."

Grace calmed a bit at Mercy's words. "Truly?" she whispered, lifting a hopeful gaze up to Mercy.

Mr. Hinton looked at the paper in his hand and then glanced at Bede with a shrug. "That may well be the case. But then I am owed my due. Your brother put up a sister in marriage against my twelve thousand pounds."

Mercy sucked in a hissing breath at the exorbitant sum and shot a fresh glare at her brother. Twelve thousand pounds! Her brother could never cover such a debt.

Hinton continued, "If I took this to the courts, you are correct. They would not force either one of you into marriage against your will, but they would honor the original wager. There were plenty of witnesses present. It's either your sister in marriage or twelve thousand pounds. Simple as that." Mr. Hinton sniffed, rubbing a finger against his unsightly nose. "Shall we put it to the test then?" His rheumy-eyed gaze flitted between Mercy and Grace. "Shall we take this to the courts?"

A long stretch of silence fell in which Mercy's mind worked feverishly for a way out of this mess. She had no wish to air this humiliating situation to the world. She would prefer not to go public, and she knew he was correct. A court would merely insist her brother pay Mr. Hinton the twelve thousand pounds.

Hinton continued in a cajoling voice, "Come now. You have two sisters, Kittinger. Surely you can spare one of them. I must confess, I tire of the whole courtship and eons-long engagement. I have done that before and been married to less than hearty lasses."

He was married before? What happened to his wives?

He fluttered his fingers and went on. "I am not getting any younger. I don't have time for that anymore. I want a bride." He looked Mercy and Grace over approvingly. "A young one that won't die on me again. I've buried three."

She held her sister in her arms, glaring at their brother. "How could you do this to us?"

They had no money to offer in exchange for that marriage contract. No sum even approaching the one Mr. Hinton had put up. This was beyond ruin.

This was total and thorough devastation.

Bede had finally done it. He'd backed them into a corner from which there was no escape. Not without consequence.

Hopelessness welled up inside her. With a final pat to her sister's shoulder, she set the girl away from her and faced Mr. Hinton with squared shoulders. "We will honor the marriage contract."

What choice did they have, after all? It would be impossible to come up with twelve thousand pounds to settle the debt. Such a sum of money was beyond them. She did not even think selling their lands would yield that much. Until she found a way out of this, she had no choice.

Grace moaned behind her. "Nooo!"

Mercy gestured toward her with a shushing hand and sent her a silencing look.

Mr. Hinton nodded approvingly. "Very sensible. Saves us all a lot of trouble."

"But you don't get her." She motioned to her sister with a decisive wave. "It will have to be me or you can take us to court. As pressed as you are for time, I am certain you don't want to do that."

Until Mercy could come up with another solution to escape this predicament, this was the way it would have to be.

Mr. Hinton took several halting steps forward until he was standing directly before her. "Ha! Is that a fact?" He looked her up and down assessingly. "I like your moxie. And you're still young enough. You'll do."

Mercy held his gaze, determined that he see she was no simpering girl. She would not cower to him.

"I like her," Mr. Hinton declared, whirling around to face her brother. "It has been a while since I had a wife." He tsked and shook his head. "They never last me long, but this one seems sturdy enough. A strong lass. Just what I'm looking for."

A surge of bile rose up in her throat. She held it back. Stood her ground. Looked between the man whom she was to marry and her treacherous brother.

She thought of Silas then, and felt keen relief to have had two nights with him. Nothing could erase that.

At least her first time would not be with this wretched man. At least she would have some sweet memories.

"Mercy." Grace grasped her wrist and stepped

close to whisper for their ears alone, "What have you done? What about Mr. Masters?"

"What about him?" She shook her head.

"He and you are—"

"No. There is nothing between us. I am unattached and free to do this."

"Does Mr. Masters know that? Certainly he will not permit this to happen."

"He has no say over any of this." He was leaving in the morning.

"I say, is anyone going to show me to my room for the night?" Mr. Hinton declared. "These bones of mine are aching for a rest."

Mercy turned a hot glare on her brother. "My brother will see to that. You can use his room for the night."

Silas occupied the guest chamber—at least for one more night. Bede could sleep on the sofa in the parlor—or out in the stables, for all she cared.

Bede blinked and looked as though he would protest the matter of giving up his room, but one look at Mercy's face quelled whatever complaint he may have been ready to lodge. "Of course," he muttered, and slinked forward. "This way, Mr. Hinton."

Mr. Hinton snatched up his coat. Grace and Mercy scooted back, eager to avoid contact with the unsavory man—who was to be Mercy's husband.

The bile was back—accompanied by a healthy dose of despair.

The man was almost through the door when he abruptly stopped and turned around, pointing a bent finger at Mercy. "Tomorrow we will work out all the details. I hope you are not partial to a large and extravagant wedding. As I mentioned, this is not my first. I would prefer something small and something soon." He looked her up and down again, a lascivious glint entering his eyes. "I look forward to getting to know you better . . . and my house needs a proper mistress to put it into order. I have all these children that need managing, too. They run wild, keep chasing off the governesses I hire." That said, he followed her brother from the room whistling a merry tune.

They were alone only a few moments before Grace started to weep.

"There, there," Mercy soothed, "you will be fine. You will have Gladys and everyone else here to help you about the place. You won't be alone."

Grace looked up, her expression horrified. "I am not crying for myself! I am crying for you, Mercy. Don't you know that? You just agreed to marry that horrid man!"

"I didn't have any other choice."

"There has to be a way. There has to be another, *better* way."

She had hoped so, too, but perhaps that had been wishful thinking. A hope to cling to as she watched her life slipping beyond her control.

"No," she said in a flat, hard voice. "Sometimes there is only one way. Sometimes life doesn't offer options. Presently, this is the only choice I have."

"Blast Bede!"

"You're getting overwrought, Gracie. Let us get you to your bedchamber." She took her sister's arm to guide her upstairs, but Mercy yanked her arm free.

"No! I *am* overwrought just as you should be!" Grace stormed from the parlor in a temper. Mercy let her go.

She let her go and then slumped against the inside wall of the parlor, rattling a framed painting behind her. Alone, with no eyes on her, no sister around for whom she needed to feign strength, she surrendered to tears. She lifted her hands to her face, and let her despair flow freely and unchecked.

Chapter Twenty-Four 🖋

The house was dark when Silas arrived, the Blankenship business thankfully well behind him.

It had not taken too much persuading to convince Amos Blankenship to keep his mouth shut. It appeared the young man was already nervous about his actions and the inevitable wrath to come if his father learned of his dastardly deeds. The bastard had gone weak at the knees when Silas threatened to use his connections to blackball him from every gaming hell and pleasure house in London lest he keep his escapade with Grace Kittinger under wraps. The lad would be carrying no tales.

Silas eased in through the front door, closing it quietly behind him. He took the stairs, mindful of his tread and the creaking steps. He did not wish to wake the household with his arrival. In fact, he was already contemplating rising early in the morning and departing before anybody else even awoke.

Cowardly of him perhaps, but he could not stomach an awkward farewell. It was for the best if he didn't have to see Mercy again. A clean cut. Less pain that way. Less chance for festering and infection.

He reached the second landing and did not make it two steps before he was unceremoniously summoned.

Glancing about, he noticed young Grace sticking her head out into the hallway from her bedchamber. "Mr. Masters! Over here. Come, come. Over here." She waved him wildly over to her door, her long plait of dark hair bouncing over her shoulder with her movements.

He advanced, assuming she wanted reassurances that everything went well with Blankenship and she was still in possession of her good name. He opened his mouth, ready to give those reassurances to her when she blurted out with: "You must stop her! She has gone mad. She thinks she can actually marry the man!" She motioned to her brother's bedchamber door.

"Whoa." He held up both hands in a pacifying manner. Nothing the girl said made sense. "What are you talking about? *Who* are you talking about? *She* who?"

She blew out an exasperated breath. "Mercy. Mercy is going to marry this dreadful man. Apparently our fool brother promised one of us to him in a marriage contract . . . He put one of us up as the prize in a game of cards." She waved her hand wildly about again. "And he lost. Of course!" She rolled her eyes in disgust.

"When did this happen?" Silas had not been gone very long. *How* had this happened?

"This all happened while you were attending to Blankenship. The gentleman is here to claim his bride. He's asleep in Bede's room. A Mr. Hinton—"

"Otto Hinton?" he demanded in outrage.

She shook her head. "I don't know his first name. He is old." She wrinkled her nose. "Very old."

Silas nodded grimly. "It is he." Otto Hinton was a seasoned gambler, and the man was certainly old. He had a history of collecting wives that never seemed to survive beyond a few years. The notion of Mercy married to such a man was unfathomable. How could her brother have offered either one of his sisters to him?

"Well, he came to claim his prize—either his bride or twelve thousand pounds, the amount Mr. Hinton had offered up in the pool."

Silas closed his eyes in a weary blink and dragged his hand over his face. "That idiot."

Grace knew instantly whom he meant. "How

could Bede have done this to us? He is a menace. He should be locked away where he can cause us no more harm."

Harsh words, but Silas did not disagree. Something had to be done about the man. Kittinger needed to be stopped. He would only continue to jeopardize his sisters. As long as he was their guardian, they would forever be at risk from all the dangerously stupid things he did.

But first . . . there were more pressing matters to address. Namely, saving Mercy from her own damn nobility. The lass would sacrifice herself on a burning pyre if she thought it would save her family.

Well. He would put a stop to that.

He nodded reassuringly to Grace. "Don't worry about any of this. She is not going to marry Hinton. I will see to that."

"But what about—"

"I will take care of it. Go to bed. Rest easy."

Without even registering a response from Grace, he turned away.

But he did not move toward his bedchamber. Indeed not. He turned for Mercy's room.

THE KNOCK ON her door sent a bolt of alarm through Mercy. She was not asleep. Of course not. Sleep was impossible. Sleep was for people at peace, and there was no peace in her life. She might very well never sleep again.

Another knock came.

"Who is there?" she asked warily, envisioning Mr. Hinton's face on the other side. If he thought he would sample his conjugal rights early, he was mistaken. She snatched up the iron poker, ready to use it to defend herself.

"It's me. Open the door."

She did not need further elaboration. She knew that deep voice instantly.

With a careful breath, she set the poker aside and opened the door to Silas, hoping he did not take one look at her puffy face and know that she had been crying.

He strode inside and faced her with hard, glittering eyes. "It seems much has happened in my brief absence."

He knew.

She gave a mirthless laugh. "Indeed. My brother is ever full of surprises."

"You cannot do this, Mercy."

Somehow he had been apprised of matters. She suspected that was her sister's doing. Her well-meaning and interfering sister. "There is no other alternative."

"There is always a choice."

That was easy for him to say. A man who would

never marry would, of course, believe marriage was a choice.

She angled her head. She did not have the luxury of choice. How could he not see that?

"It is not the end of the world." Even as she uttered the words with a flippant air, she did not believe them. And yet she said them. She *had* to say them. She had to *learn* to believe in them. Just as she would learn to live with her fate. She continued, "People marry all the time, and there is no affection or love as the foundation."

He waved an arm wildly toward the door. "But that man? Did you not converse with him? I realize you don't know him, but believe you me. You do not want to be married to Otto Hinton. His wives die as frequently as a change of season. Marriage to him very well could be the end of your world."

She lifted her chin and swallowed back the lump of emotion . . . of dread . . . clogging her throat. "Surely you exaggerate."

His eyes grew as round as saucers. "About this? I do not."

She stomped her foot. "Do not make this more difficult than it already is. I have to do this."

"Oh, you admit this is difficult then? That is something at least."

Of course, it was. Did he not see that? She was trying to be brave lest she crumble and fall apart.

He was only making it worse. "What business is any of this of yours?"

He reared back slightly as though she had slapped him. "What business? *You*. You are my business, you daft woman. Can you not see that?"

She shook her head, hard and fierce. "No. I do not see that. Why would I see that? Our time together has come to a conclusion. You said as much. You are leaving tomorrow."

"So I should just go on and forget about you? Are we not friends? Did you not say that to me?"

"Friends?" she echoed numbly.

Yes. She had called him that. She had said he was a *good* friend, but now that word somehow rang ridiculous to her. *Insignificant*. She had several friends and she had done none of the things with her friends that she had done with Silas Masters. Suddenly she wanted to shout at him. She wanted to strike him. At the very least she wanted to scream: *Go! Be gone!*

His eyes narrowed. "Yes. *Friends*. Should I simply forget you?"

"Yes!"

He ignored her and continued loudly, angrily, "Forget you and leave you to this fate you have assigned yourself?"

Mercy gulped, wondering why he was even here. He could do nothing to help her. So why was he doing this to her? The torment was real. He had said he was leaving. She was not making that up. She did not impose that upon him. It was his choice. *He* who was so blasted fortunate to have choices.

"I am doing nothing more than making the best of a bad situation." She was proud at how calmly her voice escaped.

He laughed harshly, bitterly. She cringed at the sound. "There is no *good*, no making the best of this situation."

"Go. Leave." She flipped a hand to the door. "This has nothing to do with you."

He nodded slowly, a tic feathering along his jaw tensely. "Very well. I will leave as planned in the morning."

Those words fell with finality. They stung more than they should. More even than the words she had uttered only earlier tonight, agreeing to marry Hinton.

She clutched the collar of her nightgown in her fist and nodded jerkily. "Goodbye, Silas."

He blinked slowly and turned for the door. "Goodbye, Mercy. Have a good life."

She flinched.

He left her room. Left her. As had been the plan from the start.

She stood alone, wondering why she suddenly

felt so terribly wretched—even more wretched
than when she had agreed to marry a stranger old
enough to be her grandfather.

Why did she feel as though he had abandoned
her?

Why did she feel like she was dying inside?

Chapter Twenty-Five ❧

Silas did not return to his bedchamber upon leaving Mercy's room. She might have pushed him from her life, she might have insisted she was marrying Hinton and that he had no place in her affairs, but he could not abandon her to the wolves.

He knocked firmly at Kittinger's bedchamber door where Hinton slept. It took a few moments before he heard sounds coming from the other side.

After several minutes the door finally opened. Hinton stood there, wispy strands of white hair standing up in every direction on his head. He blinked bleary eyes at Silas before recognition lit his face. "Masters! What are you doing here? No one mentioned you were here as well."

"The question to be asked is—how soon can you pack your things and get the bloody hell out of here?"

Hinton stared at him, speechless for several moments before a slow insidious smile curved his fleshy lips. Avarice filtered through his rheumy eyes. "Oh. I see. You have a vested interest here, too."

"You could say that," he agreed tightly. There was no sense denying it. He was at this man's door, prepared to barter with the devil himself to save Mercy.

"I take it one of the lovely Misses Kittinger has snared your fancy. Which one? Is it mine? The elder gel?"

"She is not yours. Your filthy hands shall never touch her."

The old man chuckled and then nodded. "Ah. It *is* my soon-to-be wife then. She is a spirited lass."

"You will never marry her. Get that notion out of your head."

"She is a tasty morsel." He paused and tapped his chin thoughtfully. "Well. I am a businessman above all else. Let us negotiate. What will you give me for her?" He eyed Silas expectantly.

"I understand the stakes of the pool were twelve thousand pounds. I'm prepared to offer you that."

Hinton waved a hand with a grunt of dissatisfaction. "That was weeks ago. Things have changed. Apparently her value has gone up. Demand has a way of doing that. She is worth more than mere money."

"What will it take?" Silas growled.

"That is a question better left to you, is it not?" Hinton stroked his bulbous nose, scratching a nail against one oozing sore.

Silas held the man's gaze for several long moments, attempting to read his intent. Comprehension finally dawned. Hinton did not want money.

That left only one thing he wanted from Silas.

Hinton appeared to hold his breath as he waited for Silas's response, anticipation bright in his eyes. "Well, Masters? What will it be?"

Silas nodded once, briskly, resolutely. "Very well. It is yours."

"Say it," Hinton directed with great relish. "I need to hear you say it, Masters."

"The Rogue's Den is yours."

The old man rubbed his hands delightedly. "What a splendid turn of events this is. We will meet in London, of course, at my solicitor's office to sign all the necessary paperwork. But for now . . ." Hinton held out his hand. "A handshake will suffice to seal the agreement."

Silas stared down at the old, gnarled hand before accepting it. It felt frail and cold in his grasp, the skin parchment thin. He should be sad. Angry. He just gave up what it had taken him years to build. But he could only feel relief knowing that cold, frail hand would never touch Mercy.

As far as he was concerned, his gaming hell in exchange for Mercy's freedom was a beyond fruitful arrangement.

Silas started down the corridor, finished with the man.

"Enjoy her in good health, Masters," Hinton called after him.

Silas paused, battling the rage that urged him to turn back around and plant his fist in the old man's face. Such a move would likely kill the bastard, and that would not get Silas anywhere. He would likely end up at the end of a hangman's noose if he surrendered to that impulse. His hands curled and uncurled at his sides as he fought for restraint.

After several breaths, he continued down the corridor to his room, content in the knowledge that Mercy was free. Free as she deserved to be.

BY THE TIME Mercy arrived downstairs for breakfast the following morning, everyone was already there. Her sister. Her brother. Gladys and Elsie. Even the detestable Mr. Hinton sat at the head of the table as though it were his right to be there.

The only person who was not there was the one she most wanted to see. Even as senseless as that might be. The sight of him would only make her pain greater.

"Good morning," she said stiffly, making her way to the food-laden sideboard.

She had no appetite, but somehow she would manage to eat. Or at least she would go through the motions of eating. She needed to put on a brave front. If not for herself, then for her sister and the rest of the staff. She cared very little about what her brother thought right now. This was all his fault, after all. He should feel terrible. Beyond terrible. As wretched as she felt.

Seating herself, she glanced around the table, still battling relief and anguish not to see Silas's face among the others. Of course, he was not here. Not after last night. Not after their words.

"Mr. Masters has already left then?" She could not help but ask the question.

Gladys cleared her throat. "Oh, yes. He left a short time ago. He seemed in quite the rush."

Quite the rush to leave here. She could not blame him for that. Mercy nodded miserably and stabbed at a bit of egg on her plate.

She did not miss the bewildered glances Gladys and Elsie sent Mr. Hinton's way. Clearly they were curious as to this man's identity and his place at their table. Apparently no explanation had been given for his presence among them. That unpleasant task would fall to her undoubtedly.

He held a scone aloft, smacking his lips in delighted approval. "I must take some of these home with me. They are so splendidly flaky and yet not overly dry."

Mr. Hinton was leaving then. Mercy looked down at her hands in her lap, a sense of bleakness rising up inside her. Did he think to take her with him? Her fate was in his hands. Desperation came over her and she had the wild urge to escape the room and . . . *flee*.

Perhaps she was not as strong as she thought. How would she endure this? She reached for her tea with a shaking hand.

"You mean to depart?" Grace asked Mr. Hinton in an overly sweet voice. "Good riddance."

The old man's expression turned decidedly peevish at Gracie's harsh words.

Mercy gasped. "Gracie!"

Grace met her gaze with a shrug. "What? Are we to feign as though he is a welcome guest here? Even he would know that is a lie."

Gladys and Elsie watched the byplay in rapt interest.

Mercy struggled for words. How could she explain to her sister that it would behoove them to be polite to this horrid gentleman if for nothing more than to ease Mercy's role as his future wife? She did not want to incur his wrath even before their vows were exchanged.

Apparently Grace understood anyway. "Oh. You are worried he might take exception and vent his spleen on you?" She shook her head. "You need not fear that."

Mercy closed her eyes in a long weary blink. "Grace," she moaned. Of course she had to fear that. Fear, among other things, was to become a condition of her existence married to this man.

"What? We need not be nice to him. You don't have to marry him anymore," Grace declared as though that were known to all.

Mercy opened her eyes slowly at that.

Gladys and Elsie simultaneously choked on their food at the mention of marriage.

"What do you mean?" Mercy resisted the hope that fluttered as weakly as a baby bird inside her chest at her sister's words. What could have changed since last night?

"Mr. Masters handled it. Just as I knew he would," Grace said pertly and rather smugly, popping a berry into her mouth.

Silas?

"Explain yourself, Grace. What did Mr. Masters do?"

"Well. I don't know all the particulars." Grace shrugged and nodded to Mr. Hinton. "Ask him."

"We reached a mutually satisfying arrangement."

Why was it so difficult to get a direct answer from anyone?

"Let me understand this. I don't have to marry you anymore?"

"Yes, much to your disappointment, I am certain." He chortled at that. "Masters made me a better offer."

"A better offer," Mercy echoed.

"No offense intended, lass, but The Rogue's Den is one of the most popular hells in London. I can always find a wife. I can't find another club like that."

Mercy stared straight ahead, seeing yet unseeing. "He traded his club for me?"

"Indeed," Hinton answered amid the sound of him eating.

"Can you believe it?" Bede who had been silent through this entire conversation found his voice to say, "Have you any notion what that club was worth? Far greater than twelve thousand pounds, I'll tell you." He chuckled, shaking his head. "And he traded it for you."

"Enough! Stop it! You should say nothing. You should say *nothing* ever again," Grace interjected with hot indignation, slapping her hand down on the table so hard her palm stung. "Mr. Masters is an honorable man. Honor, Bede. Something you would know nothing about."

His business. His livelihood. His world. All of it gone. Traded.

For her.

She closed her eyes. *No no no no.*

It was too much. It was not fair to him. He gave too much. She would never be able to repay him for such a debt.

She jerked to her feet, knocking her chair back to the floor. "And he has gone. He left," she announced rather dumbly.

"Er. Yes. I tried to persuade him to take breakfast with us, but he was most insistent about being on his way home," Gladys provided unhelpfully.

He wished to go home back to London. Home used to be the third floor of his club. But not anymore because he had sacrificed that for her.

Why?

That baby bird inside her chest started to beat its wings harder, faster, hope burgeoning within her.

She had to see him. She had to . . .

She shook her head. She did not know what she could say or do, but she had to do and say *something*.

She had to see him.

"I have to go after him," she muttered, hastening away from the table.

"You do?" Bede queried in bewilderment.

"Oh, shut up," Mercy snapped at him as she passed him on the way out.

"Yes, you do," Grace called after her in a tone that conveyed that was the most obvious course of action for Mercy. "You never should have let him leave."

For once, Mercy agreed wholeheartedly with her sister.

She should not have let him leave.

Chapter Twenty-Six ❧

*M*ercy rode like the devil himself was chasing her.

Fortunately, Silas did not have too far of a lead on her.

The broad back of him atop his mount soon appeared ahead of her on the road.

Relief expanded within her chest. She waved her hand wildly above her head in the air as though he could see her. "Silas! Silas!"

He whipped around quickly on his mount, a slightly panicked expression on his face. "Mercy?"

She soon closed the gap between them.

She dismounted and he followed suit, jumping down from his horse. She fought for her breath. It was almost as though she had been the one racing hell-bent after him and not her mare.

"Mercy, is anything amiss? What is wrong?"

She shook her head violently. "Nothing is wrong." She winced. "Well. That is not quite true. You are leaving." And that was wrong. That was the *most* wrong thing in the world to ever befall her.

"Yes," he said slowly. "We knew that."

She stared at him in anguish. "What you did for me . . . It is not right." She shook her head fiercely. "It is not right that you gave up so much. I don't deserve—"

"Don't say it. Don't say that. Of course you deserve your freedom. No woman deserves being married to that man or any man not of their choosing. You deserve a better brother. You deserve choices in your life, Mercy. You deserve . . . *everything*. Anything you want."

So he would have done such a thing for any woman? Or was she special? Was she special to him?

A sob rose up in her throat. "It's not right. It's not fair. I cannot let you—"

He seized her by the shoulders then, and his big hands on her were practically her undoing. Those hands made her *feel*. They made her feel *everything* and remember *everything* that had ever passed between them. "You did not *let* me do anything. I did it. I chose to do it." His gaze roamed her face. "And I would do it again." He paused a beat. "I would do anything for you."

Tension swelled between them.

Neither spoke for some moments.

She moistened her lips. "You are too good to me . . ."

"No." He dropped his hands away from her as though she suddenly burned him and took a step back. "I don't want your bloody gratitude."

What do you want then?

She came after him, her body a taut bow, straining toward him in longing, in need. She seized his hands in her own, hating that he had severed the contact. "What is it you do want, Silas?"

He looked down at their joined hands and took a deep breath, lifting that broad chest of his.

"I will tell you what I want," she volunteered.

"What is that?"

"You," she whispered, almost afraid to hear herself say the words that would render her irrevocably vulnerable. "I want you. However you will have me."

She knew what that meant. She knew what she was saying. She was offering him . . . *herself.* All of her.

If he wanted her. As a mistress. As a friend. As an occasional liaison.

She would take this good, honorable, beautiful man in whatever way he would have her. In whatever capacity, and she would be happy. She would be delighted and not suffer a moment of regret.

His hands tightened around hers then, squeezing, clinging to her as though she might vanish from him. "Do you know what you are saying?"

"I do." She nodded. "I love you."

He stared at her for a long moment before a wide, thrilling smile curved his lips. He snatched her up into his arms with a whoop and swung her around in a circle that sent her heart racing in her chest.

She giggled. "Perhaps I should have told you this sooner."

"Perhaps you should have." He set her back down on the ground to look into her eyes, his hands coming up to cup her face tenderly. "Or perhaps I should have told you sooner. I am so bloody in love with you, Mercy Kittinger, and I have been ever since I chased after you. I accept your offer. I will have you." He dropped to his knees before her, reclaiming both of her hands in his and pressing a kiss to each of her palms. "Marry me, Mercy. *That* is how I wish to have you. As my wife. Please say you will have me as your husband."

A sob thickened her throat as she replied, "Yes. Yes, yes, and forever yes."

Mercy flung her arms around him and pressed her mouth to his, kissing him until she could not feel her lips anymore and then she was certain that she could quite happily keep on kissing him, however much and for however long she wanted. Forever if she wanted to. Because she could. Because they belonged to each other.

For the rest of their lives.

Epilogue ❦

Six months later . . .

*P*ounding footsteps in the foyer accompanied Grace's enthusiastic shouts, alerting Mercy and Silas that their privacy had come to an end.

"Mercy! Silas!"

Silas groaned and lifted his face from Mercy's neck where he had been nibbling quite deliciously upon her skin. "She has the worst timing." He removed his hand out from beneath her skirts where his fingers had just begun quite the interesting foray up her thigh.

"She will be gone in a week and then you will miss her terribly." Mercy playfully poked her husband in the shoulder and then climbed off his lap where she had been sitting so comfortably.

Mercy would miss her sister, too, but finishing school was only for a year. A year was not so terribly long in the grand scheme of life. She told herself that for solace, and yet she knew that it was likely Grace would not ever return to Shropshire unless it was for visits. She was a bird flying free from the nest, ready to explore the world and go wherever the winds took her. Her sister was on her way, and as happy as Mercy was for her, she would miss having her with them.

"I know you're right. I will miss the little scamp whilst she is away, but presently I would enjoy some alone time with my wife."

Mercy leaned down and pressed a kiss to his mouth. "We will have plenty of that soon enough."

Grace burst in the room, waving a letter in her hand. "It's from Bede!"

"Oh." Mercy took the correspondence from her sister and seized a letter opener from Silas's desk, slashing it open.

Grace danced anxiously around her as she read it. "What does he say?"

Silas grunted, clearly uninterested in news of her brother, and returned his attention to his work. With the exception of the gaming hell, he still managed his several properties in London, and now he helped Mercy manage the farm. They had hired more staff and were expanding, growing more crops, building more outbuildings. They had even begun discussing renovating and adding another wing to the main house—a project Mercy was delighted to embark upon. Of course, there was the trip abroad, a belated honeymoon of sorts, they were planning for themselves in the spring.

Life was good. Good, indeed. In fact, she had never imagined it could be this good.

Mercy was happy. Silas was happy. Grace was happy. It seemed that everyone who mattered to her was happy. Even Gwen Cully had married. No one expected such an improbable thing. The lady blacksmith, so very stalwart in her unmarried state, had married . . . and to someone so unexpected. It was astonishing really. Quite the juicy chatter for the residents of Shropshire.

As for Bede, Silas had given him no choice regarding his fate. Prior to their marriage, Silas had demanded Bede sign over the farm to Mercy or he would ruin his name throughout London, making certain all doors were closed to him. Mercy had not protested or defended him against such a threat, even when Bede pleaded with her to intervene. It was necessary. She knew something had to be done. Bede could not be given any more chances. He had done too much damage. He could not continue on his destructive path. If not for Silas . . .

She shuddered, not caring to think what her fate

would have been. And she needed not consider it. There was only joy in her life now. There would only be joy to come.

Silas was generous enough to give Bede some money so that he could make a start of it elsewhere. Some place other than England. He permitted Bede the choice, and her brother chose New Zealand. Silas paid for his fare, sent him off with a plump purse, and that was the end of it.

"He's made it to Christchurch and has taken a position there at a school."

"He has found employment?" Grace blinked in surprise.

Mercy nodded and handed the letter over to Grace to read. The money Silas gave him would not last forever. Perhaps her brother had changed and was thinking to his future. Perhaps he had grown up. More outrageous things had happened. Things like Mercy marrying Silas Masters.

A whimsical smile played about her lips. Who would ever have imagined such a thing? Such a wild, improbable thing?

And yet here she was. In love. Married. Loved in return . . . and not just by any man. Loved by a man like Silas Masters. Beautiful. Strong. Good and kind.

Still smiling, she returned to her husband's lap, not even caring that they had an audience. She loved the man too much to stay away for even a few moments.

"Oh, you two." Grace looked at them over the letter. "Can you not keep your hands to yourselves?"

"No," Mercy responded, pressing a lingering kiss to her husband's cheek and threading her fingers in the hair at his nape. He bestowed a tender smile on her, and she smiled back at him. "We can't."

Don't miss

The Scoundrel Falls Hard

The next book in *New York Times* bestselling
author Sophie Jordan's Duke Hunt series.

Available from Avon Books
August 2022